D1010941

Praise for *Our Little Secret*

"Roz Nay's addictive debut proves that dark secrets of the past cannot be forgotten."
—*Us Weekly*

"Nay's engrossing read is told from multiple perspectives, and from its chillingly mysterious opening to the subtle brilliance with which a revengeful saga unfolds, its steamy love triangle will hook you and never let you go. It's a debut thriller that's just delicious."
—*Entertainment Weekly*

"Remarkable. *Our Little Secret* superficially resembles Paula Hawkins' *The Girl on a Train* and similar psychological thrillers that have stormed the best-seller lists in the last decade. But Nay's work transcends the subgenre. The plot is more textured and heartbreaking, and her prose contains startling turns of phrase that reveal the soul of a poet."
—*Associated Press*

"An insidious and disturbing read, *Our Little Secret* is a stunning thriller about the deadly consequences of a first love."

—*Buzzfeed*

"A cracking read . . . *Our Little Secret* builds to a deliciously dark conclusion."
—Ruth Ware, *New York Times* bestselling author of *The Woman in Cabin 10*

"Nay lures readers down a dark and tangled path that explores the aftereffects of lost first loves . . . A gripping addition to the psych thriller world."
—Mary Kubica, *New York Times* bestselling author of *The Good Girl*

"A gripping and disturbing story, which left me guessing until the very end."
—B. A. Paris, *New York Times* bestselling author of
Behind Closed Doors and *The Breakdown*

"Clever and addictive, *Our Little Secret* won't stay a secret for long—it's that good."
—Chevy Stevens, *New York Times* bestselling author of *Still Missing*
and *Never Let You Go*

"A sneaky-smart, charismatic debut that will win fans among those who enjoy the kind of duplicitous and deliciously complex psychological suspense written by Ruth Ware, Sophie Hannah, and Erin Kelly."

—*Booklist*, starred review

"Fans of Paula Hawkins and Ruth Ware will devour this twisty psychological thriller; Nay has expertly crafted a narrative that has the potential to veer in several directions, keeping the readers enthralled and guessing until the end."
—*Library Journal,* starred review

"A hugely accomplished first novel—and one which, in the guise of a page turner, poses many questions about intimacy, jealousy and the vertiginous trajectory that is revenge."
—Douglas Kennedy, international bestselling author of
The Pursuit of Happiness and *Leaving the World*

"In *Our Little Secret,* Roz Nay shows how the past is never truly past, and can be darker than we guess, especially when it comes to first loves. A most promising debut."

—Andrew Pyper, bestselling author of *The Demonologist* and *The Only Child*

"In Roz Nay's tightly woven debut *Our Little Secret* we meet Angela – a wily woman with a twisted love story, who is in quite a heap of trouble. As the story unfolds and the mystery deepens, the breadcrumbs Nay expertly leaves behind reveal a dark truth you won't see coming. Ruth Ware fans will love this compulsive, impossible-to-put-down novel!"

—Karma Brown, bestselling author of *Come Away With Me* and *The Choices We Make*

"A stunning debut . . . *Our Little Secret* is a deliciously twisted novel about a love triangle. It's so suspenseful your heart will be pounding as you hurry to the end. Roz Nay has proven she can write the thriller you haven't read before."

—Liz Fenton and Lisa Steinke, authors of *The Good Widow*

"A juicy, darkly comic tour through an unpredictable mind, populated by characters as captivating as they are despicable. If you liked *Disclaimer,* you're in for a treat with this one."

—Averil Dean, author of *Alice Close Your Eyes*

"[A] mesmerizing debut . . . Nay expertly spins an insidious, clever web, perfectly capturing the soaring heights and crushing lows of first love and how the loss of that love can make even the sanest people a little crazy. Carve out some time for this riveting, one-sitting read."

—*Kirkus Reviews*

"Captivating . . . Nay is a writer to watch."

—*Publishers Weekly*

"Heading to a cottage this weekend and need a guaranteed good read? Bring this book. Trust me: you're likely to read it in one breathless sitting. When you return to reality, it will be well past midnight and everyone else will have gone to bed. [A] winding, deceptive descent towards the truth about what happened. I didn't see it coming, and neither will you."

—*The Globe and Mail*

"Seemingly every aspiring author out there is now busy capitalizing on the trend, crafting dark psychological thrillers with unreliable female narrators and wild plot twists. It's increasingly difficult, then, to stand out in this crowded market. . . All of this is why first-time author Roz Nay's debut *Our Little Secret* is so impressive."

—*Toronto Star*

"Roz Nay keeps readers enthralled with prose that's at once lyrical and incisive. The author can make a drug trip seem poetic. *Our Little Secret* should keep readers tied to its pages."

—*Shelf Awareness*

HURRY
HOME

HURRY HOME

A NOVEL

ROZ NAY

CROOKED
LANE

NEW YORK

Published in the United States by Crooked Lane Books, an imprint of The Quick Brown Fox & Company LLC.

Crooked Lane Books and its logo are trademarks of The Quick Brown Fox & Company LLC.

Library of Congress Catalog-in-Publication data available upon request.

ISBN (hardcover): 978-1-64385-479-3
ISBN (ebook): 978-1-64385-480-9

Cover design by Melanie Sun

Printed in the United States.

www.crookedlanebooks.com

Crooked Lane Books
34 West 27th St., 10th Floor
New York, NY 10001

First Edition: July 2020

10 9 8 7 6 5 4 3 2 1

For my sisters, Jo and Sal.
Watt girls forever.

The woman holds the baby close and ghost-dances by the window. She can see her reflection in the glass. She doesn't mind being awake with her little boy at this odd, witchy hour when everyone else is asleep. This moment is a secret that only they share.

He is olive-skinned, familiar—although a far cry from her own pale coloring. It *doesn't matter*, she thinks. *He's mine, and I'm keeping him.*

Outside, the street is quiet. The mountains in the distance watch over the sleeping town. She concentrates on the cowrie-shell curl of his hand. His fingernails are tiny and perfect, little crescent moons in each one. Did she make those? In one of his hands is a worn old clothespin that he's been gripping for days.

A dog's bark pierces the silence, and the baby startles and throws out his arms.

How powerful babies are, she thinks. *How vulnerable.* She lifts her shirt and juggles him until he finds her breast. They fit perfectly together; they're made for each other.

A few moments later, the baby unlatches, frustrated, and she prods at his lips, her brow darkening. "I'm sorry," she says to him. "Shhhh." He doesn't even try to latch again. Instead, he fusses and turns his head away.

"Hey," she says, her voice louder. "It's just us now. You'll never see her again."

The baby blinks, working up to a cry, and they stare at each other for a second, old souls reconnected, like there was never any loss before and nothing ever went wrong.

"You're okay, little one, you're safe now. There, that's better."

In a minute she'll fetch him formula from the fridge, warm it up, test the temperature of it against the tender flesh of her inner arm. She knows how to do all of this. She's a natural. Finally everything is exactly as it should be.

PART ONE
THE GUARDER

ALEXANDRA

In the dream I am running and my sister is behind me. The ground is brittle, hard against my summer feet, and as with every dream, I think I'm rushing to save something, to stop it, but it's not that. It's so much worse. I can hear Ruth gaining on me—she's bigger than me—and she grazes the back of my shirt with her fingertips as I strain to run faster. When she finally grabs me, as she always does, she pulls me down into the dust and her sharp fingernails dig into the little-girl flesh of my arms. *It's just a game!* I scream, *We're only playing!*, and I jolt upright in bed, my feet pedaling at the sheets, my tongue pasted against the soil of my mouth.

I lie panting for a minute. I thought the dreams would lessen, but they're getting worse. They're always of her, or the version of her I last saw all those years ago. It's crazy to be so afraid of her; I don't even know where she is.

I tiptoe out of bed, careful not to wake up Chase, and stumble to the kitchen to get water, to put out this fire in my head. I'm so thirsty all the time. By the sink, I run cold, clear water and drink from the tap, splashing a little to my forehead.

Chase's loft is high-ceilinged and open concept, a one-bedroom that's short on doors and boundaries. Some couples might find that claustrophobic, but I don't. I find it companionable. I can just see him from where I stand by the sink: He's a muscular guy, but he breathes so softly, his tanned arm lolling against the crisp, white sheets. I've no concept of where he goes when he sleeps, but it's an opposite dreamscape to mine.

Outside, the sky is trying for an early blue. It's June, but there's still a 7:00 a.m. gray that leaks slowly into color. In this Colorado town, we're never too far from the creep of the glacier, a silent advance I can't help but find sinister. Chase, though, he loves everything about the mountains. On my way to the walk-in closet, I trail a fingertip across the tall canvas print of him by the front door, a professional shot of his body upside down on the mountain, hucking a twenty-foot drop on skis. I could never do that, wouldn't even know where to begin. But he's good in environments that I'd find daunting. He rarely ponders such things as his own mortality. Behind him, snow wisps delicately to eclipse the sun. I have to admit it's a beautiful photo.

Once I've pulled on skinny jeans and a T-shirt that isn't too crumpled, I grapple my hair into a topknot and grab my khaki jacket and my old leather satchel. I lift the satchel over my head so the strap lies diagonal across the front of me. My Vans are by the front door, and I kick my feet into them, wondering if at twenty-five it might be time to buy shoes that aren't best suited to the average fourteen-year-old boy. But my job doesn't require a corporate dress code. As a child-protection social worker, it's best if I look relatable.

Tucked away in the Rocky Mountains, Moses River is isolated in the winter months, but now the trees along the sidewalk are in bloom, the buds bulging with optimism. Locals mill about on Main Street, coffee in tall travel cups as they lean against their parked trucks. Wheels of mountain bikes hook over every tailgate—if there's bustle, it isn't work-related. *Life is beautiful* reads more than one bumper sticker. But ask any social worker in this town and they'll tell you life around here is a lot of things, not all of them beautiful. But we're trying. We're trying for the kids who don't believe the bumper stickers, for the kids who live the truth.

As I walk up Main, I think about Minerva's email from last night. It was hassled and hurried as usual, but she told me there was a report of negligence involving a little boy and his parents, a couple called the Floyds. I haven't heard the name before, but from the tone of the email, it seemed like she was familiar with them. If she wants me on board, the case must be an ugly one. It always is when there's a baby involved. A little baby boy.

Minerva Cummins used to work in Mental Health and Addictions before she crossed over to Family Services, and she's never shaken it off. Every exchange I have with her feels like she's trying to help me out of some kind of saddening entrenchment. Even as I'm solving problems, she'll sigh with her eyes closed as if I'm the cause of them. Sometimes I wonder if that's why her husband divorced her. My boss, Morris, rarely puts me and Minerva together on cases—perhaps because he knows that as one of the older, more experienced social workers on the team, she can be patronizing. *She's a mother, Alex,* Morris told me once in his office. *But don't let her mother you.*

An unexpected cold blast of air hits me as I round the corner onto Cedar Street, and I jog the next few steps to the Lovin' Oven bakery. The bell above the robin's-egg-blue door jingles as I enter, and I'm greeted by the smell of scones. The bakery is compact, with one long counter, various chalkboards on brick with the handwritten names of soups, rows of golden-fresh bread stacked on shelves behind the till, and three rough wooden tables for eating at, all of them rectangular with benches. I do a quick scan of the room as I enter. Minerva's not here yet. For all the dedication she claims to have, it's rare that she arrives on time to anything.

Once I've bought a coffee, I find a seat at the far end of the long table and wait for her. Over in the corner, two old ladies in matching knitted hats share a pot of tea. For a second, I wonder if they're sisters. The thought stops my breath.

But then the bell above the door jingles and Minerva strides toward me, corduroy pants chafing noisily as she moves. Her brown bob is still wet from the shower. It looks plastic, like hair you press onto LEGO people.

She stops in front of me at the opposite bench. "Another day, another dollar."

"Morning," I say. "Are you ready to go?" I half stand.

"Chill your boots! I need to brief you first, and you know I can't do anything without a strong coffee."

Coffee is why she wanted to meet early? I reluctantly sit back down While Minerva orders her drink, then settles into a seat as though we have all the time in the world—all the time in the world when a young child's well-being is at stake.

"So," I say, careful to hide my impatience. "Tell me about this baby boy and his parents."

"Frank and Evelyn Floyd have a history of drugs and alcohol addiction." She takes a wary first sip of her drink. "Basically they were druggies, trouble-makers before they had a child. But they've been better since he was born."

"Okay . . . So then why are we both going on this visit?" I ask. What I really want to say is *Get a move on*.

"The baby's name is Buster," she says, dodging my question. She pauses, relishing the Floyd baby's name, hoping I'll laugh at it, but I don't. "Earlier this week, they left him outside in the car while they went into the post office. Some Good Samaritan called it in. We'll go out to their house, have a quick peekaboo and that'll be it. We'll be in and out, brussels sprout."

Her phrasing catches me off guard. "In and out so fast when they left a baby abandoned in a car? How long was he alone for?"

"Come on, Alex, you know the drill," she says, shaking her head. "You can't assume the kid is in danger just because some stranger said so. I need you there with me to fairly assess things, and we need proof of abuse or neglect."

Abuse or neglect. Suddenly I can't touch my latte. "How old is Buster?"

"Oh, a year at the most, I think." Minerva looks at me quizzically. "Are you okay?"

No, Minerva, I'm not okay, I want to say. As many cases as we resolve in child protection—kids living in horrible circumstances who we rescue and give a chance at a better life—new cases pop up at double the rate. I feel like Mickey Mouse in that old cartoon, the one we had to watch as kids after school was out. Mickey's in the sorcerer's workshop, and it's flooding, and the mops are out of control, and yet no matter how hard he tries, the water keeps pouring in, backing Mickey up the stairs. I hated that cartoon the first time I saw it, but it was always Ruth's favorite.

"Can we get going?" I stand up.

"Oh, all right then," she says, exhaling. "Although it wouldn't hurt to *relaxez-vous* for a minute. You'll be on stress leave in no time, just like everyone else, if you keep trying to save the world."

I ignore her and head for the door.

The Floyd property is on dilapidated farmland off Highway 4. Minerva drives too fast out of town in our government vehicle. She has music playing on Sirius like it's high summer and we're heading to the beach.

"Hey," she says, adjusting the rearview mirror, which has been nowhere near her line of vision the entire journey. "Have you seen Sully recently?"

"What?" I stare at her. Hooked around the front of me, my satchel feels like a shield.

"You know, Sully Mills? Handsome cop with the piercing eyes. Aren't you two buddies?"

I hate how she says the word *buddies*, the way she separates the two syllables. Sully and I met a year ago through work. I guess you could say that we connected. I meet him for coffee at the Oven a couple of times a week. We're friends, not buddies. We're *just* friends.

"I don't see him that much." I tug at the seat belt cutting into my neck.

Minerva's eyebrows shift up for a second, but she doesn't say a word. I want to push her face with the full force of my hand.

A minute or two later, she says, "He's single, right?"

What does it matter to her? "Do you want me to get you his number?" I ask in a monotone.

"*Get* me his number?" She bats at her bangs, fluffs and repositions them in the rearview mirror. "You mean *give* me his number. Because you have it already. And you text him all the time."

I shift in my seat. "I have a boyfriend, you know. Remember? The guy I live with?"

"Exactly! So share the wealth, sister." She smiles at me, then moves her eyes back to the road after swerving a little. The house is up ahead. She slows down, pulls into the driveway, and jams the car into park. When we get out, we have to maneuver our way through clusters of shiny green goose shit that lead up a dirt track to the Floyd place. There's a fence and gate about three hundred feet from the house.

"Mr. and Mrs. Floyd were a gong show when I knew them," she says, turning. "But just so you know, they're the good gong show, not the bad one. There's a difference."

"Is there?" How the hell can Minerva think drug addicts make good parents? We reach the gate, which has a sign on the front: *Big Dog Bites.*

"That sign's been there since I was in Addictions. There was never a dog." She pulls at the gate, creating enough of a gap to squeeze through. A long stripe of mildew transfers to the front of her sweater. We walk up the potholed driveway together, past a bucket on its side and a couple of mismatched flip-flops.

"Oh, the house looks better," she says.

The home itself is squat and peeling, the deck ragged with rusted nails. On the porch outside the door is a cat litter tray full of crooked cigarette stubs. Next to that, a Hot Wheels car, blue, abandoned. If this is "better," then what on earth was the place like before?

She pauses on the top step of the deck. "Let's remember: even if Buster was left alone for a minute or two, when you're a mother, shit happens. You might not know that, but mothers do. Those of us with kids have all been there."

There's that card again, her favorite in the stack of superiority. I could retaliate, especially because I know about her son, know he's estranged and won't talk to her, but my heart's begun to race and my palms are sweating. The Hot Wheels car is faded and forlorn and reminds me of misery. Nothing good will come from this house. I wipe my hands on the back of my jeans.

"Okay, ready?" Minerva has her knuckles poised to knock, but the door is open. We walk into a tiny linoleum-floored vestibule that serves as some kind of pantry. Three shelves face us, empty apart from a couple of tins of baked beans, one of them opened with the ragged metal sticking up. The glass of the main door itself is busted as if someone has put an elbow through it. Duct tape crisscrosses the pane.

"Let's get on with it," I say.

"Okay. If Frank Floyd comes at us, stay calm. In the old days, he was something of a charging bull."

I nod, wipe my palms once more on my pants. Nobody answers Minerva's knock, or the second one.

"Hello?" she calls out. "Anyone home?"

The vestibule smells musty, grainy, with the pungency that always comes with poverty. It's sour, hoppy, horrific. I cover my mouth with my sleeve. From inside we hear a crash and a shout, the sound of a plate clattering in a circle as it settles. Minerva pushes the rickety door open. She steps inside as Frank Floyd rounds the kitchen counter, leading with the top half of his body.

"I'm coming," he growls. He wears track pants, rolled at the waist, and a T-shirt that swamps him despite the fact that he's a huge guy. "Can't a man take a nap in his own house?" He spots Minerva, clearly recognizing her. "Oh, for fuck's sake. Here we go again. Send in the clowns."

"Mr. Floyd," Minerva says cheerily. "I hope you don't mind the intrusion."

"I do fucking mind, and I don't remember inviting you in."

I peep around Minerva, taking in Frank Floyd's bare feet, the ashtray on the floor, the dishes stacked up in the sink.

"We wanted to make sure everyone was okay in here. How are you doing today? I'm Minerva Cummins—do you remember me? We met years ago, but I've changed jobs since then: I'm here with Family Services. This is my coworker Alexandra Van Ness." Minerva sounds like she's gritting out a smile.

I still have one hand on the door handle.

"No, no, *no*," Frank says, bashing his fist against his own hip with each syllable like a toddler in a tantrum. "You're not coming in. You're trespassing. Nobody's fucking asked you to come here."

"It's okay, Frank. It's all right." She moves into the kitchen, both palms up. "Listen, I know you don't want us here. Is your wife around? Evelyn?

12

Can we have a chat with her? We've just had a tiny little report, and we need to check up on it."

I edge into the kitchen and stand close to Minerva. The house is as long and straight as a shipping container, the kitchen sprawling into the living room, where, at the far end on a sofa with a missing cushion, a woman is sleeping facedown, wearing only an undershirt and panties. She sleeps as if dropped from a height, her limbs splayed. And it's then, only then, that I see the baby.

He's tiny and fast asleep, his face pressed dangerously against the cheap sponge of the couch cushion. He has nothing on but a diaper, the bulge of it round and tight like a soccer ball. The coloring of him, the tan and the sandy skin tones, the way his hair sticks up at the crown, the bumpy little muscles in his shoulders—it all grips me like a fist. He's a carbon copy. I have to rescue this child, just like I had to rescue another one before him.

"My wife's tired," Frank says, tracking my gaze. "She banged her head." He's sweaty around the hairline, jerky in his movements.

"Should we call for an ambulance or bring her into the hospital?" I ask. Why isn't Minerva rushing toward the baby? He's clearly not safe. I take a step toward the couch but tread on something that skids under my shoe. A cooked pasta tube squelches into the peeling floor tile.

"No! She didn't bang it that hard." Frank runs a mitt of fingers through greasy strands of his hair. "Look, everything's fine and shit. We're just tired. It's fucking difficult."

"Can we sit down, Frank?" Minerva asks. She pulls out a seat before he's responded and sits.

"What's difficult?" I say. "Is it something we can help you with?"

"Having a baby."

"Oh, steepest learning curve in the world!" Minerva says cheerfully. "I have a ten-year-old son, and I couldn't tell you a thing about the first year of his life, Frank. It's literally a blur. You probably won't believe me, but I've been thinking lately that I wish I could do it all over again."

"Yeah," Frank says uncertainly.

"Is Mrs. Floyd finding it really hard, too?" I ask.

"Yeah. I suppose. Yeah, yes. Look, okay, my wife didn't really bump her head."

"No? Then can we wake her up, do you think? It's really important that we speak with you both." I wait, still standing, while Minerva sits tidily amid the carnage that surrounds her.

"Yes, let's figure this all out together." Minerva's arms rest on the table as if she's waiting for a Sunday roast. Has she seen the state of the house? Does she really think this is a safe environment for a child?

Frank lumbers toward the sofa and pushes hard at his wife's shoulder. On the second attempt, she sits up, rubbing her eyes. Immediately she grabs Buster and he awakens, his face reddening, his arms sticking out straight, but he doesn't cry.

"The fuck are you two?" Evelyn looks from my face to Minerva's. "Who's this?"

"They're Family Services," Frank says, handing her a baggy pair of track pants he's found on the floor. "Put those on, and don't say shit."

Deep inside my stomach, I feel the grit of pitted stone, the same gnawing that hits me every time I meet liars with a brand-new child.

Frank's sweating harder now, round circles visible in the armpits of his T-shirt. While Evelyn struggles to put on the pants without letting go of her son, Buster dips and flails.

"Mrs. Floyd, good morning." Minerva half rises from her seat at the table, holding out a Family Services card that wavers pointlessly in the gap. "Do you remember me? I'm Minerva Cummins, and this is Alex Van Ness."

Evelyn doesn't look at either of us.

"We've had a report we need to follow up on."

"About what?" Evelyn sits, shifting Buster, who raises one little hand to hold on to the strap of her shirt.

Frank and I also take a seat at the table, and the four of us face each other like opponents in a quiz show, Family Services versus the Floyds. Buster starts to wriggle.

"He needs a diaper change," I say quietly. "That one looks full."

"I'll get to it," Evelyn replies. "What do you want?"

Buster makes strange little just-awake noises, a snuffling, more animal than infant. It's all I can do not to reach across and take him to my chest.

"We had a phone call," Minerva says.

"Who from?"

"It was anonymous. A woman called to say that you left little Buster unattended in a vehicle outside a public building."

Evelyn reaches back to the kitchen counter for a packet of cigarettes, tipping sideways on her chair so that the soft curve of Buster's forehead becomes visible. That beautiful skin, olive and smooth. Evelyn pulls out a cigarette from the pack and lights it, jiggling the little boy in her lap as she smokes. She's bitten every fingernail she has, just like Ruth used to. I'm flooded again by all the lies, all the nervous little tremors and tics. They're universal among people hiding things.

"What do you mean unattended? What public building?"

"Well, a bystander noticed that Buster was in your car on his own with the engine running. You were in the post office. Does that ring a bell, Evelyn? It would have been yesterday, or possibly the day before."

"It wasn't me."

"I'm afraid the bystander wrote down your vehicle license number," Minerva says.

We wait. Frank's shoulders slump. Thoughts flicker across Evelyn's face like she's assessing a poker hand.

"If it *was* me, I was only in the post office for two minutes."

"Two?" I say. "Are you sure?"

Frank elbows his wife suddenly, his voice cracked. "You fucking idiot. What the fuck were you thinking?"

"He was asleep!" Evelyn drags deeply on her cigarette and billows a long, straight plume of smoke over Buster's head.

Minerva turns to me with a look that says, *I've got this.* But she doesn't. Meanwhile, Buster keeps reaching up to his mother's face, but each time she jerks her chin out of his way.

He wants you to look at him, I think. *Why won't you?*

"He was fucking sleeping when I pulled up. All right? I didn't want to wake him. I left the car running because otherwise, the air-conditioning would shut off and it was the afternoon and hot. I'm not a fucking idiot."

"Totally. No. I get that." Minerva takes out a notebook, writes something and underlines it. "I'm a mother, too, Evelyn."

Evelyn rolls her eyes, but Minerva continues as though she hasn't seen. "I know how hard it can be to get things done with a little one in tow. But you can't leave Buster unattended. What if something happened? What if someone jumped in the car and just took off with him? You can't . . ." She searches for the most diplomatic phrasing. "Just don't do that again, okay?"

"She won't," Frank mutters.

Evelyn lowers her head. I watch as ash droops on the end of her cigarette, then falls to the floor. "Are you taking Buster away?" she asks flatly.

Oh, God, if only we could. The rules of procedure make it hard to remove a child. We need more evidence to present to court, but the second home visits are scheduled and never the same. The Floyds would have time to hide the drugs they're probably using. Minerva knows this, too, so why isn't she being more proactive?

She snaps her notebook shut. "We're not taking Buster anywhere. Absolutely not. Do you know what I see?"

Abuse! I want to scream. *Neglect! A boy being thrown to the wolves!*

"I see two people trying very hard, two people who are nearing the end of their resources." Frank and Evelyn stare at her. "We're going to offer you some support services. Ways to make this whole thing a bit easier, so you're not"—she glances around at the debris of their house—"struggling so much. And we'll do a follow-up home visit. Just to see how you're getting on."

"Do we have to?" Frank asks. "Do we have to use the services? Do you have to come back?"

"Don't you want the help?" I ask, my eyes drilling into his.

He shrugs. So does his wife.

Minerva smiles like we've all just agreed on a fabulous business deal. "Great. So we'll head out now, but we'll be in touch soon, once we organize some supports. You're doing very well. We'll just help you do a bit of a cleanup of Buster and . . . your home. And no more leaving him alone in the car."

"All right," Evelyn says. "All *right* already."

Minerva gets up. Is that it? She's the senior worker here. Why is she not doing more of an inspection? Are we really going to leave the child in this filth?

Slowly I stand. "Could I just use the bathroom?" I ask. "You can lead me there. I won't go poking around."

Evelyn sighs. "I'll take her."

Buster grips her neck as she stands. He's entirely devoid of language, a red flag in one-year-olds. We move down a skinny hallway toward the bathroom, Evelyn behind me. When I turn to look at her, her eyes are beady and granite black. In a flash, I'm back in my dream, those fingernails behind me, about to grab. Will she pull me to the ground like Ruth does? I swallow hard, and we pass a bedroom that must be Buster's. Quickly I glance in. There's no furniture at all in the room apart from a standing bassinet. One stuffy lies on the floor—a blue bunny, the ears so sucked and slimy with grime that the fur looks like it's been pulled through an engine.

"Bathroom's this one." Evelyn tugs at my jacket, and I jump. "Push harder," she says, doing so for me.

I go in and close the door behind me, moving a heavy black garbage bag away with my leg. There's no shower curtain, no soap. I breathe deeply with my eyes closed for a few seconds because my sister is *everywhere*.

There's a white bathroom cabinet over the sink, and I pull open the smudged front of it, rattling among lidless Tylenol bottles and brown-tinged Q-tips for some clear evidence of a drug habit. There's nothing. They're hiding it elsewhere. *Goddamn it*, I think.

I flush the toilet, or try to, my jacket sleeve low over my fingers. Back out in the corridor, Evelyn is waiting for me, bouncing her son. We walk in silence to the door, where Minerva is standing with Frank.

"All set?" Minerva asks. She's working herself up to a chipper goodbye and makes another attempt to hand over her business card. "So we'll be in touch. The future is bright. Don't worry: we'll work on all of this as a team."

Neither of the Floyds take her card. She sets it on the counter.

"Please call if you need immediate help or assistance." Minerva waves as she backs away down the porch steps.

We leave them both there in the doorway, Buster obscured by the sinewy arms of his mom.

In the car, Minerva turns to me. "That went well." She snatches at levers on each side of the steering wheel, trying to find the left signal.

"What?"

"That whole visit. Didn't you think? They're doing so much better. I feel we can help them."

She's out of her mind. If she thinks Buster is safe in that environment, she's nothing but another risk factor in his life. "Minerva, their house was awful. That smell?"

"What smell?" She turns the car around, making traffic slow as she swerves into the right-hand lane.

"Like old beer. Like grain at harvest." I shudder.

"Haven't you gotten used to that yet?" she asks.

"No, and I don't want to. How are you okay with the situation that child is in? There were definite signs of neglect."

"Be careful with that term," she says quickly. "Just because the Floyds are struggling doesn't mean they don't love their son, or can't look after him. They need some scaffolds around them."

I find my fingers clenching and jam them under my thighs. Minerva might have more years on the job than I do, but in all that time she hasn't figured out that *child protection* is an oxymoron. Even when we save kids or remove them, workers like her throw them back into the fray. *Safe enough* is her motto, but it isn't mine. We drive too fast in silence.

After a while, I can't help myself. "They don't even change his diapers!" I say. "I bet he has welts all over his backside if we'd bothered to look." I know I sound petulant, but I don't care. Because I'm the one doing my job properly. I'm trying to protect a child.

"You know the rules. There were no grounds for removal, Alex. They weren't high on drugs. Which, incidentally, I'm very proud about. And there were no signs of abuse. They just seem overwhelmed." Her hands whiten at the knuckle where she grips the steering wheel. "Loving someone and protecting them aren't always the same thing."

Enabler. She wills herself to see the best in people because she can't handle conflict. And she won't admit the impotence that we real child protection workers feel when we have to obey the fucking "rules"—which serve no one, especially not the children whose needs aren't being met. She sets the bar so low and refuses to see it. I stare out the window and say nothing.

The rest of day passes at the steady pace of paperwork and doleful phone calls. I have more than twenty files on my caseload, some of them reported incidents, others active investigations. That's a whole crowd of children I'm desperately trying to save. As I sift through the voice mails left on my machine—most of them from bio parents, a lot of them incoherent or hateful—I think about all the gates I'm guarding for these kids and how none of them really know it's me.

By four o'clock, I'm happy to start the walk home to the loft. When I step inside the apartment, I see Chase standing in boxers and a yellow shirt with the collar up, dicing tomatoes. He turns when he hears me.

"Hey, beautiful," he says, the paring knife still in his hand. In the living room the baseball game is on, scores from around the league zooming across the ticker. "Everything okay?"

He always asks me that. But how can *everything* be okay? To be fair, he hasn't seen what I've seen today. He doesn't know what I know. The bulge of Buster's diaper. The press of his small face into couch cushions. The utter apathy of his parents. Chase's world is much brighter than that. It's a good thing. And his brightness buoys me. It's what I love most about him.

I smile. "Most things are fine."

"Tough day?" He rinses his hands and then grabs me a wineglass from the cupboard, fetches a chilled bottle of white from the fridge. "I don't know how you do it. You could have gotten a job in a coffee shop, you know. Just deal with caffeinating people all day."

I laugh a little every time he makes suggestions like this, although I'm not sure he's actually joking.

"How was your day?" I sit on the chrome barstool at the kitchen counter and pry off my sneakers, letting each one drop with a thud. "You got in late last night. How was the photo shoot? Where did you go again?"

Chase is in marketing for our local ski hill, Powderkeg. More often than not, he's the face of all the promotional advertising—the billboards, the website, the commercials—but I can never keep up with which west coast ski resort he's filming in, or when. Most of his work is November through April, but there's always the odd shoot in the summer months to preempt the new season. It's nice to have him around more at this time of year, though. He helps a lot with meal planning.

"We just did some promo shots for next year." He inspects the wine bottle vaguely. "Inside-outside stuff in Breckenridge. They turned out great. They took a lot of head-and-shoulders shots of me, and the director was really happy."

"Of course he was. Are you going away again over the summer?"

"No, that should be it now." Chase cracks the wine and pours a generous portion, sliding the glass across to me. "Downtime."

"Good," I say. "I miss you when you're gone."

He reaches across the countertop to hold my hand, but I withdraw it—I haven't had a chance to wash properly yet. If I told him what I'd touched today, he'd be horrified.

His smile falters. "Are you hungry?"

I shake my head. "I have to take a shower first. I have to get this day off my skin."

"Oh," he says. There's a second where I imagine him taking the expensive wineglass back. "I've made a new turkey and quinoa dish. It's paleo. Full of good proteins. But we can hold off. We can eat in, say, twenty or so." He picks up his knife and begins dicing again, the knife easily severing the tomato's skin.

"That'd be great." I take a sip of the crisp wine, then slide off the stool. In the bathroom, I peel off my clothes. Social work makes me want to scrub my entire body with a wire brush every day. I wonder for a moment if Sully feels that way about his job, too. After a quick shower, I head back out, toweling my hair as I enter the kitchen. Through the open bay windows, a chickadee is singing its binary song in the street. That's when I hear a knock at the door. Chase, tea towel over one shoulder, pauses his chopping.

"Are you expecting someone?"

"No, definitely not."

I wrap the towel around my neck, then head to the front door and pull it open. I see a face more than anything, the paleness of it stark against dark hair. Long hair, familiar. Blue damaged eyes. Immediately I feel my knees might give out, like I might fall to the ground. I cover my mouth with both hands and stare.

It's her. It's Ruth Van Ness. My sister.

RUTH

We all live more than one lifetime in a life. I've always thought that. But when Alex opens the door to her fancy loft apartment, her face is still an eight-year-old's, changed only a little to fit an adult body. She hasn't lost the freckles or that startled look, as if she's just been told it's her week for show-and-tell and she's forgotten to bring in a toy. She's willowy and beautiful, though, dark auburn hair, long arms like a ballet dancer's, and yet there's a scruffiness to her, a kind of scrappy soul she's hung on to from childhood. I haven't seen her for ten years.

"Hello," I say, clearing my throat. "I thought it was time."

She doesn't do anything except gape. It's possible I'm not a sight for sore eyes; I might not even be welcome. I made a choice a long time ago, and as soon as I made it, I sealed my fate. But none of that matters now.

"Can I help you?" A man who is so physically flawless he must be a model moves in behind her. "Alex, who's this?"

"My sister," she says. The words come out as a scrape.

"Seriously?" Model Material swings the door wider, and I see him take in the ragged hem of my sweater. He's a Gap ad, all pastels and hope. "Well, hi. Wow. Alex always said that—"

"I said you're not really one to visit, Ruth." My sister gives him a pointed look. "That's what I said."

"I guess it's been a while," I say.

"It has." She pauses and then steps aside, and I move past them both, the smell of the man overpowering, like the cologne counter in a department store. The loft has vaulted ceilings, and everything's white. I feel I've just entered an art gallery and I mustn't leave a smudge.

"Nice place," I say, lowering my bag to the floor gently so the contents don't make a sound.

"Thanks a lot, yeah." The man glances at Alex, not quite knowing what to do. Then he picks up my bag and hangs it on a coat hook to the side of the door. "I got a great deal on this place. Friends in the right circles. Come in, sit down. Take a load off."

The way he's talking, it's like he knows I've been through hell, like he can see it on me. Alex, for her part, looks like she's been drained of all bodily fluid. The guy urges me to the designer couch, where I perch at the farthest edge of the cushion, frightened to make a dent. *Alex lives here?* It doesn't seem like her at all, not like the girl I once knew. None of us talk; we sit. We simply stare. A minute goes by.

"What happened to you?" Alex says finally. Her arms are crossed over her stomach as if my presence makes her physically sick.

I could ask her the same thing—*Where have you been for a decade?* But I don't.

She studies me suspiciously with her sea-gray eyes. But it's a two-way mirror: she's different—familiar and yet a silhouette of herself—the years she's spent away from me like a shroud. Maybe I shouldn't have come here, but what choice did I have? I bought the bus ticket. I got on. I ran away hoping never to look back. And yet now, the past is right in front me.

"You own this place?" I ask, rather than answer her question. "How's that?"

"I'm sorry." Model Guy leans out. "I'm Chase Kennedy, Alex's boyfriend, and this is my apartment. I mean, we live here together. Your . . . sister and me." He stretches past Alex with his hand, which I shake limply. I don't really like his fingers. "And you're Ruth? Am I getting that right?"

Another glance passes between him and her, one that makes me feel I'm a ghost that's suddenly begun to haunt. What did she tell him about me?

"Yes. I'm Ruth. I'm Alex's sister. I always have been."

"I'm sorry," Alex cuts in. "But you've shown up here rather unexpectedly. This is all kind of a . . . shock."

The way she stares at me, it's pretty clear she doesn't think it's the good kind.

Chase tries again. "Are you in town for a while, Ruth? You're welcome to stay."

Alex's back goes ramrod straight. "She probably isn't. She might not want to."

Chase looks from her to me and back again, like we're a tennis game.

"I'll get out of your hair for a minute and take a shower while you two . . . chat." He stands, touching Alex briefly on the arm, searching her face for some kind of explanation.

She ignores him, though. I can see this makes him simmer.

His neck tenses. "Take your coat off, Ruth—at least stay for dinner?"

That gets Alex's attention, but she doesn't utter a word.

"Thank you," I say.

He pauses with his hands on his hips, then disappears to the far end of the loft, behind a sliding Japanese door that's almost see-through but not quite. Alex sits stiffly.

"So why are you here? And where have you been for, you know, ages? You didn't say." Her hands are fists in her lap.

I bypass the sarcasm. "I've been out east. Here and there. You look good."

"So you've been with him. With Hal?" She can't hide the effort in having to say his name out loud.

Hal Nightingale, the lanky-legged drifter I dated, who she and Dad loathed when he worked that one summer on our farm. His car was a Plymouth Duster with a stereo so distorted the rock music blared out as fuzz. I bet she thinks I married him. She never knew why I hung out with him, except she did know. She knew all the disappointment that pushed me there, all the towering blame.

"I left him a long time ago," I say. "You do realize that was ten years ago?"

Her eyes widen for just a second. "Right. Good for you." *Liar*, she's thinking.

"Are you okay, Alex? Is there something you want to say?"

"Isn't it a little bit late for that?" she says.

My plan isn't working. "Look at this place," I say, forcing my voice lighter. But I can't help adding, "It's nothing like you."

"What does that mean?" She takes a long strand of her hair and sucks it, just like she did when she was little and someone was cornering her. We sit in silence for a minute, a stilted agony more than a family reunion. Eventually I point to the giant canvas photograph by the door, the only artwork in the whole loft.

"Who's that?" I ask.

"It's Chase. He's a ski racer. Or he was. Now he works for Powderkeg, the local mountain."

I stare at it. Who hangs a fuck-off-massive picture of himself on his own wall? Right on cue, Chase emerges from what must have been a thirty-second shower. Was he afraid to leave us alone for longer?

"I'll just get dressed," he says, "and then we can have some dinner. Take your time, no rush. You two must have a lot to catch up on." He smiles broadly and heads into what looks like a walk-in closet.

When I shift my leg to move one knee over the other, the pointy glass corner of the coffee table stabs me at shin level. I wince. Chase is only half-right. Alex and I do have a lot to catch up on, except that we don't. There's so much to be said that we can't say anything. I might not have seen my sister since she was fifteen, but I can already tell what her adult life has been, already sense the ease of it—while mine has been the opposite—and the lies behind it all, our whole family, including me, willfully forgotten. We were forged in the same fire, though. In the end, it will all come out.

"He's upbeat, isn't he, your husband? He seems to have a very sunny disposition."

Heat blotches at her throat. "He's not my husband." She looks down, notices the tattoo on the inside of my left wrist. My arrow, the end of it sharp and hard, but she doesn't comment on it. "He already told you he's my boyfriend. We're living together, but we're not married."

"Is that allowed?" I venture a smile, but it's not reciprocated. "Dad would lose his mind."

She starts a sentence and stops it again. Tries several more times.

"Do you know about Dad?" she finally asks. "About what happened to him?"

"That he's dead, you mean?" I say.

There's a beat, a twist of hurt. "So you heard." She sniffs. "It was four years ago, and I left Horizon as soon as he passed."

"I don't blame you. It was a shithole, let's be honest."

"And Mom? You know about her, too?"

"Listen, Alex, I didn't come here to—"

"How could you get my messages and not get in touch with me? Why didn't you come home?" She has bigger questions than that, though. She must have.

"You know why," I say.

Alex sits rigidly next to me on the unforgiving couch. I can feel her low animal steadiness, the precision of her breathing. "So why are you here?"

I put both hands on my stomach and rest them there, around the well-disguised curve of me. She looks down at my fingers, up at my eyes, until recognition dawns on her.

"No," she says finally. "No."

"Yes, sister," I say. "I'm pregnant."

ALEX

We sit crowded around one end of the kitchen island to eat Chase's paleo meal, our bowls almost touching. On one side of me, Ruth shovels the food in as though she hasn't eaten in weeks. She still holds her spoon like it's a bike handle. It brings me back: Dad must have told her a hundred times.

"So you're just traveling through? Or . . . ?" Chase lets the real question hang in the air.

"I don't necessarily have a plan," Ruth says. Her mouth is full, and a fleck of quinoa spits onto the marble countertop.

"She's pregnant," I say, pushing my food away. I've taken only a couple of bites. The quinoa coats my tongue like sand.

"Really?" Chase spills a little water on his chin. "Okay. Well, wow. Congratulations, then." He checks my face to see if he's responding the right way, but I'm fresh out of signals.

"Having a baby is like being reborn." Ruth puts down her spoon. "Isn't it, Alex?"

I say nothing, concentrate only on breathing quietly in and out.

"It's all about getting it right. I have to build a nursery. I have to build it while the baby is still on the inside."

"A crib, you mean?" Chase fills my wineglass, watching me.

"She's being metaphorical." My voice is as steady as I can make it. "She means she's planning to be a good mother." Has she wiped everything that happened before from her memory? If she believes she's capable of being a mom, she's blocked it all out. My hand trembles as I lift my wineglass.

Chase fills in the silence. "A nursery sounds like a great thing. And . . . where will this nursery be?"

I know he's trying to help, but he's so entirely literal. It's as if he's wandered into a movie halfway through and is trying to guess the plot.

"Your food's delicious," Ruth says. Typical, age-old avoidance.

"Thank you. It's all organic, locally sourced." Chase glances to the bay window as if the weather threatens, but it doesn't. "Alex, it's getting pretty late. Is your sister staying? Or is there somewhere we can take you, Ruth? Do you have a place to—"

I grip the wineglass. "She can stay here," I say. "Just for tonight. Then she needs a better plan."

"Thank you," Ruth mutters. She keeps her head low and continues to eat.

Later, we set her up with clean sheets on the couch and Chase gives her a towel. She doesn't shower. The bag she brought with her hangs by the front door. If there's a toothbrush inside it, she doesn't go looking for it. Once we've established that the couch is hers for the night, Chase and I can't watch television, relax, or go anywhere in the loft except to the far end, where our own bedroom is. I pack a few things in the kitchen for work tomorrow, while Ruth sits with her back to me. Our good nights are lackluster and clipped.

"She's different from anything I expected," Chase whispers once we hear Ruth pad her way into the bathroom. We can both see the light on in there through the gap in our bedroom door. I undress hurriedly, as if being timed.

"You told me you thought she was probably dead," he says.

I don't take the bait. I've got nothing to say. The last thing I'm doing is explaining myself.

He gets into bed and sits cross-legged, a child with a big man-chest. "I kind of had this idea in my head that if she was alive, she was living out of dumpsters or shouting at pigeons. But she seems . . . normal. Why do you think she showed up now?"

"Your guess is as good as mine."

"Is it? You told me she was a drug addict."

"She is. She was. She was when I last saw her." I toss my T-shirt to the ground. "Look, she abandoned my entire family. Just up and ran away from us all, never to be seen again. I didn't know what became of her. She was a mess. I just assumed the worst."

He glares at me as if I'm not apologizing enough.

"When it comes to the details of my life, Chase, you're hardly a master code cracker. You barely show interest."

"Hey, don't turn this around. Whenever I ask about your past, I get one-word answers and shrugs. And besides, I'm not mad that she's here. She's your sister, after all. She's family." His jaw clenches. "I just want to know who I'm welcoming into my house."

"Excuse me?"

"Our house." He sighs. "You've always said your sister was serious trouble. So is she or isn't she?"

"Why don't you decide? You're the one who invited her in for dinner." I stamp my pants to the ground and leave them there.

"I was trying to be nice! I didn't know what to do. You weren't offering many cues as to how I should act." He lets out a deep breath, turns back the duvet for me, and I slip under it. When he speaks again, his voice is gentle. "Look, I know this is all a shock. Let's just try to calm down and talk about this sensibly, okay? What I really want to know is why she's here. Why would she search you out now, when she's pregnant?"

Chase doesn't know that he's playing with fire. How could he?

"We should be careful," I say, hugging my knees.

Chase rubs my back roughly, a bear pushing at a tree. "Why?"

"She's done a lot of things that were kind of wild. She put my parents through hell. She put me through hell, too." The past swells in my throat, and I swallow hard to keep it down. "She claims to build things while she actually destroys them. She's hurt me, Chase. I don't want her to do that again—not to you, not to me."

He gives up on his version of a massage. "I don't really know what that means, Alex. What exactly did she do?"

"She's that kid who borrows a toy and gives it back broken."

"Yeah, but you're both grown up now. My brother used to take my ski gloves and rip them up on a tree run. But that was when we were ten."

I squeeze my eyes closed for a second, my throat tightening again, as I picture Chase's perfect family, his banker father and yoga-loving mother and Brad, his brother, who sails yachts. They live in Nantucket now, all of them, but Chase stayed on the west coast for his career. He grew up without a care in the world. It's one of the things I love about him—his limitless innocence. My own childhood was quite different.

"Ruth made a mistake years ago that changed everything for my family. And then she made a hundred more. She left because my dad disowned her. He had to."

Chase doesn't say anything.

See? I think. *You don't want to know. If you did, you'd ask why.*

He thumps his pillow a few times before settling back against it. "All I know is you do a lot for other people's families. She's your sister. And she's clearly doing better than when you last saw her. Maybe things are different now. Maybe you should try a bit, see if there's a way to help her out."

"She's a virus."

"Wow. That's pretty harsh. She doesn't look that bad to me."

He shifts so his back is against me, and I lie down, too, but there's no way I can close my eyes. *She's cleverer than both of us*, I want to say. *I don't care if that's cold. I don't care what she thinks of me and nor should you.* But I don't say anything, and within minutes he's asleep. It's like he has a sleep switch he can instantly flick on or off. I hate it. I listen to the softness of his breathing, and then the padded creep of my sister's footsteps out of the bathroom and back to the couch. For the first time in ten years, I'm lying in the dark near my sister. I lie stiffly, afraid that she's a spider that will move while I'm not paying attention.

There have been chances before this to tell Chase more about Ruth, to sketch in all the details of my family, tell him everything that happened in Horizon. But the truth is I've moved on and I don't want to look back. I've dealt with the mess Ruth left me. And it's over. I have a stable life here—I'm a social worker; I'm helping people—and I won't let her ruin that.

Out in the living room it's quiet, but I know she's awake. I still remember the rhythms of her sleep. Perhaps that's the real intimacy: to know how someone else breathes when they're asleep. To know the patterns, to predict how they'll move. In our old room as kids, our beds were so close together that Ruth and I could reach out with our fingers and touch. One time, when I was in second grade, I'd taken a treasure from the teacher's desk. It was a round piece of basalt stone, smooth as skin. The teacher used to run it under hot water and give the warm trophy to the kid who'd done the best that day. She never once gave it to me. When I stole it, I hid it in the vent in our bedroom. I was stroking a forefinger over the top of that stone when Ruth saw me.

"Alex," she said, coming right beside me. She reached out a hand and moved hair from my forehead. "I'll get you your own perfect rock. Put that one back tomorrow before the teacher notices it's gone." That was when she still had my back.

Ruth left the farm when she was twenty, seven years after she tore our family apart. Mom didn't want her to go, even if she couldn't say it loudly. Every time Ruth passed by with a new armful of belongings to put into her boyfriend Hal's stupid car, Mom touched her on the shoulder or arm, but Ruth kept going. Hal offered her a get-out-jail-free card, and she took it. He burned out of our driveway in that car, rock music blaring in Mom's face. There's no doubt in my mind he's the father of Ruth's baby. She can say he isn't, that he's a thing of the past, but there's no way. I don't believe it for a second.

Two summers after Ruth took off, Dad found Mom lying face-first in the field out back of the house. She used to walk on her own each evening. It was a heart attack, which sounds right if you're listing organs most likely to store sadness. They said it happened fast, but I know that part's a lie. It was slow and insidious, and Ruth was at the root of it all.

I've spent years sorting through the things Ruth has done, putting them away, rising above them. I doubt she's been doing the same. She definitely hasn't come here to apologize.

From the living room, I hear her stir and turn over. I push the duvet aside and get out of bed quietly, anxious not to wake up Chase. She must have heard me, too, because she whispers hoarsely into the gloom.

"Alex, is that you?"

Of course it's me. And she knows it. "Yes. It's me."

Silence. She's thinking. I'm standing at the crack in my bedroom door.

"Remember when we were little and the wind would blow against the house?" Her sentence has a smile in it. "You used to think it was lions roaring."

I was so small then, I could curl the whole of myself against Ruth's body as she hugged me. She would stay like that, a canopy over me until I fell asleep. But it wasn't just the two of us then. The memory's swift and visceral. I feel him, right there with us, curled up beside me and Ruth, so close that I can feel his little heartbeat. I know what Ruth's doing now, how she's softening me. But still I let her. I close the door to my bedroom and walk down the few stairs toward her. "We were sure those lions were right under our window."

Our voices are velvety in the high-vaulted space as I turn on the dim lamp by the television.

"That's better," Ruth says. "I can't sleep in here. It's too quiet, and the fridge keeps plinking."

I don't answer her. She's sitting, stooped like a vagrant on a park bench.

"Alex," she says again, her whisper softer. "I really need your help."

She's never said that before. Not once. Chills shiver down my back. I sit down next to her. She drags the sheet to hook it around my shoulders, but I shrug it off.

"Will you help me?"

There's a swell in the deepest part of me, a heaving undulation. She's shifting a rock at the bottom of the seabed, and I don't think I want it moved.

"You're my sister. The only one I have." She edges closer. "Anyway, I thought coming here would be good."

She reaches to move hair out of my face, just like the old days, but I dodge her.

"Good for who?" I ask. "For you?"

"Yes . . . yes, I suppose, but also good for you. After everything that's happened, Alex, I thought the timing was right. We've both made mistakes."

Both of us? Any mistakes I've made, Ruth was at their very center. How could her coming here pregnant and destitute, and wanting help, ever be good for me? I take a deep breath and remember Chase's words about family, about being there.

"Are you clean?" I ask.

She nods.

"Are you sure?"

"Yes, Alex. Yes. I've been clean for years and years." She glances across the room to the coat hooks, where her bag hangs in the shadows. "Totally. One hundred percent. I'm clean and sober."

"Okay, that's good," I say, not that I believe her. But this does feel different. In the past, she would slide away from any answer, slippery as an eel.

"Go to sleep now. We'll talk about this more in the morning." I tiptoe toward my bed again, toward the safe blank slate of Chase. Her plea hangs in the air, but I refuse to give her an answer now. I need time to think.

"Sleep tight, Alex," she says. "This could be good for you, you know."

I feel the fire surging in my belly, but I don't turn around. I don't bite. I won't dare say another word.

RUTH

I wake to the sound of a blender crunching ice in the kitchen. It's mid-morning, judging by the light streaming in through the window. I sit up, pulling the sheet around me, and see Chase by the counter.

"Hey," he says, opening the lid of the blender and poking inside with a spoon. "Sorry about that. I guess I woke you." He's dressed in workout gear, complete with an enormous watch on his wrist. "I've got an acai berry immuno-enhancer going here. You're welcome to a glass."

"I'm good," I say.

"You're missing out." He reaches up to a cupboard and grabs a glass from a perfectly symmetrical row. There are also white coffee mugs in there, identically spaced.

"Where's Alex?" It's so quiet: even with the window open, there are no sounds to suggest other people exist. I'm not used to being in such a small town anymore.

"Oh, she left at sevenish. Guess you're a pretty deep sleeper, huh?" Chase pours the purple gloop into a glass. He tastes it, then sucks a thick foamy line from his upper lip. "She works eight till four at Family Services."

Family Services? "That can't be right," I say, trying to keep my voice even.

Chase cocks his head to one side. "Don't tell me you don't even know what your sister does for a living."

"I had no idea," I say. And it's true. Alex cut off all communication after I left.

"She's a social worker. Child protection."

I nod slowly, light dawning. Child protection. The irony is astounding.

"You really didn't know?" He sets down his smoothie.

"We haven't exactly been BFFs." I get up, bunching the sheet into a ball behind me.

He takes a long draught of his juice, watching me over the rim of the glass. When he's done, he wipes his mouth with the back of his wrist. "But you were close as kids? You grew up together?"

"Oh, we did everything together," I say. She's told him nothing at all, I see that now.

"But it was a tiny town, right? Alex told me she grew up in North Dakota, but when I googled the town name—Horizon—I saw only grain silos and fields."

"That's all there is. That's the heart of it." Now would be a good time to excuse myself and take a shower or something, but I feel trapped here in men's boxers and an oversize T-shirt.

"Can I ask you something?" Chase sits down on a stool, lacing his fingers in front of him. "Why did you leave it so long to get back in touch?"

"I couldn't leave it a minute longer."

He bites his lip for a few seconds. I'm giving him the answers he wants, and still he doesn't like them.

"But you left in a hurry," he says. "You've brought nothing with you. And what's *that*—" He points at the side of my face until I rest my palm there. "There's a mark. There—by your temple. That's a bruise."

"No, it's not." I pull my hair forward to how it was last night. "It's nothing. I just banged myself against the window on the bus."

He nods quietly in the way people do when they don't believe you. He's more observant than I'd given him credit for. It's true I left in a rush. Packing would have raised suspicion, and it wasn't safe for me to stay in Pittsburgh any longer, not after what I'd done. I push those thoughts away and take a seat at the island, wondering what he'll ask next. Mostly I just want to find out more about him and Alex. I heard them whispering last night but couldn't catch what they were saying.

"If someone's hurt you, you can say so, you know." He looks down at the countertop. "I don't know much about that kind of stuff, but it would be okay."

I smile. If Chase knew the kind of trouble I'm in, he'd kick me out of his apartment right now and lock every door and window.

"You have such a nice place here, Chase," I say, diverting the subject. "Where are Alex's egg-smeared plates, her trail of toast crumbs?"

"Her what?"

"Never mind. So . . . Alex works with kids, right?"

"Yes. Kids who need help. She's really good at it." Chase sighs, part resigned, part proud. "I know she doesn't like to talk about the difficult parts of her life. I thought you might know more."

"Have you asked her about the difficult parts?"

"Yes, but she's not all that forthcoming." He scratches an itch between his shoulder blades. "I do want to know her."

I study his quarterback-stud face. Alex always went for the poster boys. This one seems like a decent-enough guy, but he has no clue who he's living with. He's completely out of his depth.

"So . . . you say you two were pretty close?" he says. "What kind of things did you get up to?"

"This and that. We grew apart as teenagers," I say. "If you have questions, you should ask her."

He takes his glass and places it into the sink, pressing it there for longer than he needs.

"What do you do for work?" There's a tone in his voice. He doesn't want a freeloader in his home.

"I wouldn't say I'm career-oriented."

"No? That's interesting. Because Alex is very driven. I have this thing where I like to give everyone I know a word to describe them. It's helpful—like a radar, or a GPS. Anyway, that's my word for Alex. *Driven*."

I drum my fingers on the counter. It's clear his word for me is less flattering, but that's okay. I'm used to sideways insults, and besides, his GPS is broken.

"So what? You don't . . . work?" he asks.

"Not presently." I don't tell him about our ramshackle house in Pittsburgh, ashtrays on tables, whiskey bottles with no caps. I don't tell him about what happened with Hal, or later with Eli. I don't tell him any of that because none of it will help me. "Alex says you're a ski racer," I say.

His whole face brightens. Bingo. He can't help himself. I'm free.

"I used to race, yes. I was kind of a big deal, to be honest, on the national team, but I blew out my knee at twenty-four, so I had to quit competing. It is what it is."

"Oh." I try to sound disappointed for him.

"It's okay, it all worked out. I took four years of school in Cali for marketing and resort management. The hill here is just starting to explode, and I'm the face of all the advertisements. It's more modeling than it is me running Powderkeg, but it's pretty cool, all the same. Right now it's my off-season, but I'm on billboards all over Colorado."

"Wow," I say because I think he wants me to be impressed. I'm tempted to ask if Alex skis, but my stomach growls and I shift in my seat. He must have heard it, too, because he opens the fridge to reveal rows of marked Tupperware and a fully stacked vegetable drawer. There's soy milk in the side compartment. No ketchup. No beer.

"Can I make you some breakfast?" Chase asks. "Something healthy?" He looks down at my belly, which I don't like. I instinctively rest my hand on the small bump there.

"Do you mean toast?"

"No."

"An omelet would be great. Lots of cheese, please. Thank you."

Chase grabs eggs and what appears to be ham, juggling both to the countertop. "So Alex said you guys grew up on a farm. That must have been pretty great. A farm in Horizon, North Dakota." He sighs as if relaxing, but I know what's coming. "Why did you leave?"

He's persistent. *Careful, Ruth.* He really doesn't know the basics of what went down. Or perhaps he *does* know, and this is a test. Maybe he wants to feel powerful, to make me say it. He's hoping my face will crease or go pale. That I'll act grief-stricken and traumatized. Is that what he wants? Is that what *she* wants? Well, I'm not playing that game: I've played it my whole life.

"There was a problem," I say. "Something happened. It was better for everyone that I leave." It was better for everyone except me.

"A problem," he says. He slices ham with a ridiculously sharp knife, shaking his head as he does so. "You and your sister have something in common, I see. Not big on sharing details from the past. I wonder why that is."

I blink and say nothing. When the omelet arrives, it tastes of cloth, and Chase isn't generous with the salt. I eat silently, and as soon as I'm chewing the last bite, he whips the plate away.

"Did Alex and you decide if I could stay here?" I ask as he stashes the plate in the dishwasher.

"You need to talk to your sister." He won't look me in the eye. "That's her department."

"Her department, but your apartment. Interesting." I cough into my hand. "I think I'll take a shower . . . if that's okay."

He sweeps one hand in front of him, a magnanimous gesture although his expression doesn't match it. "Knock yourself out."

I slide off the stool, grab my bag from the hook by the front door, then creep to the bathroom, where I kneel, unpacking everything I brought with me onto the mat. A passport, outdated. A toothbrush, fuzzed with lint from the bottom of the bag. I forgot toothpaste anyway. My purse, old-fashioned. It used to be Mom's. Eli's Folgers coffee tin that I've wrapped shut with Scotch tape. A weathered old clothespin, the wood smooth as silk with R-A-W scratched into the side, that I held all the way here on the bus. And the photo, taken on the farm the summer before everything went wrong. I'm thirteen in this picture, so Alex must be eight. Pim, my brother, he's four. It's the summer when we were all still smiling.

I stow everything but the toothbrush and the purse back into my bag and jam it into the cupboard under the sink. She won't find it. She's so repulsed by me she would probably never touch my bag anyhow. Then I shower and dress in the same clothes I wore yesterday.

In the living room, Chase is sitting on the couch reading a magazine about fit people.

"I'm going to go check out the town," I say as I hover by the front door.

He looks up but only for a second.

"Bye," he says. "Maybe later we can have another chat."

That's definitely not happening. I nod and head straight out of the door.

ALEX

I texted Sully because I needed to talk. Yesterday was a brutal day, followed by a shocking night. First, Buster. Then my sister appearing back in my life out of nowhere. After I finally drifted off to sleep, leaving Ruth in the living room, I had a nightmare about the Floyd baby, that little baby boy. He was older in the dream but still in his bulging dirty diaper. In his hand was that little blue car, and in the distance a figure beckoned him toward a ravine. I couldn't stop him from going to the stranger. And the worst part—the part that woke me with a jolt in the darkness—was that the figure in the distance was Ruth.

Sully's already at the Oven when I get there, travel coffee mug full, leaning over a book. He's never on his phone, only looks at it if it actually rings or beeps. I like that about him. The books he reads are tomes, too, great, celebrated works by writers I'd never attempt. French ones, sometimes Russian.

I buy a cup of tea and join him at the table. He closes his book, and I get that comfortable surge that seems to emanate only from him.

"How are you?" Sully watches me sit down, moves my mug while I settle so I won't bump it. "Your text message sounded urgent."

"Sorry about that."

"No, it's fine. It's just . . . what's going on?"

"It's work stuff," I say, and there's a second where he seems disappointed.

He crosses his arms, hooks each fist into an armpit. "Come on, then. Do your worst."

I exhale. What is it about Sully that's so disarming? He knows who he is, maybe, but never leads with an ego. Reliable face. Drives an old truck with one battered Van Morrison CD in it that he plays on a constant loop. Loves his dog more than most humans love each other.

"I went out to an intake yesterday with Minerva."

He nods once, like I almost don't need to say anything else.

"It was grim, Sully. Minerva kept saying it was an innocuous house call." I describe the filth, the plain-as-day neglect, and Sully listens, sipping unhurriedly. He knows this world, isn't thrown by it. He grew up here, and he's been a cop for ten years; I could probably tell him a kid was living in a box of snakes and he'd ask how many. That's why I'm here with Sully: I can speak in shorthand in a way I can't with Chase. He gets it.

"So did you remove the child? What was the intake?"

"No, we didn't, because Minerva's on her usual mission to keep families together whatever the cost. Family Services doesn't focus on what the child actually needs. It's like there are sharks in the water and we go, hey, *Let's see if the kid can swim to shore! He might make it!* But Sully, we know the truth." I swallow. "A lot don't make it." Dizziness sweeps through my head, and I pitch forward for a second. Sully doesn't notice.

"So your team's still big on the bloodline thing?"

I met Sully in a liaison meeting a year ago, where unexpectedly I ranted to a roomful of social workers and police officers about the failings of the current protection system. Sully sipped calmly through that speech, too, but after the meeting he asked me out for a fresh coffee. *You're just what we need,* he said. *But be careful you don't burn out too quickly. Text me whenever you need to talk.* And then it kind of became a weekly thing. A couple of times a week, maybe, at the most. But it's not like we've set it in stone. And he knows about Chase. This is purely a professional relationship. But I find I do look forward to seeing him. More and more. I need him. I really do.

"Morris leans toward advocating for family, yes." I stare down at the table. "But this baby doesn't stand a chance if we don't remove him." The image of a tanned boy with a toy truck in his hand pops into my mind again, but it's morphed a bit. It's not Buster anymore. He's not holding the blue car but something else: a clothespin. I shake my head, trying to rid myself of the image, of the memory.

"Minerva's a soft touch," Sully says. "She doesn't always make the right call, in my opinion. Then I have to deal with the consequences on the job. And they aren't always pretty."

"Exactly! So we have to do something. Better sooner than later." I feel relief to hear him talk like this. He understands. He knows I'm not overreacting. "God, Sully, it's good to see you."

"You too." He looks down at the table, picks at a gnarl in the wood.

"You know who else would like to see you?" I say. "Minerva. She wants your number."

His eyes and mouth widen like I'm suggesting he eat chalk. "Oh my God. Are you serious?"

"I haven't given it to her."

He shakes his head. "Good." He leans forward an inch farther, puts an elbow on the table. "I'm very selective about who can reach me, Alex. You'd be breaking protocol if you passed it on."

"Understood," I say, blushing, because there's a compliment in there for me, and we both know it.

"And about that kid . . ."

"The little boy. Beautiful little boy."

Sully sighs. He knows I'm too involved, but he doesn't press me. "Trust your instincts. Remember that case a month ago? You were right about those parents. If you feel Minerva's approaching it ineffectively or too laxly, take it to Morris. He gets what you do. You're his best social worker."

I try to protest, but he keeps talking.

"No, you are. He'd listen. Just . . . document everything. Cover yourself. We protect the ones we can, right? Breathe new life into them? But some kids suffocate, no matter what we do."

Suffocate. The truth of this hits me right in the throat, and for a moment, it's like I can't breathe.

"Okay?" he says, and he lays his palm flat next to mine, a comforting gesture. I wish he were actually touching me. I feel a surge of warmth.

"Thanks, Sully. I'll talk to Morris." I take a short sip of tea. "It's hard to explain this stuff to anyone else. At work, they just pull out the official rulebook and tell me to back away, stay neutral, do less. But somebody has to do something. Somebody has to."

"It's an important job, helping those kids. I'm right with you. And don't second-guess how good you are at it. The trick is to make sure your head's above water so you can keep going—one appalling situation at a time."

I nod.

"And as for trying to explain your work, I wouldn't even try," he says. "We're a different breed, you and I. We're ghost dogs at the gates. Most people in Moses River will never have the first clue about what we're guarding and why."

We sit silently for a few seconds. His hand is still near mine. Capable hands, curved and vital.

"What's your book about?" I ask.

"Oh, this old thing?" He retrieves and holds up a copy of *Far from the Madding Crowd*. "It's about two people who should be together but aren't."

I laugh because it's his favorite joke to summarize books in one sentence. *It's a story of two people who should be together but aren't. It's a tale of loss and loneliness. It's about a stranger who comes to town.* He puts the novel away again and watches me.

"What else is bothering you?" he asks.

The thing about Sully is he's always switched on, reading people. He's the slightly scruffy, affable guy you accidentally tell everything to at a dinner party, thinking he can't really be listening. But he is. He knows you. Deeply.

I rotate my cup in a slow circle. "Yesterday was a bad night. My big sister showed up at my door."

Now he really looks surprised. "You have a sister? How has this never come up before?"

"Probably because I haven't seen her for ten years. Her name's Ruth. To be honest, I thought she might be dead."

"Holy shit, Alex. No wonder you look . . ."

He pauses.

"That bad?" I ask.

"No, no. It's just that you look . . . I don't know. Haunted."

And I thought I was doing such a good job of hiding it.

He studies me closely. "You are not okay."

"No. Of course I'm not." I take another shuddering breath. "It's complicated."

"I can see that."

"I mean, she's my sister. But wherever she goes, she's kamikaze. You know? I don't understand what she's doing here."

"Maybe she missed you? You are quite . . . missable."

Inside, somewhere deep down, I smile at that, but I'm careful not to show it on my face. "Oh, it's not that," I mumble. My skin feels hot. "I mean, I'm not hard to find. Did she *not* miss me for all the other years she didn't bother to get in touch?"

"Right," he says, which really means *go on*.

"She's good at the sleight of hand. You know people like her, Sully. You've arrested lots of them. She'll show you *this*"—I wave one palm—"while she takes away *that*. She's up to something. I can feel it."

"Huh," he says. "Okay."

Why is he tilting his head like that?

"So you're having a hard time trusting why she's here now, is that it? You think she's come to hurt you."

I bite my lip hard, because he's put exact words to my fear.

He shifts away, leaning back into his seat. "Sorry, I probably shouldn't have said that."

"No, no, you're not *wrong*." My voice carries in the overly warm bakery. I pause, check my volume. "She knew me when I was barely formed. And she did hurt me, Sully. She hurt me in ways that are unforgivable. And yet, here she is again. I didn't say no. I didn't tell her to go away. I can't."

He nods, his eyes sad. "Sure," he says. "She's your sister."

"Exactly." I know very little of this man's private life, of his family, other than he's single and lives alone. Minerva told me that much. She also once said that he has a brother in town, although I've no idea how she knows that, and I've yet to meet him. Sully protects his privacy, but his empathy feels genuine. I can tell he's had his own struggles, too.

"Family dynamics are rough," he says. "You looked up to your sister, and now you're having to look down."

Did I look up to her? Was there a time? Something comes back to me then. First grade. I got in a fight with Grover Teague at recess and the school called my mother. In the principal's office Mom's hands worried over each other. She had such sturdy hands, scuffed around the nail beds from all the farmwork. *Why can't you be more like Ruth?* she said when she heard what I'd done. The principal sighed in agreement. Her shirt was buttoned all the way to the throat. In her hand was a viciously sharpened pencil. *It always amazes me, Mrs. Van Ness. Same gene pool, entirely different child. You might as well have bought her in a shop.* In my head, I imagined her pitching forward and impaling herself on the sharp tip of her pencil. But that didn't happen. It took years for me to understand how power works—how to build it, how to wield it. Only when I grew did I understand the long game.

Sully clears his throat. "Earth to Alex? Did you hear me?"

It frightens me that I did not. "Sorry," I say, managing a light laugh. "You'd think I'd be a better listener."

"I was saying that in sibling relationships there's always a jostle for power. There's a hierarchy, but I don't think it's always set by age. I have a twin brother who's four minutes younger than me, but he still tries to boss me around." He smiles. "Doesn't mean I let him."

I want to meet him, I think, but I stop myself. Instead, what I say next shocks. "When I was fifteen, I helped Ruth get an abortion." I blurt it out, just like that.

"Whoa." He's stunned, but only for a second.

"Sorry. God. Sorry. You were telling me about your twin brother. I swerved off course."

"No, no. The less I say about him the better. I'll ruin my own day. So, your sister, you helped her do that? When you were so young?" His eyes are soft at the edges.

"She wasn't in a good place—she'd gotten into drugs. I convinced her that she couldn't have the baby. It wouldn't be safe. We told our parents that we were going into town for a milkshake. I directed her to the clinic. She played music the whole ride and didn't speak to me."

"You were fifteen?" He moves his travel mug to the side of the table.

I just keep talking. "Outside were all these women with posters on sticks with horrible photos on them and banners about being a murderer. We had to push through them to get to the front door. She walked in pregnant and walked out not, and then we got in the truck and drove home." I glance up at him. "I've never told anyone this before."

He looks like he wants to climb over the table, but if there's more he wants to ask, he has the good sense not to. It's amazing that he knows exactly the pace I need.

Behind us at the bakery door, the bell sounds and someone comes in, but neither of us breaks eye contact.

"How does Chase feel about your sister's arrival?" He pauses slightly before saying Chase's name.

Oh, for God's sake, Alex, don't start looking for subtext.

"Chase has learned not to ask questions."

"You mean you taught him?"

He smiles, and so do I. We both know that Chase is easygoing, and I can be headstrong—but relationships are all about balance. It's one of the reasons I chose him.

"So why is Ruth really here? What does she want?"

"My 'help,' apparently," I say. It comes out fierce and sharp. "She's pregnant. Again."

When he reaches across the table this time, he places his hand on mine. His skin is warm, electric. It feels like he's transferring energy into me, an infusion of love and strength. He goes to speak, but as he does so, his eyes dart up to someone standing behind me.

I turn.

Of course. I should have known.

It's Ruth.

RUTH

"Hey, sis," I say, setting my coffee on the table.

"What are you doing here?" she asks.

There's that face again, that little girl not coping.

I look from the man she's with, then back to her. "I'm checking out the town. Spied you through the window." He's wearing a soft gray T-shirt and is leaner than Chase, although still strong-looking. Brownish-blondish hair, cropped close to his head and sticking up in places like he only just ran a flat palm over it before leaving his house. "You're not Chase," I say to him.

"No. Not even a little bit." Whoever this man is, his face stays friendly and open. He lets go of Alex's hand, sits back and stretches.

"Sully, this is my sister, Ruth," Alex says to him. "Ruth, this is Sully."

"Hi." He reaches out for a handshake that doesn't grip or linger. His hands feel like he's good at camping, like he could build a fire or a shelter.

"That your dog on there?" I point to the picture of a grizzled old blue heeler on his coffee mug. He must have got it made at a mall.

"That's Gravy. She's fourteen."

"Gravy?" I say. "She isn't brown."

"I just like the word."

"Is that my jacket?" Alex asks.

I needed something to wear, and I'd seen it on a hook by the door. "I'm just borrowing it."

There's a look that passes between Alex and Sully.

"I should get going." Sully spins on the bench, lifts his leg over to stand. He's not that tall, but his boots are police issue. So Alex is hanging out with a cop. "Here, you can have my seat." He waits while I sit, checking his pockets for keys and picking up a battered novel from where he's stashed it on the seat. "Text me later, Alex." He puts one hand on my shoulder as he moves off. "Really good to meet you, Ruth. Bye, Alex."

Then he's gone, taking his jean jacket and his phone, his novel and his Gravy mug with him. But something of Sully hangs in the air over Alex's head long after the jingly bell at the door has gone quiet.

"What are you doing?" she asks again, once he's out the door.

"What do you mean? I'm having a coffee." I place my cup on the table. "Is that a crime?"

She doesn't answer, just kind of shrugs. Neither of us says a word for a long minute.

Finally I say, "I remember a time when you weren't so keen on cops."

She doesn't reply, just grabs her phone from a pocket and busies herself with the screen.

"He seems nice, though," I say.

"Okay, let's get a few things straight." She sets the phone onto the table with enough force to squash a bug. "First off, it's not me who's had a lifetime of skirmishes with the law. So let's just skip to the chase."

"Chase?" I say. "That's Freudian." I don't know why I enjoy watching her struggle like this. Maybe it's just a leftover from childhood. She was always so easy to incense. Before, I mean. When it wasn't so risky, so loaded.

"We need to talk about your plan. What are you here for? How long are you staying?"

"Not sure how long I'm staying." Another measured pause.

"How far along are you? You're barely showing."

"Five months. Something like that. What? I'm tall. I hide it well."

She rolls her eyes like it's not the only thing I'm hiding, and I resent the implication.

"Chase and I had a good chat this morning over breakfast," I say.

She shifts on the bench as if it's heating up underneath her. "You had a chat? About what exactly?"

"This and that. One thing he did say, though, is that if I needed to stay a little longer, he was okay with it." It's a trick I learned a long time ago: Play one parent against the other. So rarely do they actually have time to compare notes.

There's a moment where she scrunches her eyes and rubs them like she used to when she was losing at Monopoly. "What else did Chase decide?"

"Nothing else." My coffee is too sour, and I search around for sugar. "You don't tell him much, you know."

"I tell him plenty."

"He wanted to know more about you. About your past."

Energy crackles from every part of her—the same fire—but she is so much more in control of it than she used to be.

"You said you needed help last night. With what?" Her teeth sound tight, as if she's clamped them with wire.

"Everything." I lean in. This is it. The defining moment. "I'm in trouble, Alex. I mean it. I'm in danger."

"You're having a baby in a few short months, you mean. And you have no money."

"It's more than that. I left in a hurry. I had to. I didn't bring much with—"

"Why?" Her eyes are a sea storm gathering. "Why did you leave in such a hurry? What are you on the run from this time?"

My fingertips drift to my temple, where I smooth my hair forward to cover my bruise. How deftly I thought I was stealing away from that house, how clever I thought I'd been. But Eli knew everything, predicted my every move, and he was waiting for me. He cared more about money than he did about me. I'd misjudged my importance all over again. Old habits die hard.

"Look, I took a bit of a wrong turn. I did something hasty—I'll admit it—and it might not have been the smartest thing, and now I'm—"

"Does Hal know you're here?" She slams down that sentence so hard that it clangs in my ears. She's stuck on the Hal thing again, looping around and around in her head that he drank too much beer when he was meant to be working, that he threw rocks at stray dogs. Never mind all the other things she constructed in her head. That was ten years ago, and she's still talking about it like it was yesterday! The truth is that Hal was never only one thing. Nobody ever is.

"No, I told you. I left him a long time ago."

"How did you find me?"

"Facebook." I feel tired. I want to lie down.

"I sent you messages years ago," she says, pointing an accusatory finger in my face to punctuate her outrage. "To let you know when Mom died. And the same with Dad. And you didn't respond. Now you show up?"

I shrug, fighting the urge to put my forehead on the table. I wasn't in the right place then to respond to her messages. What could I have done for her or anyone?

"Do you know what they died of, Ruth? Our parents?" Her eyes sear right through me. "Pain and fucking misery."

What does she expect me to say? I never meant to hurt our parents. Did *she*?

"But this is our chance to have a fresh start, to right the past," I begin. "And I think Mom and Dad would be happy to know we're speaking again. Especially Mom. She'd want this." I smooth one hand over my belly. "You know she always loved it when we helped each other."

Alex picks at a crumb of old muffin on the table. "How are *you* helping me?" she mutters, but my mention of Mom has made her soften.

I sit quietly, let the pathway widen.

"If you stay, there are rules," she says slowly.

Bingo. I'm in. "Okay."

"I'm serious, Ruth. You can't break them."

"Okay," I repeat. "Whatever you say, Alex. I don't want to be any trouble."

"Number one, you don't do anything that can harm your baby. Not one thing. You take responsibility. Agree? You will have this baby. We'll figure out the next steps from there. Do you get that? No drugs, no alcohol. Nothing."

I balk, but I don't show it. "I want this baby, Alex."

"Do you?"

"Yes, of course. I already told you it feels like a second chance, you know, a way to have a family of my own that doesn't—"

"Number two," she plows on, "you don't tell Hal Nightingale where you are."

How little she understands. I nod, a contrite agreement.

"And three." She leans forward on her elbows. "You don't talk about the past. Not with me. And more important, not with Chase. Ever."

I blink at her. What does she mean? I'm not to talk about *anything* from before? Surely she can't mean all of our past.

"The life we had is a tunnel that caved in a long time ago, Ruth, and I've no interest in digging it out."

"But—"

"You left. You left me with all of it."

"Alex, what I did—"

"You can show up out of the blue, waltz into my house, guilt-trip me with your pregnancy, and insinuate yourself into my life, but there's no way you're destroying it. Never again."

"Me? Destroy *your* life?" I can't believe her gall.

"Yes, you." She stands over me, gathering her things, yanking her satchel strap over top of her. "You, you, you. This might be a new town for you, Ruth, but I know you. I know how you operate. We're adults now. Do you know the meaning of that word? You say nothing to Chase. Nothing. Now I have to go to work. I'll be home at the loft by four thirty. Break any of the rules and you're done."

Once she's walked away from me and the door's banged shut, there's a dreadful silence in the bakery. The woman behind the counter stares at me. Then suddenly there's a collective reclattering of spoons, a general and forced murmur. I look around, my stomach churning, but I know it's not morning sickness this time. Every single person in the room has heard what Alex just said.

ALEX

It's a short walk from the bakery to my work after lunch break, but I have to hustle: as much as I've dealt with the Ruth problem for now, she's also made me late. I hurry into the elevator and press the faded button for the third floor.

As the elevator rises, clanking, I stare at the screen of my cell phone. No word from Chase, so whatever Ruth told him over breakfast can't have been too disastrous. But Morris has texted me. That's unusual. Normally he just catches me on the fly. I tap on his name and the sentence appears: Can you come straight to my office?

What has happened?

The elevator jolts, and the doors open for me, presenting with zero flourish the corridor to Family Services that I walk down every day, its walls, roof, and carpet entirely devoid of color. It's like they're trying to make the place as depressing as the work itself. The corridor is lit with strip lights that buzz as I pass underneath them, and there are cameras in murky semicircular globes, like squid eyes, suctioned to the roof. Family Services is the fourth of the cloned brown doors; once inside the office, though, it's a barrage of rainbow stripes. It's like walking into an explosion in a candy factory. There are pictures drawn by children in care on every wall, as if pinning up their work will surely slow the pace at which they replicate. I buzz myself in through the security panel.

"Is Morris here?" I ask the new receptionist.

"In his office, I think. He was looking for you about ten minutes ago. Can you tell him he forgot his toast again? He made it at seven a.m."

Morris is the team leader, British, imported here from London when he married an American. We can't always decipher him. He's a stout man in his late fifties, divorced now, gappy in the front teeth. He makes toast every morning, often leaving it to grow rock-hard in the toaster.

"Has anything gone wrong while I was out?" I ask, and the reception-ist looks at me like the question's too vast to consider. "Never mind." I head down the long corridor to my left. Social workers' offices splay off to each side, little windowless cubicles, like hutches. Morris turns when I knock on the open door of his office.

"Brilliant," he says. "You're back. Good lunch?" He pulls out a blue-cushioned chair for me to sit on. Underneath is a pair of running shoes from the eighties, cracked along the sides, and a tangerine that looks petrified.

"Have a seat," he says. The walls of his office are covered in cards, thank-you notes, and photos of himself with his arms around children. If there's a gap of more than four inches, he's covered the space with an inspirational quote or a poster with something caring on it. *Nobody can hurt me without my permission*, reads one of his latest additions. He sees I'm reading it.

"That's Mahatma Gandhi." He nods, spinning his black office chair to face me. "He was amazing."

"Wrong, though."

"Pardon?"

"Nothing. What's up? You needed to see me?"

"Right." He clasps his hands together as if in prayer. "We're in a bit of a pickle."

My first thought is of Buster. If something's happened to him, I'm going to pull Minerva's LEGO hair out by the fistful.

"Look, Alex, here's what I need to say first: You're my best worker. Hands down. The most energized one, and don't think I haven't noticed." His teeth shine, but there's something wrong. He's never normally this effusive. "Every single day, you strap on your boots and you wade on out into the shit. It's admirable, to be honest."

"You do it," I mumble, as I pull my hair forward and suck at one strand. "We all do."

"No, no, some of us retreat to the paperwork." He smiles sadly. "You never do. You've never even gone on stress leave. Do you know how rare that is? Where would we be without people like you?"

"It sounds like there's a but."

"But as much as I trust your instincts, I think that if you undermine Minerva's work, you're going to create a hostile working environment."

I jerk back as if I've been slapped. "Undermine Minerva's work? What are you talking about?"

"I'm afraid she's put in a complaint. Not an official one at this point. But one that I have to confront nonetheless. As team leader, it's my job to—"

"She was in here complaining about me? *Why?* Because I called her out on the Buster Floyd case? That's it, isn't it? Jesus, Morris, we left that child in disgusting circumstances. I'm trying to protect him. I thought that was what we do here."

He shifts in his chair. "It is. And we are . . . all . . . trying—"

"Are we? Minerva's wait-and-see policy on protection is dangerous, Morris. I'm right about this one."

"I don't know the Floyd case." He strokes his tie, a sign that he's finding the conversation stressful. "There isn't a previous Family Services file on them—I checked—so all I've seen are Minerva's notes. What I would say, though, is that when you feel at odds with a colleague, Alex, you have to try to find—"

"What did she say? What *exactly* did she say about me?" I want to go down the corridor and set fire to her office. She'll be in there right now, playing pop music and eating bridge mix.

"I think she found your demeanor adversarial. Your tone aggressive. That's a loose précis."

"This is ridiculous. Has she even opened a Family Services file on the Floyds now?"

"There's an open file so we can offer support services. There's no active *investigation* into the Floyd couple. Just to be clear. And Minerva is the lead on the case." His skin has blotched pink around his collar.

It's impossible to do my job if my coworkers pull while I push. I feel sick, like the room is spinning, and somewhere in my mind, I see that little boy again. Except, it's not him. It's a different boy. No. I take a deep breath and bring myself back to reality and the problem in front of me. What am I supposed to do? I can't work with Minerva, but I can't ask to be taken off the case.

"I wasn't being aggressive toward Minerva," I say. "I was simply pointing out that she should be more so herself."

"Righty-ho." Another tie sweep. "Listen, why don't you make some notes and send me an email?"

A jaded laugh escapes me. It's his go-to, the email request. It gets him out of all confrontation while providing him with a handy paper trail. Nobody says what they mean when they know they're being recorded.

"You know how it works," he says, then waits for me to speak. I don't. I won't. "Okay, so is that everything? Can we agree that you'll approach your coworker with a little more decorum and respect for her authority?"

I wonder if he can see the muscle in my jawline tweaking.

"She might have a different approach to yours, Alex, but it's not without merit. Hmm?"

I have to play the long game, not lose my temper. I need time to think. "I'll try harder to incorporate her ideas," I mumble. "But to be clear, I'm in it for the kids, Morris. I always have been. And I'm worried about that boy."

"I know that. I know. We're all working from a place of good intention. Best to remember that. But sometimes, slow and steady wins the race, right?"

He nods like the problem is solved. I leave his office and head to mine, where the walls are uncluttered. All I have is one poster by my desk: the Hulk smashing things. I admire his approach to adversity. I try firing up my laptop, but my hands are shaky on the keyboard. Why am I the only one willing to go the extra mile for a child in danger? I wrap a curl of my hair around my forefinger, chew on the end of it. With an open Family Services file, the entire history of the Floyds becomes more available. Confidentiality laws can be circumvented by a legal exchange of information between social workers, police departments, health administrators. Minerva might have told Morris that there's no need for an active investigation into Frank and Evelyn, and he might not have sanctioned one, but didn't he also say that as workers we all have our own approach? I grab my bag and head back toward reception, passing Minerva in the hallway.

"Oh, hi," she says, resting a flat palm on my forearm. "Listen, I hope you don't mind that I spoke with Morris about the Buster case. I just feel that as a team, we need to work together more. Be more like glue."

You're on *glue,* I want to tell her, but I manage not to.

"No problem." I move away. "We're all doing our best." *Some bests are better than others.*

"Where are you going now?" she asks.

"I'm meeting Sully." It's not true, of course, but it'll sting, and I know it. I exit through the security door and walk fast to the elevators.

Outside, the temperature has dropped and glacial air hits me as I head across town. I pass the police department, but I can't go in there. I've just spent half an hour telling Sully how frustrating it is that there's no Floyd investigation. He told me to record my concerns and trust my boss; it's not advice I'm taking. I carry on past the station. From a block away, the Moses River Health building sags in its own gray drabness, a metaphor in brick, heaving under the sadness it contains. I head straight in and take the stairs to the second floor, to the offices of Mental Health and Addictions.

The reception area is empty, but on every wall are signs about noise, about cell phones, about consideration of others' sanctity. A basket of stuffed toys sits brimming in the corner. I wonder how many kids have to spend unexplained hours in the waiting room. Next to the stuffed animals is a plastic xylophone with a bright red hammer. That's asking for trouble. A poster of a skeletal tree growing against a backdrop of uplifting green is pinned to the front of the main desk. *Pain is real,* the slogan reads, *but so is hope.* The bottom of the poster has been ripped entirely in half, but someone's attempted to put it back together again with Scotch tape. As I approach the desk, the woman behind it takes a deep, melancholy breath. She's about sixty, clearly eking out the last of her union-required shifts before she can escape into a pension.

"Can I help you?" she says.

"Hi, my name's Alex Van Ness." I reach into my bag and pull out my social worker ID, hoping to prove that I'm privy to any kind of information I require. "I'm with Family Services. We're following up on an active case, and I need the mental-health records of two of your clients."

She stares at me through the smeared lenses of her glasses. "If you want information, there's a legal process. You can't just walk in here and take files."

"I realize that. And I'll get all the legal paperwork. I was just passing by your office, though, and I thought I'd get a jump on things."

She snorts, a wet noise. "Let me see if we even have the records. What are the names?"

"Frank and Evelyn Floyd."

One finger at a time, she pushes buttons on her computer keyboard. I don't believe the *Mental Health: Let's Talk* badge she's been made to wear on her linty sweater. She's the last person I'd ever want to talk to.

"Have you got the clients' signed consent?" she asks.

"No, not yet. But we're planning to run a psych assessment. Parental capacity. Court-ordered. So we won't need their consent." There's no way I'll get a psych assessment past Morris: they cost thousands of dollars. "So can I get a quick look at the files? You know, just to get the lay of the land?"

"Not. Even. A maybe." She presses one button per word, tutting.

"Listen, there's a child in danger. It's an active Family Services file . . ." It's hard to keep my voice even, to avoid betraying my frustration at this lump, this human barrier.

"I don't care if it's an active bomb, dear. You're not touching it."

Beneath the level of the desk, I grip my own thumb and squeeze.

She hits one more button, almost with flourish, and then sits back. "The records are available. Get your paperwork organized, and then you can have them."

"Are there separate files on the Floyds? Surely you can tell me that much." Perhaps one Floyd is in worse shape than the other. I might as well hone my approach.

She exhales heavily, vacillating. Will she throw me a tidbit? She really shouldn't.

"If I'm coming back with a court order, I need to know what I'm asking for."

Another long, irritable sigh before she surrenders. "The husband's file was closed a while ago."

"Oh? And the wife's?" She watches me pick up my ID card carefully. I don't make eye contact.

"We had to reopen hers. Hers was active until about ten months ago."

About ten months ago? I try hard to keep my expression neutral.

"Thanks a lot," I say, turning. "I'll get back to you with paperwork as soon as possible."

"You do that," she calls after me.

I leave, pulling the door tight behind me. Outside, the sky's brightened and the wind has dropped. I sit down on a low wall beside a fire hydrant to catch my breath and calm down. What I've just done is, I suppose, illegal. It could get me in trouble, but already I've stumbled upon a fact that would affect any judgment of Evelyn's capacity to parent. She's been struggling much more recently than Minerva made out. My guess? With drugs. Once an addict . . . And did Minerva lie about that on purpose to make herself look good? Or does she really not know? Either way, I'm onto something now. If I can persuade Morris there's more at play here, I might find real ways to help Buster.

I reach for the cell phone in my pocket. It's not long before Sully picks up.

"Hey," he says. "Do you need another coffee already? You must be missing me."

"No, it's not . . . I mean, I am, but it's not that." I laugh a little, as if I'm not wound up. *I can do this. I'm doing the right thing. I can have a positive impact with this case.* "Sully, I need your help on something. It's about the family I was telling you about earlier."

"Anything," he says, and I hear him close a door, muffling out all the surrounding sound. "You know that."

"I just need you to put the Floyd names into your system. See if anything comes up."

"Morris has opened an investigation on them? Alex?"

"He will. If I bring him new info. Please, Sully, can you just run their names?"

Sully pauses. "Who are they?" I tell him the full names and hear him typing on his keyboard, and then he sighs down the line. "Okay, none of this is public record so don't throw me under the bus here. Not that you ever have before, but I'm just saying. There are old drug charges—quite a few of them. And, okay, there's something else."

My stomach clenches. I'm seconds away from finding out I was right, but I know I won't feel triumph.

"There was a death in the home," he says. "About three years ago. Police attended. It looks like the Floyds had another kid, just a little guy. He died in their care."

There's a long gap where neither of us say anything. White noise fizzes in my head like static. *How the hell did Family Services not know about this?* But we'd had no involvement with the Floyds prior to Buster. We hadn't—*but Minerva had.*

"Minerva hid this!" I say. "Oh my God, she was their Addictions worker—she must have known!"

"She's a piece of work. I'll get a hold of the coroner's report. You keep pushing on your end."

We hang up, and I rest one hand on the fire hydrant as it glints in the sun. Poor Buster. Time and again, it's an uphill battle to get a child any proper protection. First Ruth shows up pregnant. And now this. My stomach twists. I can't let another child down. This can't happen again. I won't let it.

RUTH

When I get back to the loft after lunchtime, Chase is watching a Roller-blading show on TV. He's sprawled on the couch in his shorts and a T-shirt with a beanie pulled far back on his forehead. I guess when he called it an off-season, he wasn't kidding. We should all be models, get paid shitloads, sit around all day.

"Hey," he says warily. "You're back."

I hover by the front door. "I met with Alex. She said that it's fine for me to stay."

His face turns into a big question mark. "You went to her work?"

"No, I saw her at the coffee shop downtown. She was having coffee with . . . she was on her way back to the office." I know enough to save some details for when I might need them.

"Well, that's good." He moves to allow me a space on the couch.

I venture forward and sit on the farthest cushion from him, next to my now military-folded bedding from last night.

"So. You don't mind if I stay?" I ask him.

He keeps his eyes on the television. "Whatever Alex wants is fine with me."

We watch the Rollerbladers in silence for a minute. It seems to be some kind of race, four athletes zooming down a ramp together, flying over huge jumps, mostly elbowing one another out of the way.

"Why don't they go one at a time?" I ask.

"Because they wouldn't crash as much." Chase smiles a little. "It's television."

It seems gladiatorial—it has that same kind of baying crowd—and my attention wanders. To the left of the huge television is a stacked bookshelf, but from where I'm sitting none of the books look like Alex's. She read fantasy as a kid and these titles are all Bear Grylls's books on things like how to survive in Patagonia without a tarp. I glance to my right at the golden-boy smoothness of Chase's skin. He doesn't look like a guy who's spent much time out in the cold without top-of-the-range gear. If he's roughly Alex's age, works intermittently but can afford this loft, my guess is he's survived under the shelter of his parents' steady handouts.

"Did you play sports as a kid?" he asks.

"Yes," I lie.

"Did Alex?"

I could fill him in on how wiry she was, how she made it a mission to beat all the boys in her grade on sports day, and how most years she managed it. Instead, I bunch my mouth and say, "Not much." Only an hour's gone by since I promised I wouldn't mention the past. Did she mean her past or mine? Did she mean everything or just the secrets? Maybe it's all the same anyhow. It might be impossible to separate one thing from the other. But nobody lives or thinks only in the present tense. Not Alex. Not me. If Chase is going to be around a lot, I'll have to be on my guard.

"Where did you meet my sister?" I ask.

He sits up straighter, smiling wide. "In the grocery store two years ago. I helped her get shortbread from the top shelf."

Shortbread. My mother's favorite.

"She had one thing in her shopping basket. Do you know what it was?"

"A chocolate bar?"

"Yes! How did you know that?" He turns the volume down on the TV. "It was a Kit Kat. Nothing else. Not a vegetable to be found."

"She always loved junk food. My mom hid cookies in the highest kitchen cupboard, but Alex would just climb for them."

I bite my lip. It's impossible. The past spills out even when I'm trying to avoid it. I have to get this back on track.

"She gave me her number in the store," Chase says. "I'd left my cell in the car, so Iwrote it on a banana with a pen I found in the bulk food section. I called her that same night. And I never did eat the banana."

Keen, I think. *And way, way out of his depth.* My sister's more guarded than that. The Alex I know would never give anything away to anyone until she's sure of them. She's created a simplified version of herself for Chase, and she's lived it for the whole time she's been here with him.

"We're happy in Moses River," he says, as if he can hear the inside of my head.

"Okay."

"Are *you*? Are you happy?"

What the hell kind of question is that? When I don't answer right away, he turns back to the television. We say nothing as the Rollerblade show cuts to commercial, and he gets up and goes to the fridge for a drink. He doesn't offer me one, and I stay tensely on the couch.

I don't know if I can do this. It's not just that Alex's strict parameters are closing in on me. It's not that I'm impetuous, that I can't keep secrets. The real problem I have—the very real fear—is everything I left behind me in Pittsburgh. And everything I brought with me here. I was only trying to choose wisely, do the right thing, but I failed again. Apparently it's my specialty. All I can do now is hope that I've covered my tracks, that Eli will never find me. If he finds Chase's front door and knocks on it, it'll be like opening the door to a flash flood.

I place a hand on my abdomen. I will do everything to keep this baby safe. Alex has to know that. My story's not as simple as she's made hers out to be, but I'm not on drugs and haven't been for a long time. If I'm a thief, I only took what was owed to me, nothing more. I didn't even take it for me but for this baby. I had nothing. I did what I felt was the smart thing, but it always goes this way: Do something good and the universe twists it, debases it, turns it into something despicable. And by then it's too late to go back. It happened in Pittsburgh, and it happened in Horizon. Even now, the town of my childhood is right here, nipping at my heels. Alex might feel she can outrun her past by refusing to talk about it, but mine's not so easily diverted. I can't escape the feeling that it's coming to get me.

ALEX

It's been two weeks since I let my sister move in, since we ironed out the rules of her stay. We're sitting in the doctor's waiting room behaving as we should—being quiet and keeping our thoughts to ourselves. I'm thinking about all that's happened lately, but the smell of the clinic we're sitting in unnerves me and rattles my thoughts. The cleanliness is too pungent, the sterility an affront. I've never been able to feel calm in hospitals. When I took Dad in for his weekly treatments, the chemical veil of bleach masking the persistence of death never fooled me. Next to me in the vinyl chair, Ruth's hands rest on her small belly, but her right foot is jiggling, just like it did all those years ago when we sat together awkwardly in a clinic that looked a lot like this one.

I know I was a little harsh on Ruth at the bakery two weeks ago, so when I came home that day and saw her on the couch watching TV, I told her that I would be there for her, whatever she needed.

"If I'm going to take you in and look after you," I said, "I'm also going to look after your baby."

In truth, it was the only way I could take care of all of us. She nodded once, like she'd expected me to react that way all along.

I took the remote and muted her show. "What I'm saying is you'll need some prenatal care. I'll make you an appointment for a checkup, okay?"

"Good, because this is about you, too."

"Me?" I rubbed one eye. "Why is it about me?"

"It's all about reconnection." She patted her belly, pleased. *Look at me,* she was saying. *Look at the gift I've brought you.* "And obviously I was going to ask about a prenatal clinic. I'm already a good mother, you know. I've been shopping for a bassinet and everything." I didn't undermine her; it seemed counterproductive.

Since that conversation, we have settled into an unsteady rhythm in the loft. Chase is the buffer: at every mealtime, he steers the discussion to happy things—topics that can't possibly veer off into conflict—for which I'm grateful. I can always depend on his positivity.

Have you ever been to Mexico, Ruth? We have, haven't we, Alex? Such a beautiful culture, although it's very important to stay within the hotel grounds. Or, *Ruth, have you made it out to Prayer Rock yet? It's a great hike. Totally doable in your condition. I could go with you. Or we could all go . . .*

Ruth says very little, as instructed. I don't know if she's more talkative with Chase when she's alone with him in the apartment, but from what I can tell, she's sticking to the rules. Chase hasn't asked me any unusual questions or mentioned anything new about my childhood. But they're definitely spending time together. I find two smoothie glasses in the sink sometimes, matching pink foam around the rims. When Chase's boss called to tell him he had a few extra shoots coming up, I couldn't help but feel a bit relieved.

I do wish Ruth would tell me more about the baby, but every time I ask who the father is, she goes silent. It has to be Hal Nightingale's, though the very thought of any continuation of his gene pool makes me sick to my stomach. I'll get her to tell me soon enough. If that man is going to be showing up at my home, I want to be prepared.

At work, things have progressed more dramatically. When I talked to Morris about the gravity of the previous Floyd son's death—as well as Evelyn Floyd's very recent substance-abuse file—he was caught off guard.

"The little boy was called Rocky," I said. We sat knee to knee in his office. "He suffocated when he was four months old. Evelyn left him unattended on the couch, propped up beside her bowl of Cheerios. She couldn't say how long she was gone for. Rocky toppled face-first into the cereal and couldn't right himself." Saying the words out loud made me shudder. I could see his eyes as he struggled, the frantic flap of his tiny hands.

"How the hell do you know all this?"

I handed Morris the coroner's report, watched him blanch as he read it.

"Did you come by this information legally, Alex? Or are you pulling strings again?"

"It wasn't hard to find." I was doing my job, and he knew it.

"As tragic as this is, this coroner's report isn't grounds for Buster's removal." He folded the paper in half, negating it. "The brother's death was three years ago, and it was never deemed neglect. It's recorded here as accidental."

"I know, but you have to admit it makes the current situation more troubling. We need to go back there. And you need to come."

He smoothed his tie flat. "I've assigned Minerva to the case. You and she can—"

"Minerva knew what happened to Rocky Floyd, and she didn't say a damn thing! Morris, I've been very controlled about that. I haven't been adversarial at all, contrary to what Minerva's told you. I haven't gone barreling into her office to ask why, *why* she would keep that kind of information to herself during an intake visit. I have to assume it's because she didn't feel it was relevant, which, by the way, is completely nuts."

"Alex, you can't throw blanket statements around like that in the workplace. It's divisive."

I counted items on my fingers like a heinous shopping list. "The previous infant died unattended in their care. The second one was left unattended outside a post office. See the pattern? When I first saw Buster, he was sleeping with his face in a *couch cushion*, with his mother passed out beside him. I mean, is it the same couch where her last son died? Has she even replaced it? The house is disgusting. And Evelyn has an open Addictions file from just months ago. *Months*, Morris!" I could feel my face growing hot. "Do you not worry what will happen if things go the same way twice? If it got out that we knew about the first instance and did nothing to prevent the second, the media would be all over us."

He sucks in air through the gap in his teeth. He's thinking. I wait.

"At the very least, you have to see for yourself," I say.

"You haven't mentioned any of this to Minerva?"

"No. I thought it for the best that I come to you first. In the spirit of not being divisive. After all, you're the team leader."

"Okay, good, yes, that's right. I certainly am. I mean, that's not an ideal working relationship, obviously. All channels of communication between colleagues should be open." He pauses. "When's the next home visit?"

"End of July."

"I'll speak with Minerva and explain that the Floyd case has caught my eye. I'll come with you. But, Alex, if I agree with Minerva . . ."

"Yes, yes, I know." I raised both palms. "I'll respect your decision. I trust your judgment, Morris. I just want you there for the visit."

So that's progress, however hard-fought.

Now, in the doctor's office waiting room, Ruth is seated beside me, still jiggling her foot. "Will you stop that?" I say. "Read a magazine."

"Everyone's staring. They all think I've gotten myself in trouble." She turns to me. "How can you stand it?"

"Don't be ridiculous. You're a grown woman. They don't think that. They're not even looking at you."

But she's right. People *are* staring. Across from us, a woman in an impeccable maternity outfit licks her forefinger and turns the page of a novel, but she's not looking at the words, only at us. She's easily in her third trimester, the cover of the book submerged in the sponge of her belly. And there are other furtive glances our way. Why are all these mothers-to-be assessing us? Perhaps it's a trait among pregnant women in an ob-gyn waiting room—the need to compare, to outdo. Who will win the prize for Best Baby, Best Mom? Or maybe they're trying to figure out how we're connected, why I'm here with her rather than, say, her husband. From our lack of affection, it's pretty clear we're not a couple.

"Try this." I hand Ruth a small book of baby names. "Might as well be prepared."

She takes the book but doesn't open it.

"What about Oscar? I've always liked that name."

She makes a noise like she's blowing a fly off her lip. "That's such a Chase name."

"What's that supposed to mean?"

"He'd call his son something posh and corporate, ready for a pin-striped suit. A name for a New York portfolio." She pauses. "Remington. Hamilton. Excalibur."

I laugh—I can't help it, even though I feel a twinge of disloyalty. She joins in, pleased.

"I thought you were getting on well with Chase." It's not a question. "You're watching TV together, sitting on the couch, drinking your little smoothies."

She ignores my sarcasm and begins to flick through pages of the baby book. "That's on you, Alex. You picked an easy guy to get on with."

I can't quite read her tone. "Chase is really good for me."

When she speaks again, her voice is lighter. "Did you know we're pre-disposed to choose men who remind us of our fathers? Does Chase remind you of Dad?"

I snort. "Dad was not an easy guy to get on with."

"I know, right?" She leans in, now conspiratorial. "He was so harsh all the time. Getting praise from him was like—"

"He was still a good man, Ruth," I cut in. I can't let her speak ill of him, especially after what she put him through. "If he was harsh, he was also fair. I learned a lot from him."

She sinks back in her chair, her expression closed, and for a moment, I'm sorry. It's her own fault, though.

"Dad took a strong line on things, but he had integrity. The world needs more of that." I keep my tone level. "Unlike your Hal."

She rolls her eyes. "Haven't you given that up yet?"

"Given that *up*?" Is she joking? Across from us, Perfect Third Trimester turns a noisy page. I feel like spitting on the floor. "He had a magnetic pull on you. It surpassed everything else."

"You don't know it all, Alex. Despite what you may think, I have actually turned my life around."

I lower my voice, but my whisper sounds hoarse. "Then why did you leave Pittsburgh?"

She hesitates. "My . . . the father of my baby. He wasn't able to turn his life around."

"Who is he, Ruth?"

She opens her mouth to speak, but just then, a nurse enters the waiting room and calls her name. Ruth stands and looks down at me, her eyebrows raised.

"You want us to go in there together?" I ask. Last time, all those years ago in Horizon, we separated in the waiting room. And we never came back to each other the same.

"Of course I do." Then she exhales as if I'm unsupportive. "Just stay with me, will you?"

The doctor's office is as white and blank as the rest of the clinic. A diagram of human anatomy above the oak desk shows sections of a body with the skin stripped back. I know it's scientific, but the sight of the muscles and bones is alarming, like a warning of what lurks beneath. The doctor himself is white-haired and stout—a roll of fat at the back of his neck folds above his collar like an extra pair of lips.

"Hello," he says to me. "I'm Dr. Richard Trevalley. Which one of you is Ruth?"

"She is." I nod at my sister, who stands in the middle of the room. "She's the one you need to chat with."

"Oh." He readjusts his gaze. "Then *you*. The real patient! Have a seat up here on the bed. And for you—" he gestures for me to sit in an antique chair beside his desk. "I'm sorry it's not very padded."

"It's fine. Everything's fine." Doctors unsettle me, too. It's their ability to find the worst things, things you didn't know, and point them out to you.

"Are you a friend, here for moral support?" His jowls droop.

"I'm Ruth's sister."

"Oh, great. That's lovely. Solid family network and such. So we're here for a checkup? Are we in the first trimester?" He seems to be speaking as if Ruth and I are one entity.

"I'm eighteen weeks," Ruth says as she sits on the bed. "Twenty maybe."

"Oh, far along. And this is your first prenatal care appointment?"

"Yes," she says defensively. "I was getting to it."

He writes notes with an expensive pen, the hairs in his nose whistling. "No, it's very good that you've come in. Prenatal care is paramount, especially with first pregnancies."

I glance at Ruth, but she won't catch my eye.

"We'll take a look in a minute and confirm your due date for you. Have you felt the baby move yet?"

"What?" she says. "No." Her fingers wring at the hem of her T-shirt. "Is that bad?"

"Goodness, no! I'm not— I wasn't . . . I'm sure everything's fine. Let's just get some facts filled in—weight, height, blood group. Could you take off your shoes, please?"

Reluctantly Ruth slides one shoe off, then the other. The doctor places an old-fashioned bathroom scale on the floor, gestures for her to step onto it. The needle creaks back and forth as it settles on her weight.

"Good. See? Very healthy." He returns to his desk and scribbles in his file. "You can hop back up there, and we'll take your blood pressure." He wraps the cuff around her arm. "Have you been feeling quite well in your pregnancy? Any dizziness? Any funny turns?"

"No," she says. "None."

"That's good." He squeezes air down a rubber tube; it squeaks with every pump. "And nothing in your medical history that I need to know about? Can we get your records transferred?"

"Transferred?" she echoes timidly.

"Yes, it's important to have all your medical records. Where could we obtain those from?"

I watch as Ruth cringes. The doctor looks up from the blood-pressure dial.

"She was living in Pittsburgh," I say. "Did you have a doctor there, Ruth?"

Her eyes dart from the floor to the doctor.

"Ruth?"

Dr. Trevalley rips the Velcro cuff from Ruth's arm, then turns to me. "Perhaps it would be easier if you stepped outside."

"No, she needs me in here." I move to her side. "Don't you, Ruth?"

Ruth says nothing.

"Regardless, I'm asking you, please, to—"

"The records are in the State Correctional Institution in Pittsburgh, Pennsylvania." Ruth's voice is a husk. "That's where I saw a doctor last. They thought I was having a seizure, but it was just a panic attack. They sent me to the infirmary."

I feel like I've been punched. Ruth was in prison? My mind reels. Part of me wants to fold her into my arms, another part wants to slap her.

"What did you do, Ruth?" I ask quietly.

She covers her face with both hands and sobs once, the sound of it startling in the sheet-white surround.

Dr. Trevalley clears his throat. "Okay, you know what? I'm going to request that you wait outside, sister. We can take it from here, thank you."

"Isn't that her decision, not yours? Do you want me to go, Ruth?"

She nods, smearing at her nose with the back of her hand.

"We'll come and get you if we need you. Won't we, Ruth?" He opens the door.

"My name is Alex," I say as I sweep past him. "I'll be out here, Ruth, when you're ready."

It's emptier in the waiting room now. Perfect Pregnancy has gone, taking her novel with her. I sit down again, but my feet are restless and my head hurts. The State Correctional Institution in Pittsburgh. What has she done? What else is she hiding? A thought flickers in my mind—I could always ask Sully. No, Ruth needs to tell me herself if we're going to make this work, if I'm to help her.

It's another twenty minutes in the antiseptic reception area and just when the thudding in my head is all but unbearable, Ruth emerges, smudgy around the eyes but clasping a small papery printout. She hands it to me without speaking. It's a murky image in sepia.

"That's my baby. There's the head." She points at a bulbous alien shape and smiles. "Isn't it perfect? Dr. Trevalley says I'm further along than I thought. I'm due in the middle of September. He says I'm going to be a great mom."

"Really?" I pause. "That soon? Well, that's fantastic, Ruth. Honestly. And, are you and this baby healthy?"

"I'm fine. We're fine. I want to get out of here."

"Dr. Trevalley didn't say he needed to see you again in a few weeks or anything?"

"Let's just go."

There's a hardness in her voice, a familiar defiance. I don't have the strength to fight it, not here.

We exit into bright sunlight. The heat bounces off the midday sidewalk, and instantly the fog that was pressing at my brain inside the office lifts and I can focus on what I need to do. We walked from the loft this morning, but I know that as soon as we enter the apartment, Chase will be there with his list of happy topics. We won't get a chance to talk about what just happened, and I need answers.

"Ruth, can we stop a minute?" I look around for a bench, but there's only a bus shelter out front of the clinic. I pull her toward it, and she follows, gripping the printout like it's a toy she won at the fair. We sit down on a hard plastic ledge molded into the shelter, our knees pressed tightly away from each other. Behind Ruth's head is graffiti of a flock of white doves taking flight, like truths escaping her.

"What happened in Pittsburgh?"

She looks down at the concrete.

"Chase and I welcomed you into our home," I say. "The least you can do is tell me who we've let in."

"For fuck's sake, I'm not a dangerous felon, Alex. I'm your sister."

"How do you expect me to believe that you've turned your life around?"

I'm trying my best, but she's not making it easy. Just like when we were kids and she'd lie outright to Dad and expect me to cover for her.

She puts her hand on my knee, leaves it there, still not speaking. But the breath she takes next is tremulous.

"It wasn't me," she says. "The trouble I was in—it wasn't my fault."

I bite the inside of my lip and say nothing. How strange it is to have the same conversation again and again with her. *It wasn't me. That isn't mine. I didn't do it.* Perhaps the only thing that's changed as we've grown up is that the stakes got higher.

"It was all Hal."

His name sends a cold spear through the very center of my throat.

"He was mixed up in drugs—you know that already. He wasn't a very good guy." She pauses as if this last statement is revelatory.

"You knew that before you left with him."

"I had nowhere else to go. I did what I had to. I survived. It's no different from anything you're doing."

I look at her sharply, at those stupid doves circling the darkness of her head.

"Hal Nightingale might not have been right for me, Alex, but he was my only escape hatch."

"Hal Nightingale tore our family apart."

"We were already torn. And you know it."

I feel sick, like I always do when thinking of that time. I press down the memories that threaten to emerge and try to focus on Ruth. "Why did you go to jail? What did you do?"

"Hal got caught dealing drugs, and I was with him. Well, I was in the car sleeping."

"You were outside asleep in his car?" She's always had her way with the truth. I can never be sure if the version of events I'm getting is the real one.

"I was high. Okay—*there*—I said it. I was high, and I was sleeping it off. When the police hauled us in, I was groggy, but I wouldn't tell them anything. I wouldn't do that to Hal. But next door, he was telling them all kinds of things, blaming everything on me. I served one year. Hal got off with a warning. I thought he'd be waiting for me, but when I got out, he was gone. I never saw him again."

"Really? This was how long ago?"

"Five years. That's why I couldn't come to Dad's funeral. And before that, I was in the thick of my mess—I didn't even know Mom had died. I'll regret that forever." A tear slips down her cheek.

Is this the truth? It's hard to tell. And yet despite my better judgment, I'm beginning to believe her. What possible reason could she have to lie now?

I take her hand. It's damp and feels wriggly.

"I would have come to the funeral if I could," she says. "Even though Dad hated me, I would have come home."

"He didn't hate you." We're still holding hands. It's the closest we've been in decades.

"That's everything I haven't told you," she says. "That's all of it." She rubs at her wrist, that tattoo on the inside of it twisting.

Of course that's not all of it. "What does that stand for, that arrow?" I ask.

She glances down at the tattoo as if she's forgotten it's there. "Oh. It's forward motion. Onward. Arrows never go back. I've tried really hard to get my life on track, Alex. I made some good choices. I did. I made some."

"That's great," I say, though I can't shake the feeling that she's holding back. For all the heartfelt cards she's put down on the table, she still has a few more up her sleeve. "You still haven't told me why you're here now."

She bites her lip in that way of hers, kicks one shoe against the other. "Eli."

"Eli who?"

"Eli Beck. The man I was living with in Pittsburgh."

"What happened?" I ask, although I already know. Ruth has a pattern with men. It's a pathway burned in her brain.

"I thought he was a good guy. He was nice at the start. It was a trick. We had jobs in the same community college—his was in the kitchen, mine was serving and cleaning up after the students."

"What did he do, Ruth?"

"He got into dealing drugs. And I didn't want any part of it. He hit me. Hard. Right here." She points a shaky finger at her temple. "I had to get out of there because it wasn't safe for my baby."

Why can't you pick better guys? I want to scream at her. *Didn't you just tell me we're predisposed to choose men like our father, and yet, you never do?* But I don't say any of that. Instead, I put my arm around her and pull her close. "Oh, Ruth, at least you got out of there. And your baby's okay. That's something."

"Yes." Her smile is limp. "Good riddance to bad rubbish. And I'm going to be a great mom."

We sit quietly for a minute. There's only one question left now. "Ruth—"

"Yes, he is," she says before I can finish. "Eli is the father."

"Does he know?" The last thing we need is an abusive drug dealer arriving at our house.

"No. I left before he found out. He doesn't know where I am."

"Good. Then you're safe from him now." I squeeze her arm. "Onward? Right, Ruth?"

She breaks eye contact and fidgets on the bench beside me, lost in her own threadbare thoughts. She's a crumpled thing, the only sign of hope for her the glossy piece of paper she grips between her fingers. I might not have given her the warmest welcome, but I'm starting to realize that she did the best thing by coming to me, by confiding in me. There are still so many ways I can help. But the first thing I need to do is take all the truth she's handed me and hold it up hard to the light.

RUTH

When I came to Moses River six weeks ago, I hoped Alex and I would be able to find our way back to each other as sisters, and despite Alex's rules, we seem to be making a start. Since the doctor's visit, Alex has warmed up to me, leaving me notes before she tiptoes out in the morning, no doubt headed for the bakery, where Sully waits. Sometimes she meets him for breakfast, sometimes lunch. But she always meets him. I don't say anything to Chase. I need Alex on my good side. Every day she suggests activities I could do, mostly things to get me out of the house, but at least she's communicating. And thankfully she hasn't brought up going back to the doctor's. I think she disliked being there as much as I did.

She leaves me money sometimes on the counter, with a list of items she wants me to buy for the baby. Onesies, little booties, diapers. I buy what she tells me and pile it into a heap in the corner of the living room. The baby will sleep out here at first, but I don't know what will happen next. Will she ask me to leave and fend for myself? So far she hasn't. She seems to be coming around to the idea of keeping me close.

There's a precarious trust growing between all three of us. I don't think Alex said anything to Chase about my brushes with the law. He hasn't mentioned it. And he has started to relax around me and doesn't ask so many questions. Each day, I wander into town, only to reconvene with Chase on the couch in the afternoons to watch some manner of competitive cool-person sport. He provides the play-by-play while I sit there, rubbing my growing belly and pretending to pay attention. His presence is becoming comfortable. On the days that Chase is off making billboards or at a meeting at the resort, I mostly stay busy by making healthy food for myself, and I play classical music loud while I cook. Chase says it's been proven to make babies smarter.

My belly is humped now—there's no disguising the fact that I'm pregnant. It was as if, after meeting with Dr. Trevalley, the whole middle section of my body relaxed and I popped right out. Days later, I felt the baby move, too—a strange, feathery feeling, like bubbles escaping into the deepest chamber of me—and it wasn't only excitement that flooded me. Before, when I wasn't physically that different, the notion of motherhood felt idyllic. Now, shit's getting real. I have moments of panic, where I wonder if—in a lifetime's catalog of bad decisions—this is the very worst of them. I won't be good enough for this child, and there's no going back now.

One night when only Alex is home, I get her to feel the baby as it's kicking. She's working on something at her laptop, but I hurry over to her, reach for her arm.

"What are you doing?" she says, and her arm goes rigid.

"Showing you. Feel!" It's like trying to grapple a joystick, but when I finally get Alex's hand to rest on my belly, a calm comes over her face and she exhales like the world is right again.

"Isn't that the weirdest shit?" I say.

"It's not weird, Ruth; it's amazing." She takes her hand back.

"No, I know, but it is a little bit weird, too. It's like there's an alien in there, trapped in a bag."

"Jesus," she says, and she goes back to her work.

I feel the baby move daily now, and the sensation is becoming more defined. Soon I'll be able to see it kicking under my skin, otherworldly, my little sci-fi plotline. I always feel happy when Chase gets home again. He continues to be more thrilled about the pregnancy than anyone.

He likes having me at the loft. He tells me that growing a baby boy takes more energy than is needed to climb to the top of Mount Everest. I don't know how he knows this, or why he assumes I'm carrying a son, but it's good that he's interested. It means he's less likely to throw me out any time soon.

"Motherhood is the most powerful thing," he says more than once. "Good things are coming for you, Ruth. I can totally tell."

"Thanks," I say, wondering if that's true. It's been almost two months now and I haven't heard anything from Pittsburgh. Maybe I really have put my past behind me. Maybe it won't track me down.

Beside me on the couch, Chase hesitates. "Alex and I talked about starting a family, but unfortunately it's not going to happen for us."

"Really?" I make an effort to sit up. "Why not?"

"She's not able to have children."

"She told you that?" *She's lying. She just doesn't want to have them with you.*

"Well"—he rubs his eye—"the doctors ran tests. You didn't know that? I guess you wouldn't if you left when she was young."

"It's so sad," I say finally, pretending I believe it, which I don't.

"No, we're fine. Don't feel bad. And don't say anything: she won't want to talk about it."

I actually meant sad for us as sisters. We're meant to have a sixth sense, to be force fields around each other. But Alex has pulled hers tight, using it solely to keep me out. It's not only that I'm suspicious that she's lied to him—it's that I might have an inkling as to why. And I can't say a word to Chase about that, because it's part of the rules.

Meanwhile, Alex places no boundaries on her own prying. She's still trying to find out more about Eli. *Is he dark-haired and dirty like Hal was? Or did you at least upgrade?* I don't tell her anything. She'll just judge me. That much hasn't changed. When Eli and I moved into the house on Lennox Street with a few others we'd met from various halfway houses, I knew that everyone living there made their money dishonestly. They weren't upstanding citizens; it wasn't a model home. But there was honor among thieves, I thought, so I took the offer of a shared room, and I ignored the fact that there were drugs around. I ignored the temptation, even if Eli didn't. Things weren't easy, but we were getting by. They only fell apart entirely when he got that job in the college, started watching the college crowd. There was a market to be tapped there. He smelled young money.

I deflect as many of Alex's questions as I can. I can't tell her the real truth of it—how Eli set us all on a dangerous path, dragging us all down with him. I tried to stay out of Eli's business, but he wouldn't let me; he beat me. In the end, all I could do was run, and from there it was a one-way trip to Alex. Where else was I going to go pregnant and with a criminal record? At first, my secrecy was to protect her, but she needed me to give her something, a kernel of truth, so I did. But that's all she's getting. Every day my life in Pittsburgh moves further and further away from me. Done and dusted. At least that part of the story's reliable. And Chase, Alex, and I, in spite of everything, we're getting on okay.

It's a golden afternoon near the end of July and I head back to the flat for whatever sports event Chase has lined up for us to watch, but as I approach the door, I see that it's ajar. Alex's voice cuts through the air. She must have gotten off work early. For a second I feel put out, as if she's muscled in on something that was mine. I go to push open the door but stop, my head by the gap in the jamb.

"It's nothing," I hear my sister say. "I don't know why you're so upset about it."

"Alex," Chase says, then there's a thump of something being set down heavily. "I never see you. You're always at work. And now I hear *this*. What am I supposed to think?"

"Sully's a friend. I meet him for coffee. We talk about work stuff." I know that tone. It's a metronome steadiness before a boom. If she were a bomb, she'd be ticking.

"He's just a friend? That you meet *every day*?"

"Oh, for fuck's sake! Did your little spy run home and tell you that? Leave it to my sister to paint me as untrustworthy. The irony is ridiculous. Meanwhile, you two are here all the time, cozying up, choosing baby names, swapping tales of how I'm cheating on you."

"It wasn't Ruth. She didn't mention him."

"Oh, spare me."

I rest my forehead onto the wood of the front door, but it sways inward and creaks ever so slightly. Chase and Alex both turn.

"Oh, look!" Alex throws up her hands. "Speak of the devil."

I take a wary step into the apartment. The atmosphere is thick, like liquid, like tar.

"What were you talking about?" I ask.

"You heard every single word, so I don't know why you're asking." Alex picks up her bag from the couch.

"Where are you going?" Chase demands.

"Out. To see my 'boyfriend.' The one I see every day. Right, Ruth?" She pushes past me, actually banging my shoulder.

Chase stands there, rubbing the stubble on his chin as her footsteps clatter down the stairwell. It's only once we hear the door of the main entrance swing shut that he speaks.

"Did you really hear every single word?"

"I heard some of them." I step into the loft and close the door behind me. "Most of them. Yeah."

"I'm sorry about that. We don't usually fight. I don't know what to do." He starts toward the bay window kicking a packet of diapers and a fleece blanket out of his path. "She's tough. You know? And it's busy in here."

"She's a slippery fish."

"That's funny. She says the same thing about you."

I bet she does.

"Do you really know something about this Sully guy?" Chase wheels around to face me. "I'm sorry. I shouldn't be asking you. The last thing you need is to be put in the middle."

He looks so sad, standing by the window, his shoulders drooping. It makes me want to hug him. Would it be weird if I did?

"Alex always comes out swinging if you corner her," I tell him. "She's been like that as long as I've known her. My mom used to call her Little Tiger because she was so fierce."

"Little Tiger," he repeats softly. "And what did your mom call you?"

"Little Owl." I swallow hard.

"Really?"

"I was the worrier. Mom used to iron out my brow with her thumb. Like this." I sweep my thumb up the bridge of my nose. Even now, the feeling transports me to a time where there were people who looked after me, and I grab on to the back of the sofa to steady myself.

"What did you used to worry about?"

"Being a big sister." I take a big breath. "At Christmas one year, I stayed awake until midnight because Alex told our parents that she was staying at a friend's house when she really went to a party. I didn't want my dad to know, but he caught me watching for her through the kitchen window. He got it out of me and called the cops.

Horizon was a tiny town. The cops pulled her out of that party and brought her home."

When she got out of the cop car, she looked like a limp piece of cloth, sucking on her hair. I blink, releasing myself from the memory, from the trance.

"But Alex is such a stickler for the rules," Chase says. "She's all about safety and the truth and doing what's right."

She is now. I realize I shouldn't have said any of what I just said. I've broken Alex's rules. Panic washes over me like a salty sea.

"Look, I only told you that story because you asked. Don't ever tell Alex you heard that from me."

Chase's forehead wrinkles. "Why not? What else doesn't she want me to know?"

"Nothing." *Everything.* "Chase. Please don't tell her."

He stares at me hard, blinking as he considers his options. I've closed the lid on Alex for now, but at least for a moment it was open and I gave him just a glimpse of what's in there. I allowed him more doubt than Alex ever would.

Any bluster he may have had dissolves, and he turns back to the window. "You have my word."

He says it so simply and with such exhaustion. I believe him. He'll keep his promise. Relief floods me. I knew it. I knew we were allies. My hard work is paying off.

"Do you want to watch TV for a bit?" I ask.

"Sure," he says, and heads toward the couch. But just then, my cell phone rings. I pull the phone out of my pocket, and I stand there, staring at the screen. The phone rings and rings while the whole inside of my head turns to a swirling wind.

"Are you going to answer that?"

"No," I say. "It's nobody important." My mouth feels dry, and I stagger to the bathroom, sliding the door closed. Finally the ringing stops, and I wait for the beep that'll tell me Eli's left me a message. Something caustic. Something radioactive. An acidic burn via voice mail. I pull open the cupboard under the sink and move away the bottled rows of organic cleaning products. There, at the back of it all is my bag. I reef through it to find Eli's coffee tin, the one I hid the very first night I was here. Stripping away the tape, I pull off the plastic lid. The tightly packed mountain of cocaine baggies rests safely. So do the bound rolls of money. It's all still there.

I might have told Alex a little about Eli, but what I didn't tell her was that I'd hit him back in my own way. I took what I was owed. I was righting old wrongs. I think of it as my insurance policy. I don't intend to do anything with the drugs—not unless I have to. The same goes for the money. I'm surprised Eli hasn't contacted me until now, but I guess he knows I'm not exactly going to pick up the phone and offer him my address. He's wily, though, Eli. He's trying to find me. There's no stopping it, just like always. I run and run and run, but everyone just pulls me back home. He'll find me one day. And when he does, he'll also find Alex and Chase. Again and again the universe pins me onto a hideous wheel, and I'm always at the very center as it spins.

ALEX

It's because of Ruth. Chase and I have never fought like that before, and it's her fault. I was naive enough to think that things could really change, but again, she's in trouble and causing more of it. He's colder with me now, less open, as if he's a season in flux. He's taken to going to bed earlier so that by the time I get there after working late, he's already asleep and there's no way of communicating with him. We jump if our feet touch in the night. Meanwhile, he and Ruth seem to be warming up more and more. I told her not to talk about the past, and so she found a loophole—she told him something about the present. She had no right to mention Sully.

It's almost a direct transfer of happiness: what I lose, she scoops up. Chase hands Ruth the TV remote whenever they sit down on the couch. It's the simplest gesture, but it feels loaded. She carries his plates to the sink. Maybe I should be glad they're getting on so well—we're family, after all. Except I know what really goes on in families, how tangled and competitive they can become. How broken. One family member's prosperity is so often another's downfall, and Sully's right: it's a jostle, a teeter-totter. I've seen enough of that to last a lifetime.

At home, I can't do anything without being scrutinized. Chase is watching me like scientists watch mice. *Interesting behavior,* he's thinking when I do or don't take coffee with me to work. *I wonder what that means*, when I check my email as soon as it dings on my phone. I don't like answering work stuff at home, but a lot of people are on vacation or stress leave and I'm covering for them. Maybe Chase is right to be disapproving. We usually try to make use of his summer schedule to spend our free time together, but so far, Ruth has gotten in the way of that. If I'm not at work, I'm running errands for her, getting her baby stuff. I've given up telling Chase that none of my work emergencies have to do with Sully. Ruth has made sure that he won't ever believe me.

The truth is, I haven't even seen Sully for a week—work's been so busy—although if I'm honest, part of me has been avoiding him. Chase is just so uptight about him. Why invite more confusion? I can't tell if I'm asking that for Chase or for me. Instead, I've thrown myself into working overtime at the office, which is ironically the calmest environment I know at the moment. At least there, the chaos is on the outside. At least there, I know what I'm dealing with.

So when I run into Sully in the corridor outside Family Services, it feels almost illicit. I'm with Minerva and Morris—the three of us are on our way to visit the Floyds—and Sully's with another cop, a young woman, who's telling him a story about her weekend. He nods at me but has to keep listening to his colleague. We gather in two awkward rows at the elevators. I press the button, and we all wait for it to arrive.

"And so we didn't get in until four a.m.!" the female cop says. "It was crazy. Who knew about this town?"

"Yup. It's full of surprises," Sully replies, then turns and opens the circle. "How are you doing, Alex? I haven't seen you in a while. You okay?"

"We're all great!" Minerva says as she shuffles forward an inch.

Sully ignores her. "Where've you been?" he asks. If I can hear the hurt in his voice, so can everyone else.

"Oh, here and there."

I feel Minerva's face blasting heat my way.

The elevator arrives, and the others stream inside. I'm about to follow Minerva in, but Sully grabs my arm.

"Can I talk to you for a second?" He draws me to the side. "Excuse us," he says as the doors begin to close.

"I'll catch up with you in a second," I say to my team. The last thing I see before the doors shut completely is Minerva looking like she wants to slice me in half.

"Hi," Sully says, once the others are gone. He's so close to me I can smell the soap on his skin. "You haven't replied to my texts."

"I'm fine, I've just been . . ." I don't even bother to finish the sentence. He'll see right through it.

"I wanted to tell you I looked into those prison records for your sister like you asked."

I debated taking Ruth at her word, but I couldn't bring myself to, not when there's a child involved. And after she told Chase about my spending time with Sully, I felt a little justified in doubting her.

Sully moves nearer to me again, most likely to be discreet, but his face is only inches from mine. It's making my heart beat faster. "Her timeline matches. She was in jail for the period you asked about. She wasn't lying."

"I guess that's something."

"Yup. It looks like they went light on actual time served. Good behavior, probably, and it was her first offense."

That they know of. "What about Hal Nightingale?"

"He's bad news. A record as long as my arm."

"I know."

"But he died two years ago. Got himself in more trouble than he could handle."

Ruth was telling the truth when she said he wasn't the father, but she left out the part about him being dead. Truth, but not the whole truth. Or could it be that she really doesn't know? Either way, I don't feel one iota of sympathy. Good riddance. This Eli guy must be real, then. I wonder what part of the truth Ruth is still hiding about him. I want to ask Sully to look into him, but I feel torn. I shouldn't be talking to Sully at all if I don't want to lie to Chase. I've got to end this. I have to leave, fast. "Thanks for doing that, Sully. I realize that was a huge ask."

"It wasn't. Not when you're the one asking." Sully doesn't back up right away.

"I should probably go. Morris will be waiting for me downstairs."

"Looks like a fun field trip." He moves off and presses the button for the elevator again. "So, just to be clear, are you going to ignore all my texts? Or just the ones I send this week?"

"I'm not ignoring you," I say, my voice abnormally light. "It's just that right now—"

The door pings open.

"Coming?" he asks.

"I think I'll take the stairs," I say. "I need the exercise."

"Alex, we haven't done anything wrong," he says. Then he gets into the elevator. I watch as the doors slide closed, leaving me on the outside. I hurry down the stairwell to the parking lot, where Morris and Minerva are already in the government car. Morris is squeezed in the back seat, maintaining his role as observer, the top of his head touching the velour of the roof. He's installed a baby seat into the space beside him. That's a good sign. Minerva sits stiffly behind the wheel.

"Come on," Morris says as I get into the passenger side. "We haven't got all day to dillydally."

"She was organizing her love life." Minerva says. She lurches into reverse before I've had a chance to put on my seat belt.

"I was not." Why can't she back off?

"Looked like it," she mutters. Her knuckles shine white on the steering wheel, and I wonder how Morris broached the idea of his joining us on this Floyd visit. It can't have gone well. Minerva's been tense all morning, and that was before Sully even arrived on the scene.

"Morris, are you coming into the house with us?" Minerva asks after a moment. "Or are you here in more of an overseeing, conflict-resolution, stay-in-the-car type thing?"

"I'm coming into the house," Morris says.

"Three social workers is overcooking it, don't you think? It'll feel like the Allied invasion." She takes a corner too fast.

"Can you watch the road, please?" I ask. "And there was a reason the Allies invaded."

She ignores me. "I want to be clear, this is not a protection case. It's a follow-up."

"Everybody's on the same page," Morris says.

"Yes, we're just following up in case there's another dead child we don't know about," I say. I can't help it.

"Alex." Minerva swivels in the driving seat. "That information was *confidential* and *had I mentioned it*, your view of the Floyds would have been totally biased, even more so than it—"

"Oh, I would have seen them as neglectful?" I say.

"Good God! Did you hear that, Morris? Alex, the death was ruled *accidental*." She hits the brakes a little too hard, even though there's no reason to slow down, and we all pitch forward against our seat belts. "I can't work in these conditions."

"Calm yourself down and keep driving," Morris says. "Alex, Minerva's right. I told you that already. Rocky Floyd's death has no bearing on his brother's situation."

I shrug because I know Morris doesn't really believe that. He knows it's more serious, otherwise he wouldn't have come with us today. Plus, he's had the forethought to bring a car seat.

"*Thank you*," Minerva says. Vindicated, her lips purse. "And perhaps if you'd stop running to your boyfriend at the police station every five minutes, your view of the case would be less warped."

Don't bite, Alex. Don't bite. If everything derails on the drive to the Floyds' house, we'll never get Buster removed. I sit on my clenched fists and we drive in silence for a minute, to the point where I consider switching on the radio. Minerva turns to me.

"What were you talking about with Sully, anyway?"

"Nothing much. He was just saying hi."

She swerves left. Behind me, I hear Morris's head bump the window. "I hope you weren't discussing any of our cases with him."

"I wasn't."

"And by the way, you still haven't given me his number."

I pick at the stitching on my leather satchel. "It might be better if I pass yours on to him. He's kind of private that way."

"Is he?"

I want to push her head into the driver's side window. Morris coughs. He doesn't ask a thing about what is going on. He doesn't want to know.

"Minerva, can we talk a little bit about the Floyds? How have they been responding to the supports you've set up?" he asks instead.

"I enrolled them in a We Can't All Be Perfect parenting program, and they're doing fabulously."

"That's good news."

"If they're doing so well, their house should be visibly improved today," I say. "If not, I think we can agree it's a bad sign. A month is more than enough time for them to get their act together for their child."

"The house will be fine. They're entirely on track now." Minerva fixes her eyes straight ahead. "For the record, Alex, your suggestion to Morris that Evelyn Floyd has an ongoing drug problem is wildly inaccurate. It's comments like that that throw us off track and give us a bad name."

"Give *us* a bad name?" I say.

"Yes. Us. Those of us who work to protect children. We're called nit-pickers, government drones, Family Stealers rather than Family Services."

"That's ridiculous," I say.

"At any rate," Morris cuts in from the back, "we'll just check in with the Floyds today, have a quick look around and make sure they're using all the supports we've set up for them. I'm sure Buster is doing well and that it'll all be fine." He smears one palm against the other. "But just in case, are there any healthy family members in the area? You know, if things start to go a bit pear-shaped?"

I smile to myself. *There it is.* I knew it wouldn't take Morris long. He's by-the-book and never strays from it. Whenever a child is removed, it's always his first step to look for a healthy relative to take custody. A grand-mother, an aunt, a long-lost cousin—anyone within the child's bloodline who's not a complete train wreck. If the birth parents don't consent to that plan, our office will organize a family conference to try to find a resolution out of court. The meetings are usually tense and rarely successful. In most cases, it takes a judge to decide where the child will end up. But for Buster it's a good sign Morris is even asking. It means that the wheels are already in motion.

"There's a maternal grandmother in Crow's Pass," Minerva sniffs. "But we won't need her."

"Good," says Morris. "I'm sure you're right."

As soon as we've parked, it's clear straightaway that the home has been tidied up, at least a little. No shoes lie straggled along the path, and although the gate still has the *Big Dog Bites* sign on it, they've turned it so it faces inward.

"It's funny, isn't it," I say, "how different a house looks when they know we're coming?"

Minerva says nothing, but marches ahead of Morris and me until she reaches the porch, which has been swept. There are no heaps of cigarette butts in a cat litter tray anymore, but they haven't replaced the broken door. Minerva gently knocks on the cracked windowpane. After a few seconds, Evelyn comes to the door with a button-up shirt tucked into the waistband of her jeans. She's holding Buster, whose diaper is entirely concealed in thick flannel pants. Both of them are overdressed for July.

"What?" she asks, looking from face to face. Does she remember who we are?

"Mrs. Floyd, hi. It's good to see you again." Minerva gestures to me. "And you remember Alex Van Ness. And this man here is Morris Arbuckle. He's our friendly supervisor."

"Why are there three of you? There weren't three last time." Mrs. Floyd shifts her grip on Buster. He doesn't seem to have grown much. His little legs are clamped around his mother's waist. I can't tell if his arms are dirty or just tanned.

"Oh, don't you worry about me," Morris says. "I'm just tagging along."

"Can we come in?" Minerva leans into Buster's face like she's going to boop him on the nose with a forefinger, she's that fun. "This won't take long."

Evelyn steps to one side, and the three of us file past the pantry shelves, which are conspicuously well stocked now, and into the long, thin body of the house. I notice the smell. It's changed. It's citrusy, the kind of acidic tang in cheap cleaning solvents that clings to the back of the throat. It's masking all the former sourness of neglect. Aside from a couple of dishes in the sink and an open packet of granola that has spilled a little along the countertop, the house appears tidy, but my gut tells me there's more to the story.

Evelyn points to the kitchen table, the same one we sat at back at the start of June. This time it's clean and polished, not a soiled baby wipe in sight. We all sit down, Minerva and Morris on one side of the table, Evelyn and I on the other. Buster wriggles in her arms, and she deposits him onto the linoleum floor, where he sits with his legs stretched out straight. I look around for a toy.

"My husband's not here," Evelyn says. "He's buying diapers."

"Oh, that's a shame. I thought we'd found a time when we could all be here," I say.

Morris keeps glancing around the room, just like I am. We're checking out standards, trying to be covert.

"Yeah, but something came up. The diapers. He had to step out."

"Well, we'll just chat with you, then." Minerva says, "Buster's doing well, isn't he?"

Evelyn coughs, long and rattling. "He's all right. He's doing good."

"He looks healthy!" Minerva smiles at me. *I told you*, she's saying, *oh ye of little faith.*

"Is he meeting all of his developmental milestones?" I ask.

"What?" Evelyn replies.

"He's approaching them," Minerva says.

"While we're waiting for your husband," I say, "do you mind if I just use your washroom quickly?" I stand up, and so does Mrs. Floyd.

Minerva fumes in her seat.

"No, it's fine, Mrs. Floyd—you stay here. I know where it is."

I slip away from the table as Morris asks Evelyn how's she feeling, if she's been sleeping any better, and I walk down the narrow hallway past Buster's room again. She's straightened that up, too, and bought him a wooden train set. The engine's on the window ledge, but the carriages spill downward haphazardly. Instead of heading into the bathroom, I go a little farther along and poke my head into the Floyds' bedroom. It's basic: a mattress on the floor, a bedside lamp without a shade. She's pulled the bedding straight, but it's filthy and graying at the edges.

I enter the room. There has to be something here. I just know it. My eyes follow the line of empty beer bottles under the window. So they're drinking. The place is a mess, clothes everywhere, plastic bags littered across the floor. I look back at the hallway, panicked. I don't have much time. I search under the bed, thinking that's surely where they'd hide anything. Yes, that has to be it. Bingo. Morris just needs to look properly. I hurry back past the bathroom, ducking in to flush the toilet, and arrive at the kitchen table. I feel a bit unsteady, as though the linoleum is rippling under me.

"Have you been using all the supports we set up?" Minerva is asking. "I know you've completed the We Can't All Be Perfect program. Was that very helpful to you?"

"It was all right."

"I'm really so happy to hear that. And the house looks amazing!"

She has no idea, but before I can say anything, Buster cries out. He's knocked his head against the leg of the table.

"You're all right, Bust. You're all right, big man." Evelyn shunts him farther away from the table. He barely cries.

"He seems very capable of self-soothing, Evelyn. That's a good sign." Minerva leans out from her chair, and I take the opportunity to catch Morris's eye. It's now or never. I gesture for him to go look around.

He takes the hint. "I'll just use the washroom before we head out."

Evelyn looks up from Buster as Morris stands and moves down the corridor. "You people don't have a bathroom at work or what?" She wipes her nose with her sleeve.

"Where did you say Mr. Floyd was again?" I ask.

She crosses her arms on her chest. "What does it matter? We've done all the shit you told us to."

"No, you're doing fabulously," Minerva says. "Just like I knew you would."

"Minerva . . .," I begin, but she's steamrolling ahead.

"I don't think we need to wait for Frank." Minerva stands up. "I'm entirely satisfied with what I see."

Just then, Morris wanders back from the hallway. He's frantically smoothing his tie flat.

"We're just getting ready to leave, Morris," Minerva says. "I'm assuming you agree that we've followed all protocols and our work here is done?"

Morris shakes his head. "We have a bit of a problem. Can you sit back down, Minerva?"

"What's going on?" Evelyn says, grabbing Buster from the floor, yanking him into her lap.

Morris smears one palm against the other. "I'm afraid I've just found evidence of serious drug use."

"What *evidence*?" Minerva rounds the table and stands by Evelyn. "What are you talking about?"

"These were in the bedroom, sticking out from under the bed." He has at least four bags of cocaine in his hand, some of them chalky and half-open. He did look properly. I knew I was right.

Evelyn's head whips from Morris to me to Minerva. "No, that's not mine. What the *fuck*?" She looks at Buster. The panic on her face makes my stomach twist, but there's nothing I can do. She did this to herself.

"No," Minerva says. She looks like she's been personally slapped.

"It's not mine," Evelyn says. "I swear to God I don't touch that shit no more."

"Mrs. Floyd, I'm afraid we're going to have to remove Buster today." Morris says it as gently as he can. "This much cocaine, this accessible. I'm very sorry, but we don't have a choice."

"You can't take him!" she wails, standing up, Buster clamped around her middle. "Don't take him from me!" Evelyn covers her mouth with one hand as if she might vomit through her fingers. I feel so sad suddenly—as I always do in these moments—but what matters most is what's best for the child.

Buster sees his mother's panic, and his lower lip begins to protrude and tremble.

"Fucking what?" Frank Floyd crashes through the door and into the kitchen, carrying diapers and a bag of groceries. "Who's doing what now?"

"They're saying there's coke in our bedroom!" Evelyn cries.

"Whoa, whoa, whoa!" Frank slams the diapers onto the kitchen counter and approaches us as if we're wild circus animals. "Nobody's using drugs in my house."

The rumble of Frank's voice frightens Buster even more, and he starts to cry, his little arms clinging to his mother. She grips him to her chest. Meanwhile, Morris looks gray in the face and Minerva is turning red. Someone needs to take control of this situation.

"Okay, listen, can we all please calm down?" I take a deep breath. "Mr. and Mrs. Floyd, our boss is saying there's immediate risk here, and I'm afraid it's enough of a reason to—"

"Who the fuck is he? I don't give a fuck about your boss," Frank says. "Get out of my house."

"Listen to me," Morris says. He's still pale, but his tone is firm. He holds up the bags of drugs in his hands, and Frank balks.

"Are those fucking yours, Evelyn? Evelyn! I thought you were— *What have you done?*"

"They're not mine!" Evelyn refuses to relinquish her hold on Buster. "It's not right! Frank, don't even say that—"

"Well, they're sure as fuck not mine!" he shouts, and Buster buries his face in Evelyn's shoulder.

"Look, we all want the same thing here," Morris says. "Of course we want kids to be with their families. Buster belongs with you. But for now it's not safe for him. I need you to understand that my goal is to get him back to you as soon as possible. But you need to work with me here."

"You're planning on just walking out with him? You can't do that! That can't be legal!" Frank shouts, panic in his eyes now.

"You need to lower your voices," I say. "The way you handle this today will impact Buster. You're frightening him. I know this is horrible for you, but if you can try to stay calm, so will he."

"But—where, where would you take him?" Evelyn looks wildly from face to face.

"We want the least intrusive measure possible," Morris says. "Minimum disruption to Buster. The best choice would be if family was available to take him while we finish the investigation. Does your mom live nearby still, Mrs. Floyd? Could we get a hold of her?"

"My mom?" Evelyn is crying.

"It's your best option." Minerva manages a small smile. "Let's call her, shall we, Frank? While Evelyn packs a bag for Buster? Let's stay calm. If you can both do that, it'll form part of our report. It'll really help you get him back more quickly."

Even though she's still placating them, it's the first time I've seen Minerva do her job properly. She's taking the problem at hand seriously at last, probably because her reputation is now on the line.

"Alex, could you help Mrs. Floyd, please?" Morris has his phone out.

I guide Evelyn through to Buster's room. She moves as if paper-thin, as if she might blow away in a breeze. Buster watches her face as she moves, nuzzles into her neck with little snuffles.

"It's okay, Bust," she keeps saying. "You're going to see Nana for a few days. You're going to have such a fun time." She swallows hard, packs T-shirts and nothing else. Tries to stuff in the toy train and a blanket, but the grocery bag she's using won't stretch.

"Does he have a favorite stuffy?" I ask, picking up Buster's grimy blue rabbit from the floor. "Should this go in?"

Buster reaches out for the toy. I hand it to him as Evelyn suppresses a sob. This is always the worst part of the job and the most necessary.

When we go back to the living room, Morris nods at me once. The grandmother has been located.

"Buster is going to visit Granny!" Morris says. "He'll stay there for a few weeks. Won't that be fun?"

"It's Nana," Frank corrects. "Just for a little while, big man." He softly touches Buster's ear.

"It's very clear how much you love your son," Minerva says, her eyes watery.

Morris glances at me, and I know what he's thinking. *All damaged people love their children, Minerva.* The question is whether they're looking after them properly.

"Next steps," Morris says, his lips dry. "The police are on their way. They'll have paperwork for you, and they'll confiscate the drugs. We'll also be filing papers with the court explaining our actions today. You'll get a copy of those. And then as part of the court process, we'll have a family conference at our office. Your mum will be there, and a lawyer if you'd like one. We can talk everything over at that meeting, figure out what's best for the little guy."

"I don't understand anything you're saying," Evelyn says.

"You'll see Buster again in a few days," Minerva says. "We'll set up a supervised visit. Right, Morris? And we'll talk all of this over really soon. Next week we'll meet up. Find the right way forward."

"Bring him back where he belongs, you mean?" Evelyn asks.

"That's what everyone wants, yes," Morris says.

I stay quiet. The best thing is to remain collected. We're so nearly there.

Morris motions for us to get ready to leave, and Evelyn passes Buster into my arms. He's warm and soft to hug. His hair smells like sleep. Immediately he reaches away from me, whimpering.

"Mama?" he says. It's the only thing I've ever heard him say.

"You're going on a vacation!" Evelyn manages. "With Nana! Remember Nana's cat? He'll be so happy to play with you!" Her voice cracks, and she smiles although her eyes are doing the opposite.

"We're getting a lawyer." Frank's jaw is wobbling.

We wait in the kitchen until we see the police cruiser pull up near the driveway. Morris directs everyone outside, then leaves the drugs on the table and the Floyds walk with us to the car. Evelyn trails her fingertips against Buster's; she's trying to smile, trying to hold it together. Morris heads over to debrief the police officers, and I notice that neither of them is Sully, which is a shame. I would have liked to have seen him right now. Instead, I strap Buster into the car seat we brought, his dark brown eyes staring at my face the whole time. He's still holding the dirt-streaked bunny.

Evelyn leans into the back seat to kiss him. "We'll see you soon!"

Frank has to put his arm around her waist to pull her out. All of it's heartbreaking, but I just keep thinking, *If you care this much, why can't you try a little harder?* Once Morris is done, he walks over and gets into the driver's seat, takes a deep breath, turns the key in the ignition. The last thing I see of the Floyds, the police are accompanying them into the house.

We drive in silence straight to Buster's grandmother, all of us breathing out stress. Even Minerva doesn't speak. Adrenaline sickens my stomach, but I ride in the back seat, dancing the bunny for Buster and holding his hand.

"You're safe," I whisper to him. "Beautiful boy."

———————

I walk home to the loft at 4:00 p.m. feeling drained. I couldn't eat much for the rest of the day—the sick feeling wouldn't go away—because as much as the Buster visit was a triumph and a move in the right direction, it's never uncomplicated. That's the nature of social work: even the banner days are underscored by tragedy.

When I let myself into the apartment, it's unusually quiet. Chase isn't rattling around by the stove; the television's not on. Ruth is sitting alone on the couch with her mountain of baby things behind her and the contents of her bag splayed untidily across the coffee table. A familiar-looking purse with an antique clasp, a passport, some loose change.

"Ruth?" I say. "What's going on?"

"He found it," she says, her eyes dull and flat. "Sorry. I tried to get it back."

"Found what?" But she's lumped there like stone. "Chase?" I call, heading toward the bedroom. He's sitting on the bed. "Is everything all right?"

He looks up, his face ash-gray. He's holding a small square of paper.

"What's that?" With a flash of dread, I wonder if Sully's written me something and Chase has intercepted it. I step toward him and stop. "Chase? Let me see. Is it about Sully?"

His eyes widen further.

"If this is about him, I've hardly even seen him, Chase. I mean, I saw him today, but only by accident when—"

"This isn't about Sully," he says, "but thanks for the extra kick to the gut." Then he passes me a creased photograph, bordered in white. It's faded, and as I squint to make it out, the whole room starts to bend.

"No," I say, my voice rough. "Where did you find this?" In my hand is an old photo of my family on the farm, a Horizon summer seventeen years ago, Mom holding a bucket, us kids barefoot, sitting on the gate, smiling. I can almost hear the sound in it, the birds singing, the laughter. I haven't seen this photo in so long.

"There are three kids in this picture, Alex," Chase says. "There's you. And there's Ruth. And who is that tanned little boy?"

I can't look at him, can't stay standing for much longer.

"Who's the third kid, Alex?"

I have my arm around him in the photo, making sure he's safe and doesn't topple backward off the gate. Both of us have skinned knees from all our fun and adventures.

"You have a little brother?" Chase spits out the word. "Were you ever going to tell me about him?"

No, Chase. No, I wasn't.

PART TWO
THE RUNNER

ALEX

There's a reason I can't talk about the past even though I'm tied to it with a hundred feet of rope. Over the years, I've learned to swallow the long coil. What happened in Horizon sits piled in the deepest pit of me: I push it down; I keep it there. But my sister found the end of the rope, yanked it with all her might. And now here comes everything, rancid and foul as it's ripped upward, pulling all of my insides out.

Chase's voice sounds distorted as if he's speaking underwater. He's saying something about my little brother. He knows his name. Pim. It's a name I haven't uttered out loud for years.

I can't stay any longer. I can't be here. I turn and make for the door, the photograph still in my hand.

"Alex!" Chase calls after me. "You can't just—"

But the door swings shut, and I clatter down the stairs, through the lobby, and out into the heavyweight afternoon sky.

———

On the day it happened, my mother finished the dishes, making sure everything was clean before she left. I stood by the fridge, peeling at an old sticker of a rainbow. Half the color was gone. Mom wiped her hands on the front of her apron, unwrapped it from around her hips, and switched off the radio. The lack of bluegrass was suddenly abrupt. The sound of the crickets outside took over. It was September on the farm, that golden part of the year when everything looks dipped in honey, and the three of us—me, Ruth, and Pim—lined up in the kitchen, barefoot and scruffy. Dad was outside. I could hear him starting up the truck.

Mom turned to Ruth. "Ruth Van Ness," she said, "you're the oldest, so you're in charge. We'll be an hour, no longer. Don't touch anything electrical. And look after your brother and sister." It was the first time she'd ever left us.

Ruth was thirteen and almost Mom's height. "I've got it," she said. "Go and have fun."

"I want to come, too," I said, because I was eight years old and the world felt wrong without my mom in it. "Why don't you ever take me?"

"You'll survive for an hour, Alexandra. Willem Van Ness, are you going to be good?" She'd christened him Willem—a nod to our Dutch heritage—but for all four years of his life we'd called him the traditional shortener, Pim.

"Ruth says I can jump off the roof if I want." Pim's big eyes were earnest. "I'm going to make a parachute umbrella."

"I never said that." Ruth smiled. "And he won't be doing that."

Mom took her wedding ring from where she had hooked it over the white china bird on the windowsill and pushed it hard back onto her finger. Then she walked down the line of us, pressing her lips to the tops of our heads.

"Goodbye, my owl," she said to Ruth. "Goodbye, my little tiger," to me. And for Pim, "Goodbye, my little hazelnut."

The three of us filed through the screen door and onto the porch. We watched as Dad helped Mom into the truck, then took off out of the driveway, bumping down the gravel road. They were going into town to buy hoses. I remember it because it sounded like a boring reason to go on a journey. Couldn't my father have gone on his own? The humdrum of their chore—a walk down an aisle in a hardware store—should never have run parallel with an afternoon like that one. It seems impossibly cruel. But that's the thing about life's tragedies: they're always hidden in something small.

It was three o'clock in the afternoon, and the sun was baking the sky. I watched the truck until it was a speck on the grid road and the diesel roar had faded.

"Come on." Ruth put her arm around me. "We can fill an hour. It'll go quickly."

"Will you play a game with me?" I asked her. There were no other farms for miles around, just rolling, empty hills seamed by gullies and creek beds.

"A board game? Sure, whatever you want. But maybe not Monopoly. You know how you get." Ruth steered me back toward the front door.

"Are they coming back?" Pim asked. He looked up at me with his beautiful eyes and grabbed my hand. He was brown from a wide, blue summer spent outside, the white of his T-shirt stark against his skin. As much as our mother scrubbed his hair in the tub, it grew sideways and dusty through every August, a mocha color that would only darken again in the fall.

"Don't worry, Pimlet," I said. "Mom and Dad will be back soon. Ruth said so."

"What game are we playing? Can we *all* jump off the roof with umbrellas? I'll go first."

"We don't have enough umbrellas." Ruth winked at me.

"But inside is *boring*!" he grumbled. "Let's play in the fields!"

"Okay," Ruth said. "But come inside first—we should put on shoes." She moved us back into the kitchen. "Put shoes on, Pim. The grass is spiky back there. And there might be nails."

Pim ignored her, of course. That summer, we had devised a game that Pim called "hurry home," and we played it endlessly from sunrise to sunset. We must have gotten the idea from capture the flag, or kick the can, or one of those other childhood games that involved defending a base and chasing off invaders. There was a patch of farmland out of sight of the house, a grassy corner behind the granary that was surrounded by trees and grew wild every summer, since it lay beyond the turning circle of all the harvest machines. While one of us guarded home—a square marked with an old wooden clothespin driven into the dirt—the other two circled as thieves, picking a moment to fly out from behind a tree or a disused tractor and steal the peg. Then the thief had to race around the grain silo and make it back to home without being tagged. If the thief made it back, they were awarded the more coveted role of guarder. *I see you, I see you!* Pim would shout as he ran. He was always the guarder and would never venture far from his clothespin.

Sometimes in my dreams, I'm caught in an endless game of hurry home, except that my legs won't run, my mouth won't open, my eyes are sewn shut. I'm always an adult in those dreams, but Pim remains a little boy. And in my nightmares, he's still so much faster than I am.

"I want to be the guarder," I said as the three of us walked out of the kitchen onto the porch, the old screen door banging behind us. The last few times we'd played, Pim always caught me and I'd had enough of that. He gripped the clothespin, his thumb on the very top. He'd scratched our initials down the side of the wood, slept with the peg in his fist at night.

"Hand it over," I said. "It's my turn. I'm only playing if I'm the guarder."

"Pim, she's right. It is her turn," Ruth said gently. "Remember how it's good to share?"

I crossed my arms, tapped my foot on the old planked porch with a feigned sternness. I loved hurry home. My favorite part was the secrecy, the hidden spots I'd developed to watch home from that were faraway and elaborate, too sophisticated for my brother or Ruth to ever spot. I was good at it: the attack was all in the timing. But my speed as a runner didn't match my sneakiness. It was rare I didn't get tagged. Even so, why couldn't I have let Ruth be the guarder that day? At her age, she straddled the world of adulthood and children. She may have seen danger coming when I did not.

"You can be guarder again next round," she said to Pim, which wasn't true because there were rules. You couldn't just break them. With a sigh, Pim passed me the clothespin, and when we reached the tree-lined arena, Ruth put her arm around both of us in a huddle.

"Ready, you two? And remember it's just a game, okay? We're just playing, and we're not staying out here for long. There's lemonade in the fridge, and the winner gets first glass."

She shouldn't have said that. Because I decided right then I wanted the lemonade. I would have it, and I would drink it all down in one go, watching my brother's face through the bottom of the glass. Ruth and Pim took off to hide. I ground the peg into the dirt, stamped on it twice to be sure. I was ready. The air hung heavy with heat, the only sound the occasional droopy peep of a bird.

With nobody in sight I waited, then edged away from home base slowly, slowly, daring myself to go farther and farther. I was inviting my siblings to take their chance at stealing the peg and felt primed for the race that would follow. But when Pim darted from his hiding place to make a bid for the win, I saw him only after he'd swooped, after he'd already grabbed the trophy from the hole in the ground. He was so quick, the lightness of his frame, his ribs visible through his T-shirt.

"I see you, I see you!" I shouted, and I took off after him, the dirty soles of his feet kicking up as he flew into the long grass, giggling. He picked a clean line through the stalky, dryer patches of land that three months of heat had turned brittle. All I knew was I was going to catch him; I was going to be the guarder next round. He wasn't going to steal my lemonade. I followed, thirty, forty feet behind, my sprinting body reflected strangely in the dull chrome of the granary walls.

At the foot of one of the grain trucks Pim stopped and turned, dwarfed by the huge black rubber of a wheel. He was breathing so hard. His little chest rose and fell, but I didn't slow down. There was a second when he realized I was still coming for him, that he'd never make it home before I tagged him. I saw a shimmy of panic run through his body as he searched for an escape route. He spotted the ladder on the side of the truck, and he scaled it as fast as he could.

By the time I got to the bottom rung, he was already on the eighth. It was a metal ladder, welded on, the dark peeling paint hot under my fingers. How could he climb so fast without shoes on? Why was he always ahead of me? The injustice coated everything inside my head red.

"Stop, Pim!" I shouted. Or maybe I didn't. Maybe I just stood there, holding the burning ladder, fuming.

I've buried the truth so deep that it's lost. It has no sound, no contour, no other details to help me verify it. What I'm sure of is that Pim didn't stop climbing until he was at the top of the ladder, where he crouched on the very rim of the grain truck, holding the edge with his fingers and toes, his body huddled like a sparrow in the rain. He was looking down at me, my little brother. My little bird.

"Pim!" I called, for certain now, a crack in my voice. I climbed up the ladder until I was near enough to reach him, stretching one arm to grab at him as he teetered on his ledge.

"No! Pim!" I yelled, and as I climbed up the last two rungs, he lost his balance completely. I remember his eyes going wide, his mouth becoming a round O. By the time I reached the top, my brother was sinking into the grain, yelling in terror and flailing. Then he breathed in the flax and the yelling stopped.

The more he moved in the silky quicksand of that flax container, the deeper he sank. I lunged out to him, I tried, but his arms were so thin, and he couldn't paddle toward me. He could only sink further. He was snot and saliva, savage, primal eyes, and I screamed at the top of my lungs, thought wildly of jumping in too, but I didn't. I just hung there, waving my hands in the air near him. Only his head was visible now, those big dark eyes looking up at me, pleading. A few seconds later, even those disappeared. I watched as the last of his hair was swallowed up. I squeezed my eyes tight, my nose and throat gummed in panic. *Please God, when I open my eyes, let everything not be this.*

I had one foot over the container edge when Ruth reached the bottom of the ladder. I think only a minute contained all the chaos, a minute where she'd heard me and ran from the tree line.

"Get down!" she shrieked, climbing rungs herself, grabbing at the hem of my T-shirt.

"Pim's in there!" I screamed.

"He's what?" she clambered past me on the ladder, treading on my fingers, straddling the rim of the container. "Pim!" she shouted. "Jesus! Pim! No, oh God!"

I gaped at her, my face red-hot. I'd never heard Ruth swear before. Earnest, steady Ruth, who kept a Bible beside her bed and brushed her hair a hundred strokes every morning. In one smooth motion, she clamped both palms over the edge and dipped her whole body down into the grain.

"Ruth!" I sobbed. "Don't!" Even though she had a grip on the rim, I was sure she'd disappear, too, and in so many ways she did. We both did.

Whatever we had of ourselves was lost in the few minutes that Ruth swished and swirled her body through the grain, hoping that Pim would grab a leg, a foot, as if he was sitting underwater with his eyes open, holding his breath. Ruth's face contorted with the effort and eventually she slowed, pulled herself back up out of the grain. She hung with her ribs over the side, heaving.

"Get down," she gasped. I descended the ladder, my knees rattling. She slid down too, facing forward, all but falling, three-quarters of her covered in a strange flax dust that had turned her clothes and skin moth-silver. Her shoes were spilling seeds, little flecks of it that we'd find for weeks in our bedroom, in folds of our clothes.

"Where are the drivers?" Ruth stammered, looking around frantically. We both knew Dad had let them all go early that Saturday, a rare moment of generosity because it was so hot, so easy just to go home. "We have to empty the truck!" She started fumbling her hands along the sides of the huge vehicle, looking for a lever there, something to tip the container upward and free Pim.

"We need to get help!" I said, following Ruth as she banged on the metal siding. "We have to call nine-one-one!"

"That will take too long! We need to tip the truck!" She ran to the driver's door and tried to open it, but it was locked. The window was partway down. She slithered in, scraping her knees, all the while her breath coming out in rakes.

"There are no keys!" she shouted, as if I were holding them, as if I could just pass them to her and solve the problem. The next second she crumpled over the steering wheel, great sobs racking her as I watched from outside the driver's door.

"Look at our clothes," I said. "Mom's gonna be mad." My voice had dulled somehow, gone flat. I rubbed at my arms and legs, which were all I knew, as I smeared dirt and dust and the tang of metal from them. Nothing else in the world felt real.

Ruth got out of the truck, stumbled toward me, and we collapsed into stalky grass.

"What are we going to do?" she cried, her lack of solutions all the more terrifying. "We need Mom and Dad."

"I chased him," I said, my hands shaking as I grabbed at her. "I didn't mean to! I chased him, Ruth, up the ladder."

She hugged me until I stopped wriggling and we sat interlocked, all of our limbs shuddering like it had suddenly turned to winter.

Fat tears rolled down my grimy cheeks, and Ruth smothered me, rocked me, our ribs knocking. The truck loomed behind us, cold and silent, a hideous catacomb. Far away on the unbending grid road, we heard the diesel roar of my father's truck coming back from town. They'd been gone only about a half hour. Ruth stood. She looked down out me, her face dirty and streaked with tears. She held out her hand for mine, and together we staggered back to the porch, through the razor blades of grass that poked and scraped at our ankles.

"I love you," she kept saying. "I love you, I love you, I love you."

"Will Pim be okay?" I asked, my voice catching in my throat.

"Just keep walking," she said. "We need Mom and Dad."

Ruth sat me on the porch steps. She wiped my face down with her cold hands, emptied her shoes into the sunny dandelions. Then she slid down next to me. The truck was getting closer, closer. There was a catch in her chest every time she breathed in, like the start of a terrible sickness.

When my parents pulled into the driveway, Ruth took my hand and brought me to stand beside her. Mom got out of the truck first, her head tilted, already knowing something was wrong because she knew us, she knew our faces. I wanted to run to her, but Ruth's grip was a vise.

"What's happened?" Mom asked. She stood, one hand on the door of the truck, the other holding a woven basket with a few groceries as well as a hose.

"We can't find Pim," Ruth said. Her chin wobbled as she spoke. "He ran off, and we can't find him."

What was she doing? Why did she say that? She squeezed my hand tighter and tighter.

My father rounded the truck. What could he see in us? My father, who never missed a trick. "Pim!" he shouted into the field, elbows sharp at his sides. "Pim!"

"Have you looked for him?" Mom's basket slanted. "Is he inside or outside?"

"He's outside," Ruth said.

"We were playing, and . . ." Ruth's fingers clenched so hard around mine that it stopped me from saying anything else.

"He was running," Ruth said. "We don't know anything else."

Dad walked briskly toward the field. "Pim!" I'd never heard his voice louder. He turned back to Ruth. "Why would he just take off?"

"I don't know," Ruth said.

"Ruth?" Mom's brow creased. "Ruth Van Ness?" She turned to me. "Alexandra, where did you last see your brother?" Her eyes were granite. My whole body shook.

"The grain truck," I whispered. Ruth's knees buckled and then straightened again.

My mother let go of the basket she was holding, the groceries spilling onto the hard-baked ground.

Dad started running toward the back of the field, to the trucks. "Lottie, take the girls into the house," he called as he ran.

Mom didn't look at Ruth. Ruth tried to wrap herself around her, but it was like hugging a statue. "Come inside," was all Mom said.

She held the screen door open for us, and we entered into the kitchen. Ruth and I stared up at our mother's face, which was flat and expressionless. By the stove, Pim's sneakers lay toe to heel, loose and abandoned. They were sky blue with race-car laces.

"He wasn't wearing *shoes*?" Mom asked, looking at Ruth.

She picked up one sneaker, clutching it to her heart as she moved to the window. Then she stood, watching the field and waiting, with her back to us. Blame began to gather like weather, pressing at every corner of the room, and there was Ruth, right in the darkening middle. But she'd lied. To everyone. She was right where she deserved to be.

RUTH

I hold Pim's clothespin in my hand, trace over our initials. I couldn't let them bury it with him. At the funeral, while Mom coughed out tight little gasps, I went to the casket to say goodbye one last time and saw it there beside his body, and I took it, hoping that somehow Pim would know that his home was always with me. I don't consider that stealing.

But I did steal the photo of Pim from the family album the summer I left the farm. They wouldn't have given it to me if I'd asked. I took it because it's happy. It's as simple as that. There was once a time when everything was okay. There were days when we weren't in ruin, when I wasn't the one to blame.

I took that photo, but I didn't leave it lying on the coffee table for Chase to find. No, he sifted through my things. Maybe I should be angrier about that, but at least he only searched my bag hanging on the hook and didn't get as far as Eli's coffee tin, which remains stashed under the bathroom sink. I'm not mad at him; not really. Rifling through another person's past is all any of us are doing anyway. And if you give a dog nothing but scraps, eventually it will seek out its own food. I tried to explain that to Alex when she finally returned home four hours later, but she didn't believe me.

"You left it lying somewhere on purpose," she all but spat at me. "You love that he found it."

"Alex! Do you think I came here just to mess you up? I'm not trying to cause trouble, you know."

"No?" she said. "Why break the habit of a lifetime?"

Perhaps she doesn't understand that everything she lost, I lost, too. There are moments even now when I'm still flooded by Pim, the smell of him, his brown-berry summer skin, his laugh. He used to join Alex and me when we snuck out of our bedroom to watch television long after we'd been tucked in.

Mom liked scary shows—*The X-Files* or *Dr. Who*—and every Friday night, she'd make a bowl of popcorn for herself and settle in front of the TV while Dad worked on a puzzle in another room. The smell of warm coconut oil filled the old living room and kitchen. Our farmhouse creaked, but at twelve years old, I'd learned all the floorboards. Alex was seven and followed in my footsteps. Pim was right on her heels. We hunkered at the threshold of the living room and took turns peeping around to watch the TV, the carpet scratchy under our knees. When the show got scary, Pim would gasp, and our gig would be up.

"Willem Van Ness," Mom would say, her words elongated. "You're too young to see this. I'm drawing the line."

Behind the couch, Alex and I watched as Pim's whole face deflated. He covered his eyes with two flat palms, dimpled at every knuckle, as if not seeing the room meant Mom no longer knew he was there.

"Don't make me come back there," Mom would say.

"Okay. I gotta go to bed," Pim would announce to us in the loudest of whispers, his dark eyes huge, his hair like alfalfa.

"You too, girls," Mom would add. "Take a handful of popcorn to go." She'd hold the enamel blue bowl high over the back of the sofa and we'd each fill a greasy palm, traipsing out of the living room in a line, back up the stairs, into Pim's oak-floored bedroom.

"You did it again, Pimlet," Alex would say, although there was never any scold in her voice. She would tuck Pim in, give him his clothespin, kiss his cheek.

Pim would giggle, and Alex and I would snuggle in on each side of him. Often on those nights, we fell asleep right there, three brown cashew nuts in a row, our joints conjoined. In the morning, Mom's warm flannel blanket was always over top of us.

I live that memory again and again, and yet the other memories of that miserable September on the farm crowd it out, block the light. Every year that followed in that house was a dirge.

Alex took what happened and turned it into fire, causing trouble every chance she got. My mom and dad spent more time in the principal's office than they ever had before, but Alex continued to push them. One winter, some kid in her class was throwing snowballs at younger kids in the school. Alex took it upon herself to teach him a lesson. She was vicious. Relentless. She got sent home for pushing him so hard down an embankment that his shoulder dislocated.

"But is it broken?" I asked Alex at the dinner table that night. I was trying to fill the silence, to normalize things.

"Ruth, don't meddle," my father said.

"But I was only—"

"Stop!" My father pounded the table with his fist, and all the spoons jumped. "Your sister got in trouble at school, Ruth, but at least, at *least* that's the only trouble she's caused."

"Joseph." My mom put a hand on his wrist.

"Lottie, she's the oldest. She needs to take some responsibility, to stop pointing fingers at everyone else. All we've had from her the past two years are secrets and lies."

"What?" I said. "How is this about me? I haven't broken anyone's shoulder."

"You've done worse things," Alex said. If she'd stuck me with a knife, it would have hurt less. There was silence then, with only the whir of the old fridge as it knocked and struggled in the kitchen. Even Mom kept her eyes on her plate, saying not even a word in my defense. I felt more alone than ever. I was back out in that field, with no one to help me home.

"You're dismissed," my father said to me. "Not you," he said to Alex. "You stay right here."

I slunk to my room. A united front, they watched me go.

By the time Alex was thirteen, she was acting out as if delivering a direct challenge to the universe. *Come and get me*, she was saying, with that kind of angry glassiness you see in the eyes of players around a Russian roulette table. She was staying out late, going to parties at the raceway on Friday nights, hanging around farm kids who were nowhere near as smart as she was. Dad didn't know what she was up to. Only I did. I couldn't stop her—she wouldn't listen to me. At school, she aced classes without studying, which pleased Mom and Dad. If her marks were good, surely everything was fine with her. But she was a pressure cooker. The tension was building up inside her, and no one noticed but me. And then, at fifteen, she got into all that trouble with boys. Her whole world burst. And I was the only one who wasn't surprised.

By then I had my own life outside the family anyway. I was done living in a house full of echoes. That's why I clung to Hal. He filled in all the sadness, made me feel safe and loved. *Fuck your family*, he'd say, handing me a pill to swallow. *Who needs them? Stick with me, baby. We'll make our own home.* Every pill he gave me back then made me feel good, let me escape. I laid myself at his feet. I didn't know then about the other side of him, the side that would sell me out, abandon me in a heartbeat when a jail term was looming. When I did, it was too late. Alex made sure of that, made sure I could never come back to my family. One lie, and she sealed my fate forever.

ALEX

I wasn't the problem child, even though that's what Ruth thinks. The worst thing I ever did was go to a party when I was fourteen that my mom and dad didn't know about. It was the height of my sneakiness, which was pretty mild compared to what Ruth was getting up to at the time. Through her last years of school, she stopped trying entirely. She flunked classes, didn't even show up to most of them. At home, she was quiet and secretive. Mom and Dad didn't know what to do with her.

She started smoking weed in eleventh grade. I could smell it on her clothes and in her hair. She hung out with kids in trench coats who drew their eyebrows on in pen. Dad was always getting calls from his friend in the police about her being up to no good. The more she disappeared into that world, the less she held on to any lifeline at home.

But she still thought of herself as my great protector, and whenever I did anything at all that a normal teenager does, she squealed. She caught me sneaking out to that party, and when Dad's cop friend brought me home, Mom and Dad were right there on the front porch, and she was behind them, her arms crossed, smug.

"You carry on down this road, Alex, and you'll be ruined in no time. You're better than that." He turned to look at Ruth momentarily, whose face crumpled a little. "You want to end up like your big sister?" He paused, then carried on. "Like *her*? Be a lion, not a sheep. And don't lie to me anymore."

I couldn't help it. I started to cry right there on the front porch, and I ran to my mother.

"It's not so bad," she said, enfolding me in her arms and kissing the top of my head. "Just don't do it again, LittleTiger."

"I won't," I promised. "I won't."

I looked at Dad. He had tears in his eyes, too. I let go of Mom and went to him, my hands limp by my sides. He hugged me, his rib cage bony under my shoulders. Behind him, I could see Ruth glowering.

It was only a few weeks after that that Hal Nightingale showed up in our lives. He was fixing a broken fence with Dad, and Mom told Ruth and me to bring them sandwiches and a jug of iced tea.

"All that's for me?" Hal said, taking off his cowboy hat and wiping his forehead with the back of his sleeve. He had a deep tan and crinkles around his eyes, like he'd spent a lot of his life squinting into the sun.

"Hal, these are my daughters," Dad said. He took a sandwich from the plate and ate half of it in one bite. "Don't talk to them."

Ruth and I headed back to the house, but Ruth kept turning around to see if Hal's eyes were still on her.

"Does he work hard?" she asked Dad that night over dinner. He was chewing and stared at Ruth until he swallowed.

"No. He's a layabout. And he's temporary. He'll be gone the second I find a decent worker. Why are you asking?"

She shrugged, looking down at her plate instead of at him.

"What about that other boy?" Mom asked. "That Tommy kid you hired."

"He's green, but he's good," Dad said. He put down his fork and pointed a thick finger at Ruth. "*That's* a boy to ask questions about."

Ruth snorted into her glass of milk.

It didn't take long for Hal and Ruth to connect, probably because it was the one thing that my father had forbidden. Dad was right about Hal: he was good for nothing, just a drifter who got by on fake charm.

Ruth secretly met Hal most nights, his Plymouth Duster parked fifty feet down the grid road where it bent to the left, and the two of them would sit on the hood, passing a whiskey bottle or a joint back and forth. Or so I heard from Tommy Gunnarsson.

The first time Tommy ever spoke to me, I was sitting alone on the top step of the porch, watching the wind sift the trees. He was just coming in from tying hay bales out in the fields. He had a streak of dirt across one collarbone and his blond hair was dusty but tidily cut.

"How's it going?" he asked.

"Okay."

"I'm Tommy." He offered me his hand to shake.

"I know who you are," I said. His fingers were strong and confident.

He lifted the lid of his lunch box and glanced at me. Then he pulled out a bent dandelion and handed it to me. "I got you this."

When I took it, I'm sure I blushed, fully and bright red, a color you can only get to when boys are brand-new.

"I know it's a weed," he said. "But who gets to decide what's pretty and what isn't?"

He stared right into my eyes, and I knew he wasn't talking about flowers.

"Thanks." The yellow head of the dandelion drooped in my hand.

"I'm buying a Chevy Silverado. I'll take you for a ride in it sometime. But until then, maybe we could go for a walk some evening."

"Okay," I said.

He tipped his hat at me, and I watched him walk all the way out to the back field. Every few minutes, he checked if I was still watching him. And I was.

After that, I started spending a lot more time with him. He'd come by the house and ask, *Would you like to take a stroll around a field, Miss Alexandra? Would you care to take a turn about the road?* Dad approved, and I enjoyed the attention. Ruth rolled her eyes and called him a choirboy Bible basher behind his back. But, as with all things, she was wrong about Tommy.

A couple of weeks before my fifteenth birthday, we were walking out at the far end of the property where the fence line bordered the trees. It was a pretty night, bugs skimming the wide-open flowers, and Tommy pulled at long strands of grass as we strolled.

"Your dad's land goes on forever," he said, looking out to the farthest reach of the field. I followed his gaze, too, and squinted. Because there at the edge of the field, rammed hard against a wooden fence, my sister and Hal Nightingale were standing with their pants reefed down. Ruth had her back to us; her hands were on Hal's shoulders. Mostly I remember the shocking white of the tops of Hal's thighs, the strange bucking of his hips, the way he kept licking his lips with effort.

"Holy Moses," Tommy said. "Is that your sister?"

I stared, motionless. From forty feet away, Hal saw me, but he didn't stop what he was doing. He didn't even slow down. He smiled at me, opened his mouth so I could see his tongue. The noises he was making grew louder.

"Come on, come away." Tommy pulled at my arm. "We shouldn't be here."

We stumbled back to the farmhouse, both of us awkward and quiet. As we neared the porch, I said to Tommy, "Don't tell anyone what we saw, okay?"

"I won't," he said. And he didn't, although I know the whole scene had him as rattled as I was. And for my part, I never said anything either, not to Ruth, not to my parents, not to anyone. But it was an image that was hard to unsee.

The day I turned fifteen, Tommy came by the house and brought me proper flowers, from a flower shop. "Happy birthday," he said as he presented them to me. Then he took me out for our usual walk.

"How did you know it was my birthday?" I asked him when we were out of sight of the house.

"I found out." He took my hand. "I'm trying hard to find out about you."

I blushed, thinking it wasn't that difficult.

"So," he said, suddenly standing still. "What else do you want right now for your birthday?"

I looked up at him, unsure.

He leaned in, stopping with his mouth very close to mine. "I'd like to kiss you, if that would be okay."

I nodded, swallowing fast. He pressed his lips to mine, his hat knocking against my forehead. He smelled clean, like when Mom dried freshly washed sheets on the line. After a few seconds, he pulled back and waited for me to look at him.

"Happy birthday, Miss Alexandra," he said.

I think that was the moment I fell for him. Or it might have been later that evening. But the moment was there—real, and fluttery, and transitory—like everything when you're only fifteen.

In the weeks after that birthday night, I thought more and more about what I'd seen Ruth doing in the field. We shared a room, and I lay awake each night long after she snuck back in smelling of booze and pot. She'd fall sleep quickly, but all I could think about was how reckless she was being. What if our parents found out about her and Hal? What if she got in trouble, the really big kind? I was sure we wouldn't survive another family crisis, but I couldn't ask her about it or warn her to stay away from Hal. All I got from her by then was derision. So one Friday night when I heard Dad's rocking chair creaking on the front porch, I went down to join him. Mom was already asleep.

"Why are you sitting out here on your own?" I asked, curling up next to him in my nightgown.

The crickets screeched in the bushes. He sucked his teeth so his lips curled. "I'm waiting for your sister. Went out hours ago and hasn't yet come back. I'm going to tan her hide and skin whatever rat of a boyfriend she's with."

I knew I shouldn't say anything. I didn't even want to, but I kept thinking about how Ruth had taken it upon herself to laugh at me and Tommy. Every breakfast, she asked if I'd had good dreams about him, as if she could see into my head and knew all my thoughts. She knew nothing. She had no idea what was in my head. She had no idea what I'd seen.

"Dad," I said then. "Are you mad because of what she does with Hal in the back field?"

He turned to stone next to me, his eyes hollowed out by disappointment, but he thought I didn't see it. "Hal Nightingale? What do they do in the field?" he asked, his voice too measured to be nonchalant.

"I probably shouldn't say. It was . . . sinful."

Dad's head dropped into his hands. He looked completely worn out.

"I'm sorry, Dad. Maybe I shouldn't have said anything."

"Go on to bed."

"Are you sure? I don't mind keeping you company."

He put a hand on my shoulder. It felt warm for a moment. Then he drew it away. "It's okay," he said. "Go."

I left him and went quickly to bed. It was three o'clock in the morning when I woke up to shouting outside. At first the noise sounded like thunder, but it was the rumbling of my father's voice.

"I know what you did! I know what you're doing!"

My sister's voice was whiny and plaintive. "What? Who told you that? I *like* him, Dad. He's not a bad guy."

"I heard he deals MDMA to minors. That's chemical drugs! Are you high right now?"

"No, Dad—"

"All summer you're telling your mother one thing and me another. We won't be lied to again!"

There were sentences I didn't catch then, words spoken too fast and too angrily.

"Like *you'd* know," Ruth said in a storm of defiance. "You washed your hands of me a long time ago. You make snap judgments about people all the time, and then they're *dead* to—"

There was a crash of glass breaking as Dad hurled something against the wooden siding.

"You're done!" Dad bellowed. "Go to bed. You won't be seeing him again."

He left the porch before Ruth did: I heard his heavy tread as he came upstairs. She sat down there alone for ages, creaking back and forth in Dad's rocking chair. When she finally came up to bed, I pretended I'd slept through the whole thing.

Dad fired Hal the next day, but Hal still lingered out by the road, waiting around for Ruth to see him. All day long, he was out there while Ruth remained grounded inside the house. He tried to get my attention a few times, talk to me, probably wanting me to send a message to Ruth. He hung around after that first day when he thought Dad wouldn't be there. Mom was watching Ruth closely by then, a new development for which Ruth blamed me entirely.

"Thanks a lot, *golden girl*," she'd say to me when Mom moved away from the kitchen table at lunchtimes. "Just wait till they find out what *you're* doing."

But I wasn't doing anything, except trying to avoid Hal Nightingale lurking about the farm. Each time I saw him down by the road, I felt electrified, and terrified. Then, one day in town, he whistled at me. I couldn't tell Ruth—she'd never believe me—and if I told Dad, there'd be a homicide. So instead I went to my mom.

"Hal Nightingale did what?" She dropped her wooden spoon in the pudding bowl.

"I really hope he's not following me, Mama. He's skulking around all the time."

"Has he touched you? Alex Van Ness?"

The image of Hal and Ruth in the field filled my vision. I felt a deep pull in my pelvis, and I didn't know what it meant. "No, he hasn't . . . touched me," I said.

My mom grabbed my hand, her skin rough like used paper. It was unexpected how quickly she lit. "You've done the right thing by speaking up. I'm telling your father."

"Mom, don't. Ruth will be—"

"Ruth must realize what she's done, what danger she's put herself in and, now, her little sister, too."

"Please, Mom. It's not like he did anything, not really. I don't want Dad to worry."

She went silent. I don't think she told Dad, in the end. In hindsight, I wish she had. I wish Dad would have threatened him even more. Maybe Hal would have given up on Ruth once and for all and things would have ended differently. Differently for Ruth. And differently for me.

RUTH

I was so caught up with Hal and the life we were planning together that I didn't realize how far Alex would go, how far gone she already was. In the weeks after I was forbidden to see Hal, she'd made Mom her confidante. She'd made Dad her pet. It was as if she saw the opportunity to benefit from my being in trouble—she almost relished it—and try as I might, there was nothing I could do to make the pendulum of our parents' favor swing back my way. I didn't want to leave home; I was too afraid. And I still believed that surely they'd forgive me and come around. So when the shit hit the fan— Alex's shit, for once, not mine—how was I to know that, even then, they'd take her side? One way or another they'd all find a way to make it my fault.

One day, just as summer was starting to fade, I came back from a secret visit with Hal and walked into the kitchen. Mom was sitting at one end of the table, and Alex was at the other. Neither was speaking.

"What's going on?" I asked.

Mom looked at me, her eyes a strange watery hardness, like pumice stone at the bottom of the bath. "Do you know about this?" she asked, gesturing to a form on the table.

"She doesn't know," Alex mumbled.

I picked up the form and read it. It was a clinic form, parental consent for an abortion. An abortion? I had to read it twice to actually believe it.

143

And when I realized it was for Alex, I almost wanted to laugh. Imagine it: all those years spent pointing at me for being the family fuckup while Alex was the one to get herself pregnant.

Her face was streaked with tears, desperate. I felt bad for wanting to laugh. Despite what my family thought of me, I wasn't the bad one after all. I wasn't the monster.

Alex looked at me then, and I saw the same little girl standing on that ladder the day Pim disappeared. *Do something*, her face said. But I couldn't save her. Not this time. What she did with Tommy was her choice.

A part of me that had been closed for so long opened up. I wanted to reach out to her, hold her, but I didn't.

"Does Dad know?" I asked. At the mention of him, Alex looked down into her lap.

"Not yet," Mom said. "Good God, hasn't that man gone through enough, lived through enough agony for a lifetime? Haven't we all? And now. Now, this."

"Mom, you can't tell him. He'll disown her," I said. "He'll burn down the Gunnarsson homestead. He'll shoot Tommy himself."

"Don't!" Alex said, and suddenly her desperation and sadness transformed into rage, all of it focused on me.

"Ruth, I need you to drive your sister into town on Thursday," Mom said. "You can do that for her, at the very least."

"But, Mom, I—"

"You *will* do this. For me. For your sister." She said it with such viciousness, she was practically spitting at me.

Another bucket of trouble thrown into the air, and somehow it was all still landing on me.

———

The outside of the clinic was horrible. Hordes of red-faced, sweaty women with banners shouted at Alex and me as we pressed through. I shoved a few of them. Jesus. It's hard enough without that kind of baying in your face. Alex had been quiet on the ride in. She'd even apologized to me for having to come with her. I'd tried everything to distract her: music on the stereo, chitchat, sympathy. None of it worked. Once we got inside, she handed in the consent form.

"Is this your mother's signature?" asked the nurse, flicking at the page with a glittery fingernail, her voice one bored straight line.

"Yes, ma'am," Alex said.

"Do I need to call her and check?"

I cut in. "It's our mom's handwriting," I said. "And besides, I'm her big sister, and I'm twenty. Mom asked me to come here with her. In loco parentis. Can we please just sit down?"

We found seats next to each other in the waiting room. They deflated like sighs as we sat down. The whole room was stark and blank and smelled of acid.

"What are *you* looking at?" I said to a guy across the aisle who was staring at us. He buried his face in a magazine.

Alex was sucking the end of her hair, that nervous habit she'd developed after our lives turned to hell.

"How far along are you?" I asked gently. I didn't even know this much. She'd refused to speak to me in the days leading up to this.

"Six weeks."

"Have you told Tommy?"

Silence.

"You can't just let him off the hook, sis. And he deserves to know. This is his fault, too."

Her eyes did that thing again, turning from sadness to red-hot anger in a flash. "If it's anyone's fault, it's yours," she said.

"*Mine?*" I felt like I'd just been slapped.

"If you hadn't—" Just then her name was called, and she stood. "Don't come with me. I'll do this on my own. Like with everything else."

She walked away from me then, and I was left in the waiting room, sweating. Why on earth did she feel this was *my* fault? Because I'd been caught up in my own world and didn't really notice what was going on with her? Because our parents had practically disowned me? Because I was a ghost living in their house?

I sat miserably, staring at the shoes of the other people in the clinic. Were all the paths they trod as bumpy as mine?

The abortion was quick. She walked out on her own, refusing my help, her own arms wrapped around herself. All the way home in the truck, she stared out the window, looking both younger and older than she had on the ride in. What had happened to my little sister? Was it that day in the clinic or years earlier that she had disappeared? Guilt made me nauseated. I'd let her down. Again.

I parked in the driveway and got out of the truck. Mom was on the porch squirreling one hand over the other. Something was very wrong.

"Mom?" I asked. Alex got out of the truck slowly. Mom was crying when she went to Alex and opened her arms.

"My little tiger, I am sorry. I am so, so sorry. I didn't realize. I really didn't know." Mom cried on Alex's shoulder, her breath coming out in rakes. Alex's arms went around her, and she began crying, too.

"Mom!" I said, stepping closer. "What's going on?"

She pulled herself away from Alex's embrace. Her face was on fire. Never before had I seen her look so fierce.

"Your father's gone after him."

"Gone after who? Tommy?" I asked.

"No, Ruth. Not Tommy." Next to her, Alex was gripping Mom's sleeve. She looked just like a little girl. Her expression was strangely blank, despite the tears that ran down her cheeks. When she spoke, it was without inflection.

"I left them a note," she said. "Before we left for the clinic. I told Mom and Dad what really happened."

She began to walk to the porch steps. Mom helped her up them.

"What are you talking about? I don't even know what you're saying." It took me a beat to catch up. "Wait, what? You're not suggesting . . . No. No!" Every cell of my skin started to prickle. He would never, ever lay a finger on her. "Alex!" I yelled. "You're not suggesting *Hal* got you pregnant?"

Alex turned slowly, Mom's arm still around her shoulder. "Ever since the day Dad ran him off the farm, he's been following me," she said. "One day, he put his hands on me. I couldn't get away." She started to cry then, great heaving sobs that racked her, each one folding her with pain. Mom pressed her again into an embrace. She began to cry, too.

"Alex, no. It's not true! Hal wouldn't do that. He wouldn't."

She moved a half step behind Mom.

Mom spoke for her. "You're oblivious, Ruth. You don't see the truth. You've created all the trouble this family has ever known."

Suddenly Dad wheeled into the driveway in his truck, but he didn't stop by us, he drove straight to the barn. We all watched him, wide-eyed. He got out, his legs and arms angled and tense.

"I've been looking all over!" he yelled to Mom. "Now I've found out where he is." When he got back in the truck again, he was holding a baseball bat. His eyes were stone-hard on me as he peeled back out onto the grid road.

"Stop!" I shouted at him. The earth beneath me began to shift and slip. I was gulping for air, drowning. "Stop him!" I pleaded at Alex. "Tommy did this to you, not Hal!"

"Mom," she sobbed. "It's not true. Ruth is a liar."

It wasn't Hal. Not my Hal. If anything, he'd been kind to Alex, always. She probably let Tommy do it. Then when this happened, she had to find a way to make it not her fault. I stumbled up to the house and pushed past them, letting the screen door swing shut.

"Ruth!" Mom called out. But I climbed the stairs, grabbed a bag, and rammed everything I owned inside it. Mom came to the bottom of the staircase. "Please," she called up, but without conviction. She didn't mean it; she didn't climb the stairs; she didn't want me. None of them had wanted me, not since Pim died. Hal was the only one who understood me. Who made me feel any sense of happiness, who made me feel like I belonged.

When Hal pulled up at the end of our driveway a couple of hours later, his face was busted up, lip bleeding, left eye swollen shut. I put everything of mine into his trunk, and I slammed it shut. What else could I do?

"Are you going to be okay?" Alex had the gall to ask me before I got into his car. I laughed right in her face.

Mom came out and stood on the porch, not waving as Hal and I pulled away from the farm and roared south toward the highway, the house and my family a dwindling flicker in the dust of the rearview mirror.

PART THREE
THE THIEF

ALEX

It's late now, but still I can't bring myself to go back to the loft. Chase will have too many questions; I don't have the strength to answer them. I sit for a while on a park bench watching the moms with their little kids. At the top of a slide, a girl of about five waves at me as she gets set to go. *Look at me,* she's saying. *I can do this; I'm this brave.* For a second I worry that she'll topple backward. But she's done this before; she has a good grip on the metal siding. I wave back but can't muster a smile. Every minute that passes, I fight the urge to text Sully. Already I'm so muddled. If I tell Sully anything, I'm in danger of telling him everything, and it doesn't seem fair to Chase.

When I finally get back to the loft, Chase is showering, but Ruth is sitting on a stool in the kitchen. She turns when I come in and all but pounces.

"It wasn't me," she says immediately. "I don't know how many different ways I can tell you. I never showed him that photograph of Pim."

I don't answer. I can't play this game anymore.

"And you know what?" She shifts in her seat, jabs a forefinger in the air. "Your rule about not talking about the past was crazy. Nobody lives like that. It was an impossible thing to ask."

I sigh and close the front door. "Well, apparently it wasn't a rule you took seriously anyway."

"No, because it was stupid. Here, let's try it: You tell me a story about yourself, Alex, and none of it can be about anything that's happened to you. Go." Her right knee is jiggling. As usual, she's the one who's angry when I'm the one who's been wronged.

"I'm really tired, Ruth."

"Do you believe me?"

"No, I don't." I walk to the fridge and open it, my back to her at the counter. "I think you love that Chase found out and is mad at me. You had something over me. I think you saw that as an opportunity to hurt me, and you took it."

When I glance back, she has her palm flat against her chest, her mouth outraged at the slander.

"It doesn't work on me, Ruth." I pull a container of some kind of pasta from the fridge and open it, put it back again. "This whole *poor me* act you have going. You know what you've done in your life, all the things you chose. And you chose them for *everyone*. No one else ever had a say."

"What are you talking about?"

I slam the fridge closed. "If anyone has a right to be mad, it's me. But look at you! You're trying to steal that from me, too."

She sits up so straight it's like the chair has turned electric. "I've done a lot of work on myself, Alex, and I've come to terms with a shit ton of things. I think it's time you did the same."

"Oh, spare me." My voice is rising now, but then to my left I'm aware that Chase has come out of the shower. He's standing in his shorts, his hair tousled.

"Hello," he says. He looks scared more than anything, as if the floor is full of land mines.

"Chase." I walk toward him. "I'm sorry I took off. I needed to clear my head. Today has been awful, start to finish. I'm sorry."

"Okay," he says. "It's okay. But can we talk?" He looks around as if only just noticing there's nowhere private in this condo. "Can we go somewhere on our own right now?"

"I'd like that," I say.

"Are you hungry? You must be. Come on, I know a place." He throws on a T-shirt he's left on the couch, grabs his keys from a hook by the door. "Will you be all right, Ruth?" he asks.

"I don't know," she says, standing.

"She'll be fine," I say. And then to her: "Don't wander off."

The last thing I see before the front door closes is Ruth helping herself to the pasta from the fridge.

We take Chase's car because it's quicker. The town is deserted and closed up for the night, but he knows a wine bar that's attached to the Snow Ridge hotel on the way out to the ski hill. The hotel itself is fancy—the kind of place moneyed weekenders would stay at before returning to their corporate jobs in Denver or LA—and the wine bar's still open, jazz blaring from the sound system. It sounds frenzied, wailing, upsetting.

"Have you been here before?" I ask. Never before have I seen so many suits and Rolexes in Moses River.

"I come here all the time." Chase waves at the bartender. "I get a special rate because they know me."

"When do you come here?" I ask, and he looks worried again.

"For work things," he says. "If marketing associates come from other resorts, we always host them here."

"Oh, okay." It's the first time I've ever wondered if there's anything else I don't know about him.

We sit in the quietest corner, if that's possible, since all of them are spot-lit by expensive lighting, overhung by speakers, hemmed in by plush cushions and low, polished tables. When the barman approaches, Chase orders a gin and tonic, but all I can stomach is ginger ale. Neither of us speaks until the barman leaves.

"Where were you all evening?" he asks.

"Just walking around."

"On your own?"

"Yes, Chase. I swear." There's a long silence. "You can ask me, you know. You have a hundred questions, I can tell."

He exhales. "I really only have one. Why couldn't you tell me earlier about your brother?"

I lower my hands to my lap. "How much do you know about him?"

"That he died in an accident on the farm when he was really little. It's awful, Alex. I feel horrible for you. And I don't know why you didn't tell me."

A pocket of stress is swelling in me, spreading out as it rises. It's a pressure that has to get out.

"The truth of how Pim died is hard for me to think about, even now. It happened so long ago. My parents were out, and he fell into a grain truck. Ruth was the oldest. She was in charge."

The bartender brings drinks and leaves.

"But . . . was she to blame?" Chase asks.

I wait a beat. "Like I said. My little brother's death was an accident. But Ruth was supposed to be looking after him. She knew better than us, and she failed. She didn't keep him safe at all. It's the worst thing she could have done." I move my drink farther away from me on the table. "I was close with my mom and dad until my brother's death left this big brick wall between us. We never got past it."

"Wow," he says, rubbing his smooth chin. "That definitely explains why she's been so secretive. Everything I ask her, she clamps like a vault."

"You couldn't have trusted anything she said anyway. She's a revisionist storyteller. She changes the details of the past to suit herself." I take his hand, interlace my fingers with his. "I'm sorry I didn't tell you any of this before. It's not a place I go to if I can help it."

"I get it," he says, rubbing the side of his glass with his thumb.

"Some people are wired wrong," I say. "And sometimes they end up in your family."

Chase picks up his gin and sips it. "You know," he says, "I think this is the most you've ever talked about yourself."

My throat tightens, and I fight back tears. "It's not that I don't trust you, Chase, or don't want you to know me. I'm not trying to be inaccessible."

"You've just lived with secrets for too long."

"Yes," I say. "Yes."

He leans across the table and touches my cheek, my neck. "So what now? Are we kicking her out?" It's sweet how supportive he is. But kicking Ruth out won't help anyone.

"No," I say, kissing his hand before he withdraws it. "She's my sister. She's destitute and seven months pregnant. I can't kick her out, however complicated she is."

Chase nods, commiserating. "My brother and I didn't speak for half a year when I beat him in a ski race. I still remember it. I was miserable. But when he needed me to help train for the next season, I couldn't say no."

I'd like to have had his life, the surface depth of his trauma.

"The important thing for me is to make sure Ruth's baby is safe," I say. "You know, what I've learned in my job is that so often damage is cyclical. It just perpetuates generation to generation. I don't want that for Ruth's child. Her baby deserves a shot at happiness."

"We can look after her, make sure she's eating right, keep her spirits up," Chase offers. "But you realize, no matter what, she's the child's mother. There's no escaping that."

I smile. Is he right? Maybe. Maybe not.

He glows at me across the table.

"It's big of you," Chase says. "To accept this responsibility for your sister. I love you."

"You've taken my sister in. It's big of you, too."

He shrugs. "Alex, I have to ask you—straight up—do I need to be worried about this Sully guy?"

"No!" I say quickly, "God, no! There is absolutely nothing going on there. I swear, Chase, I don't even think of him that way. He's a colleague, and anyway, he's really aloof. We're thrown together by work. That's all it is."

Chase looks restored. He smiles at me, then notices the nuts in the bowl are all gone and jumps up to get a refill. On the way past, I pull him back for a kiss.

We stay longer in the bar than we need to that night, order a couple more drinks, until we're the only two left in the whole place. I watch Chase as he tells me some story about his week. He's animated, jovial, relieved. We're a team again, and he's entirely on my side. She doesn't own him anymore. I've got him back.

RUTH

Things are not going well. Alex and Chase are letting me stay in the loft still, although for the life of me I can't think why. She's so terse with me that it's obvious she continues toblame me for the big Pim reveal. We've stopped talking about the photograph—there's nothing more I can say about it.

She's cold, distant, and uninvested. So why is she even bothering to help me, to let me stay with her? Maybe with sisters, even when you're mad at each other you love each other. Meal times are tense, though, and she makes sure she's never there in the morning when I wake up. Chase is always there, like a loyal dog. But there is some wariness in how he approaches me. When he catches himself smiling at something I've said, there's a moment of panic in his eyes as though he's just remembered he's not meant to like me. He doesn't make me smoothies anymore.

Added to my general sense of unease is the fact that I'm now really worried about Eli. The message he left on my cell phone was razored and ominous: *Come out, come out wherever you are,* he said, a singsong meanness in his voice. *You took something that doesn't belong to you, Ruthy. Didn't your mama ever tell you that's wrong?* It's not the only message he's left me, although they vary in degrees of menace. I don't answer any of them and try not to look at my phone, but it dings repeatedly. Glows at night like plutonium. I pray to God that he won't find me, because the truth is I can't find his coffee tin. I've turned over the apartment, and it's fucking nowhere to be found.

At first I thought I'd moved it so far back in the bathroom vanity that it was simply impossible to see. I knelt down low, squashing the hump of my belly in front of me, clawing my hands into the darkness of the cupboard space. But the tin is gone. It has completely vanished. I toss and turn at night, trying desperately to remember if I've moved the hiding spot and just forgotten, what with baby brain and all. Or has Chase found the tin and disposed of it? Or did Alex? And if either of them looked inside and found the drugs, why hasn't one of them said anything to me? Nothing makes any sense.

"Have you seen any of my things in the bathroom?" I asked Alex earlier this week as she was writing an email on her work laptop.

She looked up, hassled. "Things?"

"Doesn't matter," I mumbled. It wasn't like I could be any more specific. Later the same day, I tried Chase. "Have you seen a coffee tin kicking about?" I asked him airily. "Folgers?"

"You bought us coffee?" He reached immediately for his organic version above the stove. "We usually drink this. It's got fewer chemicals in it."

Neither of them had a clue what I was getting at, which begs the question: Where the fuck are my drugs and my money?

It's a Sunday in late August, and the day is breaking into an idyllic, cloudless, ceramic-blue sky. I lie on the couch, heartburn fizzing and nauseous. There's an inescapable sense that I'm panicking for two now. I wanted to feel differently about motherhood, even with what I knew of the world; at the start, I was so hopeful that it might begin a better chapter for me and for Alex. But these strange, angular sweeps of the baby's head or elbow under my skin tell me everything is so frighteningly imminent. I stare at my midriff under the sheet, expecting a fist to punch outward, a foot. I feel more anxious now than ever. What will my baby learn about me as soon as it's out? That I'm an idiot who lost thousands of dollars' worth of drugs? That I ruined my own insurance plan? Invited violent crime into our home? I count down the days until September 20. I should be excited to give birth, but the date fills me with dread. I have to fix things before the baby gets here, before Eli shows up, although I'm starting to think his arrival will be sooner.

Your sister lives in Moses River, he said on his most recent message. *That's a long, expensive bus ride, Ruthy. I'll have to take it out of the cash you stole.* He knows exactly where I am. He must have paid more attention than I thought when I spoke about having a sister. Has he already sent a henchman to steal the drugs back? Is that why I can't find them? But deep down I know he'll come himself, if only to inflict maximum damage. I jump whenever a car pulls up outside the window. What is this stress doing to my baby?

I hear Alex and Chase get up and enter the kitchen. I pretend to still be dozing, but it's pointless. I'm so worried that I have to say something. I slowly get up from my bed on the couch.

Alex and Chase are eating at the kitchen island. Chase has made them smashed avocado on toast, although there doesn't seem to be a portion for me. Alex pauses midsip of coffee when she notices me standing by the couch.

"What?" she asks. "Did you want some breakfast?"

"Oh, I'll make you one." Chase stands. "I didn't know if avocado would make you feel queasy. I read that with pregnant women, it's all kind of a texture thing."

Both Alex and I stare at him.

"I have to tell you something."

Chase looks uncertainly at Alex. She puts down her toast, rubs crumbs from her fingertips. *What now?* she's thinking. *What the hell could you possibly do next?* Shame swells in my throat.

"I might have—I might have gotten us all into a sketchy situation."

Chase's eyes widen, but still he's waiting for pointers from Alex.

"How sketchy?" Her voice is so tired of me.

"When I left Pittsburgh, I was in a panic. Eli and I had gotten into this big fight, and he was trying to make me do things I didn't want to do. But when I said no, he—"

"What things?" Alex says.

I look at my bare feet, at my toes as they turn inward. "Sell coke. To college kids on campus."

Chase has a mouthful of toast but has completely stopped chewing.

"So I ran away from him. I ran away. But I had no money. Right before I left, I grabbed a tin of Eli's stuff. Of Eli's drugs, I mean. And cash."

Chase and Alex look at each other, shocked.

"He owed me money anyway, and I figured if I was absolutely desperate, if you sent me away and didn't take me in, then at least I could survive for a few months."

"You fucking . . ." Alex says, "stole drugs and cash from a dealer. And brought them here? *Here*, to our apartment?"

"I didn't mean to put you guys in danger. Honestly, I didn't."

"But why steal drugs?" Chase's voice is quiet. "What good are they to you? You'd have had to sell them to . . ."

"Yes. It would have been a last resort. And I didn't use any of the drugs. I didn't touch the coke or the money—because of you. You both saved me from that life. But . . . I didn't get rid of the stash."

Alex starts to pace. "Where the hell are they, Ruth? Where are the goddamn drugs?"

"That's the thing. I put them under the bathroom sink. I hid them right at the back."

Alex turns to Chase. *See?* she's saying. *One thing after another. It never, ever stops.*

"You put drugs in the bathroom vanity?" she says.

"Yes, and a shit ton of cash, if I'm honest. Like, probably ten grand. I'm really, really sorry."

"*Ten grand?*" Alex says, dumbfounded. "Stolen from a violent dealer and hidden in our house? In what fucking part of your brain did you ever consider that to be thinking like a *mother?*" Her jaw is chisel-stiff.

"The drugs are in our bathroom?" Chase rubs his forehead, as if trying to figure out a puzzle.

"They were, but I can't find that tin," I say.

Alex's head tilts.

"And there's another problem." I press my hands in front of me like a prayer. "Eli's coming."

Alex looks at Chase and back again. "What do you mean, he's coming? Did you give him our address?!"

"No, of course not! But he's . . . he's clever, and he figures things out. And I thought I could just send him away with the tin, but it's not where I left it. It's . . . gone. . . ." I trail off, not sure what else to say.

"Jesus Christ." Chase stands up, knocking avocado toast onto the floor.

"Let's look for the tin," Alex says grimly.

"Alex, a *drug dealer* is coming to the apartment," Chase says, desperately sweeping up the mess on the floor. "Don't you think we should call the police, right now?"

"I heard what she said, Chase! It's news to me, too. And I agree! This is a whole fresh wave of shit she's dumping on top of our heads, none of which is your fault or mine. But first, we need to find that fucking tin. And then you"—she points at me with steady, incriminating finger—"you are going to tell the police exactly what you did."

"If you call the cops, they'll arrest me for sure. Is that what you want?" I ask. They ponder the question for too long but eventually shake their heads.

"You left the tin in the cupboard under the sink?" Alex says, standing. "And you never moved it? You're sure about that?"

I nod. My breathing is shallow; I feel hot, far too hot. All this anxiety can't be good for anyone.

She strides to the bathroom, anger in every movement she makes. I drift after her on flimsy legs, Chase two steps behind me. She yanks open the cupboard under the sink, tossing facecloths, toilet paper, bars of soap behind her like a dog digging a furious tunnel. "What did the tin look like?" she asks, peering to the back of the space.

"It's a Folgers coffee tin." I put one hand on the doorframe to try to steady myself.

She shakes her head, grunts as she gets even lower to the ground. Behind me, Chase is shivering like a Chihuahua.

Alex, kneeling on the ground, stops searching. "It's not here."

"Who's moved it?" I wail.

"Not me," says Chase. "I wish I knew where it was, but I don't."

Alex sighs. Her hands lay limp in her lap.

"Could someone have gotten into the loft?" Chase asks suddenly. "Has somebody broken in? Or is it possible that maybe Eli's been and gone?" His brow lightens at the prospect, the poor sheltered boy.

"Chase, do you really think a dealer would just tiptoe in and out?" Alex asks.

Chase glances out the bathroom door, to the huge TV, the expensive stereo system, the easy technology scattered around the apartment. His shoulders sag again.

"She's right," I say quietly. "If I can't find it, I'm in big trouble. Eli will want to punish me." My whole body is flushing with stress.

Alex stands up, kicks the vanity door shut, and turns on me. It's all too close, too claustrophobic, all three of us still in the bathroom. "Is this real, this whole drugs-in-a-tin story?" She moves in close to my face. "Or is it another one of your attention-grabbing schemes? Are you looking for more ways to disrupt our lives? To spread a little more fear?"

"What? No!"

"Or is it that you want us all to feel sorry for you again? To huddle around you protectively?"

"Aren't we doing that already?" Chase asks.

"Maybe someone else in the building got in here? Is that possible?" I ask. "You don't always lock the front door."

"That's true," Chase says.

"Stop it!" Alex shouts. "Nobody who lives in this building has come into our loft and gone straight to the bathroom vanity! Can you hear how ridiculous that sounds?" She sidesteps Chase and pushes me so that I stagger back a step and almost fall over.

"Alex!" Chase yells. "*What the hell?* She's heavily pregnant!"

Thick clouds begin to wash across my vision.

Chase grips me at the elbow. "Ruth, are you okay? Ruth?"

The world is turning. It's turning so fast, and I can't keep up. I can't stay on my feet. All I hear is Chase's terrified voice.

"Alex, help me," he says. "She's bleeding."

My head droops downward, and I see a thin trickle of blood rolling past the hem of my shorts, down my thigh, toward my knee. More follows, pooling onto the white of the bathroom floor by my foot.

"Jesus," I hear Alex say, but blackness swirls deeper in front of me, and I surrender to it, falling onto Chase, finally finding a pit that blocks out all the sound.

ALEX

"*Rest and simplicity,*" the doctor says. "That's what your sister needs. And the more of it the better."

Simplicity is next to impossible, given the situation she's in—that we're now all in.

"Tell that to her, Doctor. Not to me," I reply.

All the tests they run conclude the whole episode is stress-related. Ruth is kept overnight for observation. It was a light bleed, nothing more, nothing dire. I sit in a slippery chair by her bed while she sleeps. It's exactly how I sat with Dad through all those last days and nights. Even the royal blue of the cushioning is the same. Ruth sleeps like she did as a child—effortlessly, soundlessly, so completely elsewhere in her slumber that it's as if she's switched dimensions. I leave for home at dawn before she wakes, and find Chase in the kitchen making coffee.

"I couldn't sleep," he says. "I know she's your sister and everything, but Christ, Alex. I don't think I'm okay with her coming back here. She brought drugs and stolen money into our home."

I move straight toward him and hug him. "I know, I know. But, Chase, what you're not getting is that she makes a lot of things up."

He pulls back, his face young and trusting. "You're saying she's lying about that? Why would she do that?"

"To destabilize us. She creates chaos. She's been like that since we were little kids. If there's a button, she'll push it. Don't ask me why."

"Huh," he says. "You shouldn't have shoved her."

I keep my eyes low. "You're right. I shouldn't have done that. It's just that she's just so . . . frustrating sometimes."

"You can't go pushing a pregnant—"

"I said I get it. I regret it."

He pulls me in against his chest. "So . . . okay. And you really think she's making it up about the drugs and this Eli guy?"

I lean up and kiss him along the jawline. "I think Eli's real, but I doubt he's coming here. I'll get the police to check on that, ask them to keep an eye out. Okay? Honestly, Chase, I don't think there's anything new to worry about. If there were really drugs, they'd be in the apartment."

He's quiet for a minute, then nods.

"I have to go into work for a little bit today. Do you have time to pick up Ruth from the hospital?" I ask.

"I thought you had today off," Chase says. "We were going to spend some time together."

"I do. There's just something I need to check on." Buster's family conference is today, though Morris waved me off when I volunteered to attend.

"It's probably better that you take a rest from this one," he said. "Take Monday for yourself. The Floyd case seems to have worked its way under your skin."

"What does that mean?" I asked.

"Just that these meetings are fraught at the best of times. We need diffusers in this room, not . . . the opposite. We've got Frank, Evelyn, their lawyer, the maternal grandmother, and me. That's plenty."

Minerva's missing it, too. She's off on a three-week trip to Paris.

"Can't you reschedule it, Morris?" she asked, the day before she was due to fly out. "I really feel it's important I'm there in the room."

"It's been a month, Minerva. That's long enough," Morris said. "We won't get anything sorted anyway. You know how these things go."

He's right. Family conferences are an unnecessary emotional stepping-stone on the inevitable road to a day in court. So rarely do birth parents show up to family conferences with an evolved, selfless outlook and agree that their child would do better growing up with a relative. Mostly the meetings just create more turmoil. But still, Morris refuses to sidestep them, and I feel the need to be in the office for this one, just in case.

"Okay," Chase says now, sipping his newly made coffee. "I can get Ruth."

"Thank you," I say. "She's being discharged at one p.m. I love you. Don't worry."

Honestly, though, I should be saying it to myself. With Ruth's due date looming and Buster's family conference, I have way more on my plate than he does, way more to worry about. There are moments when I wonder how I'm managing to keep going.

I haven't seen Buster since the removal, and I haven't been privy to any of the supervised visits. As lead social worker on the file, Minerva attended them all, but Morris assured me Buster was doing great. *Smashing*, was how he put it. *Don't worry, Alex, Granny's got it covered. Buster is thriving.*

An hour later, I hurry out of the loft and into the office, timing it perfectly so that I hear Frank's voice as they enter. Nobody knows I'm here, especially not Morris. I peek through the crack in my door as the key players walk down the hall, toward the conference room. Frank and Evelyn look rough and bedraggled as they enter, as if they've spent the month without their son sitting under a leaky drainpipe. The grandmother creeps behind them, her hair cropped close to her head and bright orange like she's dipped it in paint. She's bony, spindly old legs in bejeweled jeans, the skin of her face stretched veiny and tight around sharp cheekbones. She must have left Buster with a friend while she attends the meeting—nobody ever brings kids to these things in case the meetings go sideways. I wonder for the hundredth time if Buster's okay and indeed thriving, but have I to trust Morris's judgment. I withdraw into my office and listen through the cheap plywood wall to Evelyn's pleading, her tearful, panicked resolutions. I can hear every word.

"But we've done everything you said," Evelyn sobs. "We've done the forms and shit, and the drug tests. Didn't we, Frank?"

"Yes and they came back clean." Frank's voice hides latent rage. "Clean, Mr. Arbuckle. What do you have to say about that?"

"No, that's great, that's fantastic." I can imagine Morris flattening his tie. "And let's just recap that we all want the same thing here. Granny—how are you getting on?"

"My name is Janeen." The grandmother's voice is tight. "And they weren't on drugs. I could have told you that from the get-go. They've fought a very hard fight, Mr. Arbuckle. I think people should be given well-dones for that, not punishments. I love Buster, sir, don't get me wrong. But he needs to be with his mom and his dad."

"Yes," Morris says. "I'm very happy that the tests came back negative, but it's not quite as simple as that, though. Evelyn, Frank, to be clear, are you saying that you won't give consent for Buster to be in his grandmother's care ongoing?"

"No, I fucking won't," says Frank. "No offense, Janeen."

"None taken," she says.

"I'm afraid it becomes a matter for the court, then," Morris says. "We'll let the judge ruminate on the facts."

Leopards don't change their spots, my love, I imagine him thinking. I'm so glad I got him on board.

Only once the Floyds have left the building do I emerge from my office. I'm almost to the front door when Morris catches me.

"Alex?" he says. "What on earth are you doing here?"

"Nothing. I just . . . I left my—"

"You were listening to the whole thing, weren't you?" He shakes his head in amazement. "You couldn't help yourself. It's not normal, you know, to *seek out* work when you've been told to relax at home."

"I know. I'm sorry. It's just that—"

"You care too much. That's what it is. That's good and everything, but I can't have you disregarding my instructions. You're lucky Minerva's not here."

"Sorry, Morris."

"Go home. Take a breather. God knows we all need a little self-care."

I pause at the security screen and turn.

"Yes, Alex," he says, rolling his eyes, even though his tone is warm. "The family conference went well. Buster's set for a court date, just like you wanted."

"It's not just me who wants—"

"Go home, or I'm firing you."

"Okay. Okay, sorry. I'm leaving now."

When I get back to the apartment, it's empty. Chase must be at the hospital picking up Ruth. We'll need to keep a steady vigil on her at home. I'm worried about my sister, about her fitness to be a new mom. Obviously it's a bad sign that's she's fainting and bleeding from stress. She's not coping, and the baby's not even on the outside yet. It's going to take a village to raise her child.

By the sink, I pour water into the coffeepot, relax into the quiet of the hour I have to myself. It's rare to be in this apartment alone, and the silence feels restorative. But just as I'm unfolding a new filter, there's a rap on the door. It's lunchtime. Nobody ever knocks on the door. When I open it, a man is standing against the doorjamb, picking at his molar with a fingernail. He's long and thin, his jeans baggy around his sneakers. He looks sallow, as if he hasn't seen sunlight in a while, his blue eyes pale and cold, cropped hair more beige than blond.

"Oh, hi," he says, smiling. "Is Ruth here?"

I pause, my mouth getting drier. Is this him? Eli Beck, woman beater, drug dealer, father-to-be? So he actually tracked her down. I underestimated him.

"Who are you looking for?" I say, looking him right in the eye, trying to hide that my heart is picking up pace.

"Ruth Van Ness," he says. "Isn't this where she lives?" He leans farther in the doorway, overly casual, but with the look of a hungry puppy, a runt, the one that never got fed.

"Sorry. I don't know anyone by that name. Who are you?"

"You're her sister." He smiles. "You're the clever one."

We both know he's not complimenting me. I take a deep breath, try not to let it show that my hands are shaking. I've dealt with his type before. I've taken away children from degenerates just like him.

I decide to come clean. "Ruth has been staying with me. She's out right now."

"Can I come in?" He moves his foot like he'll barricade the door anyway. *You don't have a choice, sweetheart*, he's saying.

"Sure. I'm making coffee. Would you like one? I don't know when Ruth will be back, though." I leave the door open and walk toward the kitchen, my mind racing. I can hear him behind me, the skid of his shoes on the floor. "She's out with my husband." Is my voice level? "He shouldn't be long."

"You know who I am?" Eli's looking around, just like Ruth did when she first walked into this place.

"You're the man my sister left behind," I say.

"Oh, so you do know me." He touches his hand to his chest as if flattered.

"She doesn't want to see you. What are you doing showing up here now?"

He's wiry but strong. I wonder how many real fights he's been in, though. By the stove is a heavy china mug. I move it closer to me.

"She told you that?" he asks, and he pulls a stool out from the counter and sits on it, crossing his arms. "Ruth, Ruth, Ruth."

I wonder, did my sister really leave before he found out she was pregnant? The coffeepot starts to sputter and gag behind us.

"Look, is there something I can help you with?" I keep my eyes on him.

"Funny you should ask. She took something from me. I want it back."

Fuck. There it is. "I'm afraid I don't know what you're talking about."

"Liar."

I set my jaw but move my fingers to the handle of the cutlery drawer.

"You're sisters. You know everything she knows."

"I do not," I say. "You couldn't be more wrong about that."

"You're shaking," he says, and he stands up.

"I am not. I'm not afraid of you."

"No? You should be." He rounds the corner of the countertop, moving toward me in a fast, straight line.

The knife I grab is the small paring one, Chase's favorite for dicing vegetables, the one he keeps extra sharp. Eli thinks he's quicker than me, but I've lived among these lowlife scum who think they have power. He grabs at my shoulder but I bring up the knife and the blade catches him under his chin. Both of his hands go there, and he stops in his tracks, his pale eyes wide.

"What the fuck?" He checks his fingertips for blood. A tiny stream has opened up, changing the neck of his T-shirt to crimson. He starts to back up, his right arm out front of him like a barrier.

"You think you can come in here and terrify me?" I keep pace with him, the knife high and glistening. "You don't know who you're dealing with. You don't know what I'm capable of." He's retreated so far now that he slams into the wall by the front door, his elbow splitting the middle of Chase's ski canvas, ruining it. "I could cut your throat and watch you drown, and nobody would ever question it." I push my arm into his chest, pin him there, the blade pressing so hard against his Adam's apple that the skin bulges around the silver. For so long I've wanted to push the lowlifes and the wasters down, and finally I get the chance. Blood rages through my body.

"Get out of my house and stay away from my sister." His eyes show me nothing but fear. He's all bravado, a sham, just a weak, beaten dog.

When I release him I keep the knife high like I'll stab, and he scrambles for an escape, runs for the hallway, clatters down the stairs. I hear the door at the front entrance slam behind him.

As soon as he's gone, I throw the front door closed and bolt it. It's silent again, and I stagger toward the kitchen and wash off the knife in the sink, frantically clean the drops of blood on the floor, rinsing it all away in the sink. I look at Chase's ruined picture. *Holy shit. That escalated so quickly.* I head for the bed at the far end of the loft and sit down with my palms on my cheeks, legs shaking. Will Eli come back? Should I call Sully? I close my eyes for a minute and try to steady my head. At least it was me who was here when he came. If it was Chase, it would have ended differently. If it were Ruth . . . The thought makes me feel sick. *It's okay,* I tell myself. *You did it. You did everything that needed to be done.*

Along the skirting board to the left of the bed is a large vent, the screws of which I removed ages ago, although Chase never noticed. I bend low and pry off the front cover at one corner, lay it gently to one side on the floor. In the gap behind the vent is the Folgers coffee tin, round and shiny, the tape wrenched from the lid just like it was when I found it under the bathroom sink. Inside is everything Eli was looking for, everything Ruth thinks she's lost.

If you want to keep something safe, you have to do it yourself. That tin was a time bomb. I peel open the lid and run my hands through the silky little baggies, liking the way they move and yield around my fingertips. The rolls of tight money are all there. Safe and sound. Eli's gone, and he didn't hurt anyone. And nobody is the wiser but me.

I tuck the whole thing back into its hole and replace the metal grill in the front. Back in the kitchen, I pull my hair into a topknot, take a breath, then pick up my cell.

"Alex?" Sully answers on the first ring.

"Hi," I say. "What are you doing?"

"Nothing. I'm off duty."

"Can we meet? I need to tell you something."

He pauses. Possibility fizzes down the line. "Sure. Are you okay?"

"I'm fine. I need to talk to you. It's about my sister."

RUTH

It's Thursday afternoon, and I've just woken up from a nap. I haven't heard from Eli since Monday, the day I got back from the hospital. His silence is almost worse than his threats. Is he waiting to take me by surprise? Around the apartment, I jump every time toast pops up in the toaster, and feel like at any minute I could cry.

When Chase and I got back from the hospital, Alex had prepared a nice spot for me to rest, vacuumed the floors, and polished every surface. But something was different in the apartment; something felt blank. It took me a minute to figure out that the massive ski photo by the front door was missing, the canvas leaning torn and face-in by the coatrack.

"What happened to my picture?" Chase asked. "Did it fall down?"

"I'm so sorry." Alex moved to him and gave him a kiss on the cheek. She looked hot, like she'd been running. "I stumbled into it while I was vacuuming. I'm afraid my elbow went right through it."

Chase swallowed, his brow creased. "That's too bad. I really loved that picture."

"I'm so sorry. Maybe I can get another one made?"

"Maybe," Chase said.

I let them commiserate for a minute, saying I needed the bathroom. For the fiftieth time, I checked in the back of the vanity, but still the tin wasn't there.

There's an explanation—there has to be. Somebody knows where the drugs are. But neither Alex nor Chase has spoken of them since I got back. Alex must have told Chase I was lying about the whole thing, that the tin isn't real, that I'm making everything up. But why would I lie? Recently she seems distracted, or at least so involved with her work that she's not really here. Other times, I think she sees me as one of her cases, one of the people she has to fix. Just another burden. I know she's trying to make me feel at home, but I feel weirdly ignored and smothered at the same time.

I hear a noise behind me and turn abruptly to see Chase folding laundry.

"Oh, hi," I say. "How long was I asleep?"

"An hour or so. You were making weird noises."

"I was?" I move hair from my face, which feels sweaty.

He pairs socks and doesn't comment. He's keeping his distance, staying busy.

"Where's Alex?" I ask, starting to work toward standing.

"At work. Maybe you should lie back down."

Complete bed rest is what I've been told. He's right, but I roll my eyes anyway. It's raining outside, a hard end-of-summer rain, and heat is rising up from the asphalt. I can smell it from the open window. As I settle back onto the couch, my phone buzzes and I dig for it in the cushions. Oh God, is it Eli? My heart is pounding as I open the message.

Give me back the tin, Ruth, and we're square. I don't mean any harm. I'm in town for a few more days.

Twice I read it, three times, my heart returning to a steady beat.

I expected him to be even more upset—that's his way. Short-tempered, gathering speed, his rage driving like an engine until he lashes out, like he did the night before I left him. But this text feels different. It's oddly civil. It's so foreign, it's unnerving.

I stare at the screen for a while, unsure how to respond.

Can we meet tomorrow? I type. I can explain. I want to sort every-thing out.

It's mere seconds before the phone vibrates. Bus depot, 10 a.m., he writes. Don't bring your sister. She's a fucking psycho.

One hand goes right to my stomach. What? He met Alex? My head begins to swirl.

You came here? I text.

Again, a response within seconds. Yeah. Your sis is fucking nuts.

I haul myself up, one arm on the back of the couch. For a second or two I watch Chase folding a shirt. Chase. Of course. I have to get him onside. Even if I'm breaking Alex's rules and speaking of the past, I can't let her be in charge any longer. She's met Eli, and she's hiding the fact. Chase doesn't even know.

And then, that's when I think of it. I walk toward him, as if I'm head-ing over to help him with his chores.

"Steady," Chase says. "You shouldn't be moving too fast." He doesn't look at me and won't.

Carefully, Ruth. Tread carefully. I stop just short of him, straighten the angle of the kitchen stool for him until it's perfect. "Chase, I wanted to say thanks for everything you've been doing. You're really looking out for me and the baby."

He pauses, his eyes narrow, the T-shirt in his hands. "You're welcome. I'm glad you noticed."

"It won't be long before you get to meet the little one," I say, patting my belly. "Do you want to feel it move? It feels a bit weird, but I've gotten used to it. I kind of look forward to it now."

He smiles but guardedly. "I'm okay, thank you. But it'll be good to have a baby around. A couple of weeks to go, right?"

"If it's on time. They say with first pregnancies it can lag."

"I know," he says. "I've read up on it."

I ease onto a stool that he isn't using to pile clothes, my belly facing him. "You'd be a good dad, I think. If you ever choose to have children." I pause, eye him. "I mean that genuinely."

He softens. "Thanks, that means a lot, Ruth."

Now's my moment. "It's too bad Alex can't have kids."

He immediately stops folding.

I pause. "Oh, you do know why, right?" I say, because it's now or never. "She was so young. It was hard on her then, when it happened, and I guess the impact just never goes away."

He looks at me, confused. "When what happened?"

"The abortion." It comes out of me so suddenly, like poison expelled.

"What are you talking about? What abortion?"

"Nothing. My mistake. Forget I said anything."

There's a moment of heavy silence.

"I don't know anything you're talking about."

"I'm concerned about Alex." More silence. "She never told you why she might be infertile?"

His eyes are wide, shocked. He shakes his head.

"She was only fifteen." I try to keep the desperation out of my voice. I will sound calm and collected. "Chase, maybe it's not my place to say so, but don't you think it's odd that there's so much she hasn't told you? Doesn't it make you wonder if . . ."

He licks his lips. "If what?"

"Nothing. Never mind." I get up from the stool and take a few steps toward the couch as if we're done with the conversation. That's when he draws me back.

"We had a good talk last month. She opened up and told me a lot of things. She even explained about Sully. It's just a work thing. She promised not to be in touch with him after hours. So it's not what you think. She's private, for sure, but she's not . . . you know. We're close, and she wouldn't keep something like that from me. Not something so . . . so formative, and upsetting. She would have told me."

"Are you sure?" I said. "Do you really think I'd make up something like that about my own sister?" I stand in my place, feet planted, strong. "Sacred Heart Medical Clinic, in Horizon, North Dakota. There's only one such clinic. September 2009. I took her there myself."

He's stock-still, stress beating out of him like a pulse. I let him suffer while I look at my phone.

"Also, Chase, I think this guy who's after me, Eli Beck, he came here, to your loft, and Alex was home. She didn't tell us. Not you. Not me. Are you sure Alex broke your canvas painting while she was vacuuming? My sister is not that clumsy."

He looks so young and bewildered. I hand him my cell and let him scroll through Eli's texts. "I haven't lied about Eli, Chase. I haven't lied to you about anything. But Alex has."

He reads the texts, then gives me back my phone. "I need to . . . I can't . . .," he says. "I don't know what's going on. Why would she hide that? Why? It doesn't even make sense."

In my mind, over and over, I'm pleading with him to believe me. *Be the very first one.*

"Chase, where did those drugs in your bathroom go? Did you find them? Did you take them?"

He looks at me with disgust. "No! Of course not," he says.

"I know," I say. "And I didn't take them, either."

I can see the wheels in his mind turning. His eyes are round and sad.

"I need your help, Chase. Alex needs your help. Something's not right."

Behind us both there's the sound of a key in the front-door lock. Chase visibly panics, moves two steps away from me as Alex lets herself in. She turns, takes in the thickness of atmosphere in the room. In the silence, the rain hammers outside.

"Hi. What's . . . what's going on?" She looks from my face to Chase's and back again.

"Nothing," we say in stereo sound. Her face is sweet, but there's something scribbled under the surface of her, a more jagged outline in red, like anger. It reminds me of her at fourteen, acing tests while she acted out, angelic to everyone who wasn't looking properly. But I've always seen through her. Always.

"C'mon. What were you two talking about?"

"We were just having a chat," Chase says. He doesn't go to her. He doesn't touch her, doesn't kiss her.

Alex moves toward me by the couch. "That sounds nice. Ruth, you should be lying down. The baby, remember?" Her voice is altogether too saccharine, but I sit down. She's about to say something else, but her phone dings. She pulls it out of her pants pocket. Her eyes dart to the screen as she sets it on the coffee table. Quickly I shoot a look at Chase. He's barely keeping his head above water.

"So what else have you—" she begins, but the phone dings again.

"Who's texting you?" Chase asks.

"I've no idea. It's my work phone, and I'm off duty."

"Then let me see it," Chase says, his hand out.

"Chase." Alex swipes the phone off the table and puts it in her back pocket. "It's just work. Calm down."

"Is it really work, or is it Eli?" I ask.

She sets her jaw, her cheeks gathering fire. "What are you talking about?"

"Was he here?" Chase asks quietly. "Did this Eli guy come to our apartment?"

"No," she says, crossing her arms.

"He was here," I say. "I know he was."

"He texted Ruth about you," Chase adds.

"And I'm starting to think you know exactly where that coffee tin is," I say, emboldened by Chase's support.

Alex's face is blotching. "What the fuck is wrong with both of you?" she says, but she doesn't move. It's a pathetic defense, and even Chase realizes it.

I hand her my phone and show her his texts; she reads them, her lips silently shaping the words. For a second I wonder if she'll whip the phone across the room. "So some drug dealer says he came here. And you believe him? Are you really that dumb? And Chase"—she turns to him and he bristles—"I expected more out of you. Is this what you two have been conspiring about?"

"She told me that—"

"Of course she did!" Alex snaps. "Haven't you listened to a single word I've said? I warned you all along that she was trouble! She's driving us apart, Chase. Can't you see that? She'd do or say anything to steal my happiness."

My heart is pounding again. Chase looks contrite. I need him on my side. I won't let her win this fight. She's won too many of the others.

"I think I'll tell Sully everything," I say. "Seems to me this is getting serious, if Eli is coming to the house and threatening my sister. And if my sister isn't saying he was here. And where did those drugs go, exactly? It's a mystery I just can't solve alone. I think I need to get the police involved."

"Do you really think Sully will believe you over me? Did you ever consider that he might arrest you for harboring illegal drugs in the first place?" she says.

Her eyes start to tear up. I know it's rage, but she's so good that it doesn't look that way. This is her last-ditch effort to gain Chase's sympathy.

"Do either of you know what I do all day?" she says. "At home, at work, with you, with Buster, with Sully? I'm constantly trying to *save everyone*! And this is how you repay me? By calling me a liar? I'm protecting *you*, Ruth! That's what sisters do."

"You're protecting me how, exactly? By confronting Eli? That's really dangerous, sis. And why won't you tell us about it? Why?"

I try to move in front of her, but she's too fast. She's leaving. By the time I'm standing, she's already walked out and slammed the door.

For a minute there's silence. Then Chase turns to me, his face more determined than I've ever seen it.

"I believe you," he says. "Tell me everything you know about her. And don't leave anything out."

ALEX

The streets of Moses River are mostly deserted because of the rain. It's coming down hard, making the sidewalks smell sour. I move quickly, my body fueled with an anger that's white-hot, my head burned clear. How dare she? How dare she threaten me with Sully? She doesn't even know him. And now she's drawn Chase into the fight! I thought I could trust him—thought I'd handled that—but clearly he's weak. Ruth has always been devious, and she never did play by the rules, but now she's messing everything up.

As I cross the bridge, I pull out my phone and read the texts Sully sent me, the ones I couldn't look at just now in the loft. I need to see you, he wrote. And then, I mean professionally. And also not. I don't reply; I just keep walking. It's a good thing I didn't let Chase see my phone.

I've only been to Sully's once—last Monday, after Eli showed up—but I remember the way. Here, trees canopy the road and the houses are solid and older. As I unlatch the front gate, Gravy watches me from the window with her handlebar ears. She barked the first time I visited, suspicious of me, I'm sure, but now she is oddly silent. I knock at the door, and it's not long before I hear Sully's footsteps. I can picture his body as it moves.

"Oh," he says, holding back the dog, who lets out a low growl. "Gravy, calm down. It's just Alex."

"Don't you remember me?" I try my most winning smile. She sniffs my hand, then wanders off, and I turn to Sully.

"I'm sorry to surprise you. I hope it's all right."

He smiles cautiously. "You're always a good surprise. Are you okay? Come in. You're soaked through." He urges me in, helps me take off my coat. I'm so close to him that I can smell his skin. I want to lean into it, nestle my head into his neck and cry. But I won't. I will be careful and make things right. I will fix everything.

My stomach feels fluttery. I move past him into the front room, which smells of firewood and coffee. He waits, watching me as I kick off my sneakers. He's freshly showered, his shirt clinging to his shoulders where he hasn't dried properly. When I turn, there's an awkward second or two when he doesn't know whether to hug me or not. He's not quite sure of the parameters.

"What's happening?" he asks. "Has Eli come back? You look rattled."

"He hasn't, no. I'm okay. But could we have a glass of wine or something?" I ask.

"Sure. Of course. Follow me." He heads for his kitchen, the walls of which are a patchwork of reconstituted wood and brick, the whole space lit with pot lights. He pours two glasses of red wine.

"Alex, I put out feelers on Eli like you asked, and we're tracking him. He's a lost boy, a product of the foster-care system. In and out since he was seven. You know the drill. He did time in a Penn state penitentiary for narcotics trafficking and there's some gang history. He's lost *and* he's dangerous. There are warrants out for his arrest."

"Wow," I say, because men love a damsel in distress. *He's nothing*, I want to say. *Nothing but a beaten dog.* "That's terrifying. Do you think you'll catch him soon?"

"I'm certain we will. Don't worry. I'll keep you safe." He passes me my glass of wine, and his fingertips touch mine with a jolt.

"Is that what your text was about?" I sit down at his kitchen table. "Why you needed to see me?"

He blushes, and when he chooses a seat, it's the one right next to me, not the one across the table. That's a good sign. "It might not have been the only reason." Our thighs are aligned. It's like we're on a date at the movies.

"Thanks for looking out for me, Sully. You're the one I trust most."

He frowns for an instant. "I still think you have to report the Eli attack," he says. "You can't have men like him coming to your home. It's a police matter."

"I can't. I told you—Ruth. She's vulnerable."

"But reporting it will help you *and* Ruth. It'll keep everyone protected."

I reach across and take his hand, interlace my fingers with his. Warmth floods me, as if he's a liquid I'm sinking into. Last time I was here, it began like this, too. *Did Eli hurt you? Are you okay? Do you feel unsafe?* Sully's brow was so worried, his hands reaching out for me, and I'd nodded, even though I didn't feel unsafe. Because I wasn't. But that's the thing about Sully: he's always looking for someone to rescue. He's a good guy. His every move is predictable. And I knew he wanted to take things further, but I couldn't let that happen. Not then. Not when it wasn't necessary. Now it is.

Holding his hand, I feel a sense of rightness. It's like a transfer of energy, a download of pieces that fit. Everything is coming together. I trace my thumb over ridges of his knuckles, lean a little into him.

"How come you're here?" he asks. "If it isn't about Eli, what did you need to tell me?" He's holding his breath, hopeful.

I need to be careful; this answer is trip-wire-loaded.

"It *is* about Eli, though," I say. "I mean, I haven't seen him again, but I've found out why he's in town. Why he came to the loft, why he attacked me."

"He wasn't looking for Ruth and the baby?"

I give him my widest little-girl eyes. "He's looking for drugs and money that Ruth took."

Sully sits up straighter. "What drugs?"

"His and Ruth's drugs."

"What?"

"Ruth owned up to it all this evening. I saw her trying to hide a tin in our bathroom. I caught her red-handed, and I made her open it up. It was filled with drugs and money."

I can literally see heat reddening Sully's face. He's a policeman, bottom line, and I know it. He won't be able to let this one go.

"Okay, this is getting out of hand. You have to see that. This is dangerous, Alex." He stares at me for longer than I'd like. Can he see the moves I'm making?

"If I report it officially," I say, "Ruth will get in trouble. She can't go to prison while she's pregnant. You know what that will be like. We have to think of the baby."

"You will report it to us officially"—his voice is firm—"*and* you'll tell Morris."

"Morris?" I gape. For all my incredulity, I've had this conversation a hundred times in my head. This conversation and all the next ones.

"Ruth's out of control!" Sully sits forward on his chair. "She shouldn't be anywhere near guys like Eli Beck. She shouldn't be bringing drugs or drug money into your home. There's more than you and Ruth to consider. There's a baby. You know this—and I get that it's complicated when it's your own family—but telling Morris now is the right thing to do."

"Is it?" I ask doubtfully, as if I've never once considered the notion.

"Listen to me: Morris trusts you to do your job. They'll be all over you when this blows up—you know how this works. You have a duty to Ruth's child, Alex."

"That's true."

"We protect the ones we can. You know I'm right about this."

It's like the clicking of cogs: all the pieces falling into place, the whole wheel turning so smoothly. I knew it would go like this. I've known it since I first opened the lid of that coffee tin, but I make sure to nod slowly, as if I'm ingesting this new idea fully. "Maybe I'll outline my concerns to Morris in an email?"

Sully smiles sadly. "I think that's a good plan."

"Please don't report her to the police just yet. I'm asking you as a friend. As my closest friend."

He looks down at both of our hands, curves his fingers softly so that they match the shape of mine. "I think that under-describes me. Don't you?"

I sigh, lean in. "I hate all this."

"Me too." He wants to kiss me—but he's battling it. "I'll hold off saying anything for now. But not for long. We have to deal with this."

I nod and find tears coming to my eyes. "It's just hard. She's my sister."

"I know," he says. "But Morris will help. He'll do things the right way."

He shifts, and I feel the muscles in his hand twitch.

"I saw him in court today, by the way. Morris. It was the custody hearing for your Floyds."

"I know. The verdict's tomorrow. I'm planning to be there for that."

He takes a deep breath, perhaps happy to be on safer work-related ground. "You know, they weren't at all how you described them."

I look up at him sharply. "The Floyds? What do you mean?"

"To be honest, the Floyds were . . . kind of gentle. I mean, struggling, obviously, but they didn't strike me as monsters. They looked like people well on the road to recovery."

"Maybe they present better publicly." I pull my hand away, take a sip of my wine.

"Right," he says, watching me. "Maybe that's it."

But there's a sliver of doubt in him, a shadow. I let a beat go by. In his kitchen, a clock ticks. Outside, the rain is letting up. "It's good to see you, Sully. To be here. I've missed you."

"Look, Alex, I have to ask you: What's happening with Chase?" He's shy, primed. He's been thinking about me all week.

"We're breaking up," I say, studying my hands, folded now in my lap. My voice shakes. "If we don't have trust, we don't have anything. You're the only one I've got, Sully."

It's a silent, smooth movement when he pulls me toward him, his arms around me. His face is inches from mine. We stare at each other for only a second before he kisses me, and this time we don't stop. We're urgent and heavy, pulling at each other's clothes. When I pictured this moment, I knew it would be exactly this. That it would build between us and it would flood, the cascade perfectly timed. I planned for it all along, kept him close for a reason. There's no way Ruth can get to him, not when he's entirely with me.

We tumble from our seats to the floor, the cold tiling beneath my bare shoulders a shock. We're moving so fast—it's out of control—except all of it is calculated precision. I exhale into him, making all the right sounds, and our bodies relax and spark at exactly the same time.

"I love you," he says, and I believe him. "I've loved you from the first time I saw you in that meeting, so worked up."

I smile into his lips. "You have?"

"Of course. And I asked you out for that first coffee together. I knew even then that you and I are cut from the same cloth."

"We are." I pull him closer. "Do you love me no matter what?"

"No matter what," he repeats.

I take his head in both of my hands, hold his face above mine for a second. "I did a bad thing when I was younger. I haven't told you everything."

"I don't care about that." His mouth is hungry, his hands full of desire.

"But if you talk to Ruth, she might—"

"I *love* you," he says again. "I love you, I love you, I love you."

I pull him toward me and kiss him again, relaxing into the feeling of both of us washing away. I have everything I came for. Everything I need. And there's nothing Ruth can do to change it.

RUTH

It takes me a long time to untangle Alex's lies for Chase, all of our past, our history—Pim, her abortion, how she made my boyfriend the one to blame and how my parents believed every word she said. It's dusky outside the window as we sit together on the couch, the clock ticking toward nine. Chase's legs are splayed in front of him, his body slithered halfway down the cushions like how they show exhaustion in a cartoon.

"So what now?" he asks. "God, I can't even separate anything in my head."

"I have to meet with Eli."

"You're not really planning on doing that, are you?" He lolls his head toward me. "I read the ten a.m. rendezvous text, but you'd be nuts to go."

"What else am I meant to do? I don't know where the drugs are." I sigh, exhausted, too. If ever I've needed a drink it's now, and I have the feeling Chase would join me.

"So that's your plan? You're just going to show up and tell him you're sorry?" He runs a heavy hand over top of his head. "I'm not a master planner, Ruth, but even I know that's a shitty one."

"I think I have to do that. Or he'll never go away."

"What if—" Chase sits up a little. "What if the drugs are here? What if Alex has hidden them?"

"I don't think she'd take that risk. Plus, where would she hide them?" I look around. "There aren't many secret spots."

"It's worth a shot." He heaves himself up and starts opening the kitchen cupboards, messing up the neatly ordered contents inside. It's unlike him to be this chaotic, to allow such disorder.

"Chase. Stop. Hey, slow down for a minute." I want to help him because he's so clearly in pain. And all of this is pointless. I know Alex too well to really believe she'll leave anything unguarded in the loft.

"Do you think she's at Sully's right now?" Chase asks as he kneels on the kitchen floor, ignoring me, continuing to dig into a cabinet.

"What do you think?" I stand slowly and move toward him, bending as far as I can to see what he's doing. There's nothing inside. When I straighten, a jab of pain hits my back. "They're thick as thieves."

He slams the cupboard door shut, strides to the bedroom, and begins rifling through the dresser. Apparently when the shit hits the fan, Chase is all about action. I follow and sit on the bed. After twenty minutes, the entire contents of their room are heaped all over the floor.

"Nothing's here," Chase says.

"Thank you for trying." I smile sadly. "But she's keeping secrets, just like she did before, when she was a kid. Maybe you should just have a glass of whiskey or something. You've had a bad night."

"When she was a kid," Chase echoes, then lifts his head. "When you lived on the farm in Horizon, would she ever hide things?"

The rock, I think suddenly. *The basalt stone from school.*

"She had a hidey-hole behind the vent in our bedroom," I say.

Chase is already up, moving toward the wall across from us, to the grate there. It looks innocuous enough, but the screws unwind easily. I move closer. Chase loosens the last screw and lowers the front plate, and there—in horrible triumph—is the tin. The proof of my sister's deception hits me hard, and I stagger. How many times has she denied the tin was real?

Chase peels off the lid.

"Holy cow," he says, taking in the bags of coke, the rolls of money. "This is it, isn't it?"

I nod. The contents look like they've been rifled through, so it's hard to know if everything's there. Has Alex helped herself to the cash? Or worse, used some of the drugs? It would explain her skittishness.

"Why would she hide it?" Chase asks finally.

"I don't know." I really don't.

The one thing about Alex is that she always has a plan. She's purposeful; she's always about the finish line. What that is in this case, I'm not sure. Something doesn't feel right. I reach for the tin. "I'm taking it back to Eli," I say. "At ten o'clock tomorrow morning. I'm going to end this."

"I'm coming, too," Chase says confidently. "We'll go together, drop the damn thing off, get out of there as quickly as possible. Okay?"

"Okay," I say.

He gets up then and heads into the kitchen, where he finds a half-empty bottle of Scotch and takes a swig, straight from the mouth.

———

It's almost 10:00 a.m. and we're on our way. All of Chase's drunken confidence from last night seems to have faded. He's nervous and twitchy on the drive over. His voice is high and squeaky. Chase parks the car at the bus depot but doesn't switch off the engine. He sits bouncing his knee so that the coins in his pocket jangle.

"Are you sure about this?" he asks.

"We have no other choice." I grip my bag, pressing its hard contents into the sponge of my belly. The whole front of my pelvis is heavy and aching today, like the sucking pull of a tide, a pain that's new and unrecognizable. I shouldn't have come here; I'm supposed to be on bed rest. But if I can just get through the next half hour, then go home and lie down, maybe every-thing will be okay. All I want to do is get to my due date and meet my little boy or girl. I feel a kick. My baby wants to meet me, too.

Chase turns to me. "So . . . you'll stay in the car, like we said, and I'll bring Eli to you. You figure out your business. Then we get the hell out of here."

I nod. I'm actually grateful Chase is here with me. I check the bag, see the tin, the torn shreds of duct tape like a fringe around the lid. The digital clock on his dashboard is blinking toward ten. My pelvis tweaks and twinges. I stare at the bus depot windows that glint impenetrably, but the only people outside the building are two haggard-looking women smoking cigarettes, their inhalations the most luxury they know.

"He's not here," I say.

"What? He has to be."

"He's not, Chase." I look around at the small-town slowness. "It's not like Eli to be late, either."

"Maybe he's waiting inside. I should go in there and check, right?" He hesitates, one hand on the door lever. "I'll bring him out to the car, and you'll give him the tin. He's skinny, blond hair, baggy clothes, right?"

"Maybe I should be the one to go in."

"No." He pushes his shoulders back. "You need to stay here. If this goes sideways, Ruth, I'm calling the police." Chase opens his door and gets out, pats the side of his chino shorts to make sure he has his phone. Pungent, hard heat sweeps around his body into the car. "I don't care whose side you think Sully is on."

I watch him move unsteadily across the parking lot, his hair uncharacteristically flat on one side of his head. He couldn't have slept well last night. Alex didn't get in until long past midnight, and she was gone again by seven a.m. She hasn't replied to a single text message. Chase pulls open the bus depot door and disappears inside. I wait, my hands shaking. Is Eli actually in there, or is he watching this car? Any minute now, will he yank open the passenger door and pull me out by my hair? I try to take a calming breath and stretch out my legs, but my belly is so heavy, it's a sackful of sand on my lap. And there's that spike of pain again, making me gasp, as if overnight my baby has grown sharp metallic edges inside me.

"It's okay," I mutter, rubbing one hand over my stomach, clutching my bag with the tin in the other. "We're going to be fine."

Two achingly long minutes go by while I crane my neck and peer through the windshield at the front entrance. But when the doors open and Eli comes out, it's not Chase he's with. My heart drops. There's Eli, fifty feet away, baggy jeans, white skateboard sneakers, his elbows sandwiched between two police officers who are escorting him to a parked cruiser at the far end of the lot.

"Oh my God," I say out loud. Where the hell is Chase? The pain in my pelvis begins to drag now as if everything inside me is suctioning downward. But then the bus depot door flies open again, and Chase comes hurrying out, tripping a little on the front curve of his flip-flop. He's ten steps across the asphalt, eyes big as dinner plates, when out of the building emerges Sully Mills.

Chase is coming my way. I open the door for him. "I walked right into him!" he hisses as he throws himself into the driver's seat.

"Go!" I shout. "Just drive away!"

"Hide *that*." Chase motions to my bag and I kick it to the floor as he fumbles with his seat belt. But Sully has arrived at the driver's side window and is motioning for us to lower the window. Chase presses the button, and Sully bends and looks in.

"Hi," Sully says.

"Yep," says Chase.

"Mr. Kennedy, I'm Officer—"

"I know exactly who you are," Chase says.

Sully bends lower. "Ms. Van Ness. How are you?"

"Fine, thank you." I try to ease the bag closed by my foot, without looking down, but the fabric is floppy, and I don't know if I've managed it. Inside my chest, my heartbeat is frantic.

Sully's eyes are steady on me. He's flooding heat into the car through the window. "Eli Beck is in police custody. I thought you'd want that information. My colleagues are taking him back to the station now."

A fresh spear of pain cuts into my midriff, and I press my fingers to my hip. Alex has even told Sully about Eli.

"I need to ask you something." Sully rests an elbow on the window frame.

Chase and I glance sideways at each other.

"Beck's given a statement. And, to be frank, some of it's . . . concerning."

"In what way?" Chase asks.

Sully pauses, then says, "He claims there was an incident in your apartment, Mr. Kennedy, last Monday morning. That he was physically attacked there around noon. He has a knife wound that corroborates."

Alex.

Chase exhales as if all the air is leaving his body.

"We weren't there," I say.

"I know," Sully says. There's hurt in his eyes. "Alex was." He studies our faces for a few seconds. "I realize there are drugs in play. Ruth, if you hand them over to me right now, I'll try to keep you out of trouble."

"Eli is lying!" Chase says, his voice so bubbled that he has to cough to clear it. "There aren't any drugs. She doesn't have them."

"Alex told me Ruth hid them."

Every synapse inside of my head is snapping. Alex knew about the drugs, hid them from Chase and me, but *told Sully* about them? All while denying their existence to Chase?

"Ruth, you're harboring drugs for a dangerous felon. You're having a baby with him. And she caught you red-handed with the drugs in a tin."

"Jesus," Chase says, as the realization stings us both like a slap. She's trying to destroy both of us. More pain gathers inside of me and it's so hot.

"Is that true?" Sully asks. "I'm just trying to understand what's going on. Because there are some things about this that . . . don't add up."

He's staring into my eyes, but I hold his gaze. "I brought the drugs home. But Alex found them and hid them for weeks, not me. They were in a vent in her bedroom. And Chase and I found them. That's the truth." The words come out as a gasp. My view is blurring.

"It's true, it's true!" Chase adds in a nervous flurry.

"Where are the drugs now?" Sully is asking. "And why did you come to this bus depot today?"

The pain in my middle explodes, and then there's a viscous, briny liquid that's flooding my thighs, spreading into a warm pool on the car seat.

"We were going to return the drugs and money to Eli," I say. A shocking pain sears through me, and I slump toward the gear stick.

Chase is on me immediately. "Are you okay? Ruth? Take a deep breath. There you go. And another," he says, his calmness fake.

Pain submerges me as a fresh aching pull surges, so much stronger than the last, creating sound in me I've never heard myself make before. It's primal and bewildered, like the bellow of cows Dad helped butcher on the neighboring farm. I scramble for the strap of the bag and pull it up to my lap, dig for the clothespin in there—Pim's pin—the one I hold when

I'm the most afraid of anything. Finally I grasp it. The wood of the clothes-pin is worn and smooth.

They are talking now, but it's as though they're so far away. Chase tells me to breathe. I hear Sully's voice saying he'll follow us.

"No, I don't want him to," I pant, but Chase is already taking off, driving out of the parking lot and fast through backstreets. Trees streak by in hard lines of green, and I can't think anymore, I can't think.

ALEX

I'm so close to the finish line now that my fingers are trembling on the keyboard of my computer. The office is quiet. That's good. *Keep going*, I tell myself. *It's all for the best*. I read over what I have so far.

> Morris,
>
> I'm worried about my sister, Ruth. I haven't spoken to you about her before, but she's about eight and a half months pregnant and has been living with me since June. The man she's having a child with is Eli Beck. There's a criminal history there—violence, abuse, and drug use—and he's here in Moses River to be with Ruth. My sister has been in jail, a fact that I learned just recently, and I have reason to believe she has an ongoing issue with drugs—and maybe some other concerns as well. I'm worried for her child, Morris. Can we chat later this morning when you're in? I don't want to be alarmist.
>
> Alex

I pause, bite the fingernail of my thumb. Every move I make has to be perfect. There's so much to do today. I didn't sleep well last night—thoughts rattling in my head—although nobody was awake by the time I got back to the loft, and Chase didn't stir as I slid under the covers. But today is crucial. It's when everything comes together. I crack my knuckles and press Send on the email. It swoops away from me, a gentle bird in flight.

I grab my satchel, hook the strap across the front of me, and glance up at the clock on the wall. It's just past nine o'clock. Right on time. The Floyd decision will be well underway.

Morris suggested that I avoid the hearing today; Minerva, newly returned from her trip, outright forbid it. *As far as I'm aware*—huge pause for her nostrils to flare—*you're still not the lead on this case.* But I'm invested in it. I rescued Buster—*I stuck my neck out, not her*—and I have every right to be there for the verdict.

I walk through the tunnel that connects our building to the courthouse and climb the stairs to the main level, where everything smells fusty and sour like the wood of old church pews. Court is in session. I slip in at the back and take a seat. At the front of the room are Morris and Minerva, and then up high is the judge—it's Vickers, a no-nonsense woman in her sixties. That bodes well. I couldn't have picked a better judge myself. To the left, I can see the bulk of Frank Floyd's shoulders and the bony little rack of Evelyn. Janeen must have stayed home with Buster.

Judge Vickers is midflow in her monologue. "Overnight I've again reviewed the minutiae of this case, including the testimonials given yesterday and all the various reports. It is a case full of conflicted opinion, riddled with struggle, overshadowed by doubt. The finding of drugs in the home is, however, quite certain. It is a fact, and it is troubling. With that in mind, it is my decision that the child will be best served by remaining in the care of the maternal grandmother until such time as Family Services can find him a forever home. The court is thus awarding continuing custody of Buster Kevin Floyd to Family Services."

At the back of the room, I close my eyes and smile. There are families all over the state hoping and praying for a low-needs child like Buster. Fresh parents—healthy ones—who will give him a clean and safe home, who will take him to speech therapy, buy him fresh diapers, give him more than one toy in his room. By the time he's five, he'll barely remember that he lived any differently. I did it. I saved that little boy.

Suddenly, I hear Frank roar from the front of the court. "This is bullshit! People change! We're clean!" His fist thumps the top of the table.

"I would ask you to improve your language, Mr. Floyd. If you are unable to control yourself in my court, you will be forcibly removed—"

"You're all in it together!" he bellows, his shoulders clenched high near his ears. "This is a conspiracy!"

Judge Vickers motions toward the security guard, and he leads Frank from the court. I slip through the back door of the courtroom and wait in the foyer. When Morris emerges a few minutes later, I step out and wave. He heads straight my way.

"What are you doing here?" He looks sweaty, and his tie's off-center.

"I just came to hear the verdict. Great result," I say. "Buster will be much better off now."

Morris bites his lip. "I hope so. But it's a strange case. And Mr. Floyd, he's an angry individual for sure, but I'll tell you what, he wasn't high. Through the whole thing, he and his wife aren't what we usually see. I found them surprisingly likable."

"The Floyds? Likable?" I ask, swallowing. "Don't be so easily fooled."

He looks up sharply, goes to say something more, but just then, Minerva approaches. Her corduroy blazer is about to burst its buttons. "The judge ruled," she says. "In your favor." She glares at me, but I let it roll off me.

"I did my job, Minerva." *I did what nobody else would.*

The three of us walk back in silence, and as soon as we reach our floor, Morris swerves right toward the kitchen and pours himself a coffee. He takes a long, wretched sip. Any minute now he'll check his phone and read the email I sent him. I head for my office to give him a little space, while I pull out my own phone and text Sully.

Result! Buster removed from parents. And I'm telling Morris about Ruth. I wait for a few seconds. He usually texts me back instantly. But there's nothing. Aren't u pleased? I type.

I look down at my phone again. No new message. I miss u, I type. Had a great time last night. No reply.

There's a tap on my door and Morris's head peeps around. "Can we have a quick chitchat?" he asks. "In my office."

I follow him down the hallway, pleased. Once we're inside, I close the door as he moves papers off the extra chair so I can sit down.

"You've read my email," I say. "Haven't you?"

He raises an eyebrow as he sits and steeples his fingers in front of him. "The thing is, Alex," he says, "I'm onto you."

"What?" Blood rushes to my neck and throat.

He drums one finger against the other while my mouth gets tackier. "You can try to play things down all you want, but the fact that you've written that email at all tells me the situation with your sister is serious."

I exhale in a rush of held breath. "You're right. Maybe I should have come to you sooner."

"With family, things can be . . . very . . . murky. We often give loved ones more credit than they deserve." He pauses so the lesson drives home. "I suspect you're too loyal to Ruth to really describe the depths of her problem. That must have been a hard email to write."

When I speak again, my voice cracks. "It was hard to write. It really was."

"And the baby is due very soon. Let me ask you this: Is there a likelihood of future harm to the child?" He doesn't let me speak before he flaps a hand at me. "Obviously there is. The father's history of violence and drugs. Her past history."

"Yes, you're right, Morris. There is a likelihood of harm here. In fact, I have to tell you I've also mentioned this to Sully. He investigated Eli Beck, discovered he's a fugitive. He's keeping an eye out for him and will arrest him if he's seen around town." I pause. It's all in the timing. "But my sister. I'm worried she'll get caught in all this."

"Isn't she already?"

"Yes. She's involved with the drugs. But her baby shouldn't have to pay for her sins." There. It's done. No turning back now. "And there's one more thing I need to tell you. She's hidden drugs in my house."

Morris pales. "Do you know where they are? Are we talking a lot of drugs?"

"Yes. Thousands of dollars' worth, and cash. I'm afraid it's enough to classify her as a dealer."

"Good Christ, Alex. Does Sully know that part? Did he confiscate the drugs and the money?"

I stand up and pace in the tiny room. "I probably should have come to you earlier, Morris. But I . . ."

His face softens. "You were frightened you'd get your sister into more trouble, that she'd be another pregnant mother in custody. So you didn't go that far with Sully."

"Yes." I stop, cover my mouth with a palm. "I hope I haven't made a mistake. I'm worried there's not enough time to do the right thing."

"I'm sure there's still time." Morris holds out a Kleenex box, waits while I sit back down and dab my eyes. "The first thing we have to do is report the drugs. Do you know where they are?"

I nod, burying my face in my tissue for effect.

"We removed Buster Floyd for much less. Alex, you have to know what this means. You do, don't you?"

He thinks he's leading me. I look up at him, my eyes steely and real. "Ruth's child is in danger. And he's my blood. He's mine. I'm ready to accept that now. I hear you, Morris." I let out a shaky breath. "We have grounds for removal."

Morris reaches out his hand, places it on the papers in front of him. "I know this is hard for you. But we have to move quickly. Those drugs need to be confiscated, and we must put a birth alert out at the hospital, let them know a child is due to be born who will need protection."

"Okay," I whisper. "Can we go and get the drugs ourselves, though? Rather than call the police? It just seems so much less intrusive that way. And, honestly, Ruth's a bit of a flight risk." *I've come this far. I have to finish this myself.*

"It's not really procedure, Alex, but for you I'll make an exception. We can do this subtly, keep our footsteps light. We don't want her disappearing. That's the worst-case scenario for the child."

"Exactly." *Exactly what I knew you'd say.*

"You've done the right thing in coming to me." He stands. "I applaud your commitment."

"Thank you." I open the door and walk out in front of him, concealing my smile with my tissue. I check my watch. It's just after ten. If I read Ruth's text message right last night, she should be meeting Eli now. The house will be empty, unless Chase is there, but I can deal with him. "Should we get going now, Morris?"

"Yes, I think that's a good idea. Let me just tell Minerva we're popping out for an hour or so."

Morris drives at a measured pace, following the mirror-signal-maneuver rules of the road, hands at two and ten. Every now and then, he gives me a sympathetic smile. Neither of us speaks. We don't turn on the radio.

When we park in front of the apartment building, I notice that the bay window of the loft is open, but that doesn't mean anything. Chase leaves it open day and night through the summer whether he's home or not.

"Will anyone be in?" Morris asks.

"Ruth's on bed rest, so yes," I lie. "Chase might be keeping her company."

"Well, I'll take the lead. You can let me do the talking. I'll keep things vague."

Perfect. I walk Morris in through the main entrance and up the stairs to our front door.

"Deep breath," he whispers as I slide the key into the lock. But as the door swings open, it's obvious there's nobody home. Ruth's couch sheets are neatly folded, and both her and Chase's shoes are gone. I was right. And he must have gone with her.

Morris looks around, raises his eyebrows for a second as if surprised by the designer loft on my social worker's salary.

"Wait here," I say. "I know where she's hidden the drugs." Quickly I move to the bedroom and close the door. I crouch low and ease off the front panel of the heating vent, but when I put my hand into the gap and feel around in there, it's empty. I strain lower, reach deeper. The tin is gone. *What the hell?* I think, blood starting to thrum in my ears. *Who's moved it? Who knows?* I turn a full circle in the bedroom, kick the chair so it rams into the wall. *Shit, shit, shit.*

"Alex?" Morris calls from the living room. "Is everything okay in there?"

I take a deep breath and walk back out of the bedroom. "The tin's not here, Morris," I say. "Ruth's taken it. Maybe she's hidden it somewhere else."

"Oh, that's not good." Morris frowns.

I grab my cell and call Chase. But the call just rings and rings. Eventually it goes to voice mail. I lower the phone and stare at the screen in confusion. Is Chase ignoring me?

"I think the best thing to do at this point, Alex, is to notify the police and have them do a full-scale sweep of the apartment. It's standard procedure. We need to follow the rules. They're in place for a reason."

"Yes," I say, distracted. I check my phone. Sully still hasn't gotten back to me. What the hell is going on? Just as I'm putting the phone back into my pocket, it rings. I press the cell to my ear without looking at it.

"Hi, Chase," I say quickly, but it isn't his voice on the line.

"It's Sully."

"Oh, sorry. Hi," I say.

"Your sister's in labor," he replies. His voice is cool, clipped.

"She's what? She's not due yet."

"Her water just broke. I'm heading up to the hospital with her and Chase."

"You and Chase are at the hospital *together*?" There's nothing but silence on the other end of the line. "Is the baby all right?" As I'm talking, Morris moves to the bay window and takes out his phone. He's calling in the birth alert. Good.

"They're both doing fine," Sully says. "I gotta go."

"Wait! Sully—" But there's a click, and the line goes dead.

Morris finishes his call, then looks over at me.

"We need to get to the hospital now," I say, heading toward the door. But when I turn, he hasn't moved an inch.

"I know you're desperate to see your sister," he says. "But you can't, I'm afraid."

"What do you mean?"

"If we're going to remove a newborn from a mother's custody, we can't have you—her sister, and a social worker in our employ—on the scene. It's a conflict of interest. Remember: by the book, okay? I'm so sorry."

"But, Morris—"

"You're an excellent sister. Truly dedicated. And you're doing the right thing. Come on, let's get back to the office."

I follow Morris out to the car. This is the one turn of events I hadn't planned for, and it puts everything in jeopardy. The drugs. The baby. Everything. I reach for the cell in my pocket and dial Sully back. It rings and rings. I hang up and try again. The realization wheezes like a flu in my chest. He's refusing to answer my call. All the way back to the office, my brain scrambles to figure out why.

RUTH

There's a din in my head that sounds like wailing. It takes me a moment to realize the sound is coming from outside of me, that it's beyond my pain. Chase drives me through the town as Sully leads us, carving a path through traffic to the emergency room with his siren on and police lights flashing. Everything about me feels about to burst. *What are we going to do?* I want to yell at Chase, but I'm woozy, and the words won't take shape. My bag lolls at my feet with the tin of drugs still inside it. Chase skids to a halt behind the police car as three nurses come running, easing me out of my seat and onto a gurney, rattling me fast toward the main entrance.

"I'm right behind you," Chase shouts, but I'm not ready, I can't go, Sully is going to find everything out. The last I see of Chase, he's hooked my bag over one shoulder and is hurrying to lock the vehicle. Then the main entrance doors sweep close behind me, and I'm rushed along vinyl yellow hallways, ceiling lights streaking above me like comets. Flat on my back, I battle not to pass out.

The nurses wheel me into a private room and transfer me into a bed just as a fresh stab of pain hits and I begin to cry. For Alex, for me, for this baby. For everything that's happened that I can't undo. More than anything I want my mom, to have her kiss me on the forehead like she used to, and love me again. *My little owl*. But I can't think about Mom for too long: nothing about her memory is steadying.

"It's all right, dear," a nurse says, strapping a heart monitor around the bulk of me. Another nurse jams my finger into a plastic clip. Machines begin to beep at the side of my bed.

"What's happening?" I ask. "Is my baby okay?"

"You're doing fine," the nurse says, her eyes kind. "Deep breaths. Nice and steady. Have some of this." She hands me a cup of ice chips, but another wave of pain breaks over me, and I bat her fingers away, the ice skittering into the corner. The beep of the heart monitor hammers like a boat motor.

"I need to talk to Chase."

"Chase? Is he your husband, love?" The nurse reads monitors as she speaks.

"I need him. I need my bag!"

She pats me once on the knee. "I'll go find him for you." As she leaves, she passes a doctor in the doorway. "This baby's coming fast. No time for an epidural."

The doctor glances at the monitors at the foot of my bed, then looks up at me. "Let's get ready to push, Ruth."

He says something else, but it's like I'm watching him through glass: I can see his mouth moving, but I can't fathom any of the sound. I'm all grit and sweat as I grapple to bear down. Then Chase is there, and I grab at his hand.

"Chase, my bag."

"I've taken care of it," he says. "Concentrate on this now."

I squeeze his hand as another contraction rips through me. He flinches, but he doesn't complain. *You're doing great*, he mouths encouragingly, but his face is tight.

I push and push, curling in and in on myself, forgetting everything else around me, trying to survive. Every now and again, I slide out of the present, as if I'm somewhere else in the room, wake-dreaming through these moments and other, older ones. I see Pim on the gate. His little knees beside me. Then, as another contraction rips through me, I blink feverishly at the sight of Alex beside me, switching off all the monitors. She's wearing a surgical mask, only her eyes showing above it, and she's moving in toward the lower half of me, a scalpel in one hand. I scream out loud and the outline of her shimmers away. *It's the pain*, I think, grimacing through the dream fever, trying to keep a grip on what's real.

And then there's one last effort, so strong that my lower half feels galvanized—a stinging, savage heave that splits my body in two—and everyone's crowding my knees, all eyes above masks are smiling. I peer down to see. They've got a towel around little legs, little arms, dabbing at a face as they check it. The doctor passes me a bundle in a raspy blanket.

"Congratulations, Ruth," he says. "You have a baby boy."

And he's in my arms. My little boy. His face is squashed, but he's warm and perfect. His hair is mocha brown, his skin olive; it's Pim all over again. A perfect copy of my little brother rests in my arms, and everything I know about the world changes and aligns. He's here, my son, my boy. And I know exactly who I am. I know the very thing I was meant for.

"Hi," I say, my fingertips shaking at the edge of the towel. He snuffles, pushing at his button nose with a tiny knuckle.

"Well done, Ruth," Chase says as he stands to the side of the bed, but his voice is cracking.

"This is Will," I say. "I'm naming him after my brother. After Willem. After Pim."

"He's beautiful," Chase says, his eyes teary like mine.

When I start to drift off, the nurses take Will, swaddle him, and place him in a little see-through crib next to my bed, and I sink into a sound-less, heavy sleep.

It must be late afternoon when I wake. The beeping of machines sounds less severe. They've left the overhead light on in the room, so every-thing feels brighter. I move carefully onto my side and watch my son in his crib, his tiny swirled head in a soft cashmere hat now, fists in little mittens. Here we are, alone in the quietness, and everything about me is smiling. *So this is what it's like*, I think. *This is happiness.* But then I see the chair on the other side of my room—flat on the seat, is my bag. Chase must have brought it in. But it's floppy and empty-looking. There's no way the tin is still in there. I lie rigid, concentrating on Will, trying to believe in nothing but the new beginning of him, while I think over and over again about the possibilities. *Where is the tin? Who has it? And worse: Where is my sister?* Through the fade of the afternoon, I sleep fitfully, and even in my dreams, I imagine the worst.

Chase comes back the next morning holding a balloon on a string. It's blue with the word *Congratulations* written across it in stretched cursive. He ties it to the end of my bed. "How are you feeling?" he asks.

"Like I can't believe I did it." I'm holding Will against my chest and he's awake, gazing up at me. "Look at him. He's beautiful."

"Here, I found this on the floor of the car." He holds up Pim's clothes-pin. "I thought you'd want it."

I take it from Chase, wrap it in close to Will's body in the muslin. Immediately his little fingers curl around the wood.

Chase stands for a moment, watching the baby, as an easy summer light floods the room and the balloon above my bed sways gently.

"It suits you," Chase says. "Motherhood, I mean. I've never seen you look calmer." But there's something flat in the way he says it. Something's wrong.

"Have you seen Alex? Where is she?"

"At the loft." He runs a palm across his jaw.

"Good," I reply. She can do less damage from there. When I came to Moses River, I wanted to believe in her, but she clearly didn't believe in me. She took all the truth I gave her and twisted it into a weapon.

"She's—" Chase begins, but then the door to my room opens, and Sully walks in. My grip around Will tightens. Sully's out of uniform, wearing a faded Rockies baseball T-shirt and jeans.

"What are you doing here?" I ask.

"I invited him," Chase says, shifting his weight.

Feathery panic brushes the inside of my head. "Chase, what have you done?"

"Sully has the drugs now." His words come out in a torrent. "I told him everything about Pim, about Alex, and her web of lies, and I gave him the tin. I didn't see another way out, Ruth. So I told him the truth."

My eyes lock on Sully. "I should never have brought those drugs into their house, but I'm telling you, I never moved them. They disappeared. Then reappeared somewhere else. And there's only three people who live there—me, Chase, and my sister."

Sully takes a step forward. "You're not in trouble. Eli's in police custody, and he hasn't said anything about the drugs—probably doesn't want to incriminate himself. I've submitted the tin to the police as seized."

"Seized from who?" I ask warily.

"That's what I'm trying to figure out. Alex's version of events doesn't match yours and Chase's. She acknowledged the drugs existed, but she didn't bring them to me. Chase did."

"But they weren't *mine*," Chase says, his eyes wide. "The only person who could have moved them was Alex. What I want to know is why."

Sully eyes Chase for a long time with a look I just can't understand. "I've always been a good judge of character," Sully says, breaking the silence, "but everyone can make a mistake. She asked me to check into your past, Ruth. And I did. She also said she took you for an abortion when you were both young. I checked the records on that, too. But it wasn't you who had the abortion. It was her."

I glance across at Chase, who's fidgeting under the balloon.

"She releases the parts of her life that are too heavy to carry," I say. "She got herself in trouble as a kid, and it's no surprise that even that story got twisted into being about me."

"After Chase told me about Pim, I found the death records. It was labeled accidental, but there was a description of that day. I can't imagine what that was like for you, his sisters. It made me realize why Alex . . . does what she does." He looks at Will sleeping on my chest. "And why this baby is so important. To both of you."

I'm trying to sift through what he's saying, to figure out whose side he's on, but I can't. "What are you going to do about the drugs, Sully?"

"I'm going to find the truth. It's one thing to get into trouble, but it's another thing to cause it on purpose. My job is to protect people, and right now, I think you need protection, Ruth. You and your son."

As he's speaking, his phone rings. He pulls it out of his pocket, stares coldly at the screen. A look passes between him and Chase that's hard to decode. Then he shuts off his phone.

"Was that my sister?" I ask. "What does she wa—"

But I'm cut short when the door opens and a man and a woman enter. The woman is holding a baby seat, which she puts down onto the tray table. Something about their energy instantly makes my heart beat faster.

"Can we help you?" Chase says. "I think you must have the wrong room."

But beside him, Sully whispers, "Morris."

"You know these people?" I ask Sully, a sickness gathering in the pit of me. "What's going on?"

"Hello, Ms. Van Ness, my name is Morris Arbuckle." The man in front of me holds out a card with an insignia. I stare at it blankly until he sets it onto the side table, smooths down his tie. "This is my colleague, Minerva Cummins. We haven't met before, but Minerva and I are child protection social workers."

"Child protection . . . like Alex." The pieces slide into place and I turn to Sully. "What's going on?" I jab a finger at him. "You knew about this, didn't you?"

"Morris, I can guess why you're here, but this is a mistake." Sully's voice is low like a growl, but the man holds up one palm.

"Ruth, I was called here because there have been reported concerns about you and your baby's safety and well-being."

"No, that's not true," I say, gripping Will tightly. He's fallen asleep in my arms. I can feel the steady rhythm of his breathing against my throat.

"From who? Who called you?" Chase says, stepping to my side.

"I'm afraid that's confidential," Morris says. "At this time, we need to assess if it's safe for your child to remain in your care."

My voice catches in my throat. "Alex is lying. You can't trust her."

The woman behind Morris won't look at me. Sully cuts in front of Morris. "What has Alex told you, Morris? Whatever it is, it's not as simple as she's making it out to be. I know she's one of your team, but there are . . . discrepancies that you don't know about. We have to slow down here."

Yes, I think, *yes, investigate further*, the way that nobody ever did for me before. Somebody finally help me.

"Officer Mills, please stop making this harder. We just need to follow things through," Morris continues. "Ruth, your baby has been cleared for discharge. It was a fast labor, but without complication, and so he's leaving the hospital today, and we're placing him into a safe-care home. The investigation process will take thirty days, but you'll have visitation rights throughout, and we'll meet again at a conference in our office at the start of October."

"No!" I shout, and Will wakes up. He lets out a cry and grips the front of my hospital gown. "I'm his mother. He's safe with me!"

"I know it's upsetting, but we're doing our jobs and what's best for your child," the woman says, reaching for Will. "Let's try not to upset the baby."

I twist away from her arms, but my body is sluggish and sore. Will is crying harder now, his little voice shrill and scared.

Chase is wide-eyed with panic, looking from face to face. "You can't just—"

Sully takes my hand, his eyes steady on me. "This is a mistake, Ruth. Someone's set it in motion, but we'll get to the bottom of it, I promise you. Right now you have to be brave."

Brave? My sister has betrayed me yet again, and I don't know who I can trust. Tears roll down my face, and I scream as the woman takes Will out of my arms and straps him into the baby seat. He's clutching the clothespin in his hand.

"Where are you taking him?" I sob.

"He'll be in a foster home for a month while we can find everything out," she says.

"Do something!" Chase says to Sully.

"You're getting it wrong, Morris." Sully has both hands on his hips, but he still lets him pick up the baby seat, lets him leave the room with my baby, my son. The sound of Will fades down the corridor as I sway in bed, my vision flooding with ink-black stress, my throat jagged with bile. Chase puts his arm around my back to steady me, but my shoulders give out and I fold against him, darkness sweeping in like a sedative. All I can see is the sad balloon Chase brought me earlier, floating above our heads.

ALEX

I've been pacing in front of the bay window for an hour. Still there's no news from the hospital. Morris promised me he'd email when it was done, so what is taking him so long? I stop, press the heels of my hands into the sockets of my eyes, and exhale. *Relax, Alex. Be calm.* This part of the plan is inevitable. There's no stopping Morris when he's following the rules.

I take a long, restorative breath and check my email again. This time, when I refresh my screen, the phone dings. It's happened. Morris has come through. Relief floods me, and I all but sink to my knees.

Suddenly the front door bangs open and Chase barrels into the loft. He's sweaty with hurry, his clothes crumpled and creased, a blond mess of stubble all over his chin. He's so far from the smooth guy I first met in the grocery store that it takes me a few seconds to register him.

"What have you done?" he shouts from the doorway. He's demented and angular, completely unhinged.

"What are you talking about?"

"Is this why you wouldn't come to the hospital with me this morning?" He slams the door behind him, and the whole loft shudders. "Because you knew what your boss was going to do? How could you do that?"

"Slow down! How could I do what" I say.

"Have Ruth's baby taken away from her. Your boss just waltzed into the hospital room and took him." He swallows, devastated. And he's right: It is upsetting. For everyone. He's just had so little experience of this kind of thing.

"I haven't done anything wrong."

"You planned this." He points at me while he heads to the tap and drinks water straight from the faucet. "I'm getting the hang of you, Alex. You've had this planned all along."

"You make me sound like a criminal mastermind. I'm a child protection worker, Chase. I knew Ruth couldn't look after a baby the minute she announced she was having one. And I will always prioritize the safety of a child. It's my job. I know you think the world is a beautiful place, but it's not. You have no idea of the things I've seen."

He smashes the faucet off. "Ruth told me everything about you. Your whole 'good girl' story about your past—and the wildness of your crazy, drug-addled sister—all of it was lies. I know you got pregnant at fifteen and blamed it on the wrong guy. I know you had an abortion, and that's why you can't have kids. And that all happened to you, not to your sister. You lied to me."

"Chase," I say, reeling as if slapped. "You've been listening to the wrong—"

"Stop it," he says, his voice breaking into two. "Stop playing this game with me. Don't you care at all about who I am? I wanted to build a life with you. A forever one."

He's visibly shaking. I had no idea he'd come at me with such force.

"You've ducked and you've dived," he goes on, "given me slipperiness and half-truths while I . . . I handed you everything. You know what I've realized, Alex? *You're* the virus."

"Excuse me?" I say, both hands on my hips now. "Have you completely forgotten what she did? She stole cocaine, Chase, from a felon, and she brought all of it into our home."

His eyes brim with hurt. "You denied moving those drugs. But you did it. And you threatened some guy who came to our house, Alex. You *hurt* him."

I can feel the heat gathering in my cheeks.

"I wasn't lying," I say, but Chase only groans. "I wasn't! I thought she'd made the drugs up, but then I saw her with them."

"If that's true, you've known about them for a while. Why didn't you report them sooner, if you were so worried about her fitness to parent?"

"Oh my God." I venture a few steps toward him. "How many times do I have to tell you? I don't have all the information on everything she's done. I saw her with the tin just this week—that's why I reported it now. And that's why they're placing the baby with me, here, where he's safe. It was Morris's call, not mine."

He blinks at me for a few seconds like I've grown a second head. "What? *You're* the one taking Will? You're the mystery foster home?"

"*We* are. It's your home, too."

He seems to stumble and has to steady himself with one hand on the countertop. "How can you—? This is your *sister* you're doing this to!"

"Exactly. You don't know this world, Chase," I say, inching closer again. "You're only freaking out because you're out of your element."

"I'm not doing this to Ruth. My apartment isn't available as a foster home. Get out of my house," he says.

A line in the sand. Who'd have thought he'd stand up to me like this? Well, it's not that easy, I'm afraid.

"You can't kick me out," I say. "If I don't have stable accommodation, Will goes to a random family in the foster-care system. He'll likely get bounced around all over the place. Do you really want that to happen?"

Chase stands tall, his jawline set. I can almost see his mind whirring.

"Look, I don't want to fight with you," I say, edging forward a little more. "What I'm doing may look harsh to you, but it's all for my nephew. The child comes first. It's just like the Floyds at work and that boy I saved, Buster. Those parents were drug users, too. Unreliable people do and say unreliable things. And the child has to come first."

Chase pauses, and his shoulders relax a little. He's getting it. He's catching up. For him it must be such a difficult leap into a cruel world.

He looks me right in the eye. "Whatever happened to that baby? What happened to Buster?"

"Simple," I say. "I saved him."

A strange look comes over Chase, a look I've never seen before and can't interpret. "I never realized how far you'd go . . . to protect these kids."

"If I didn't, no one would." I lower my head, wondering if I can round the counter yet and hug him.

Chase scratches at his stubble. "I guess it's hard to pick out the reliable people. I'm not very worldly that way. It leaves me wide-open." His face is so sad. Maybe he's finally seeing the world for what it is.

"It's a tricky business," I say, moving forward until I'm standing in front of him.

He puts his arms around me. Yes. I've got him. He's with me still.

"I'm sorry, Chase," I say. "I'm sorry you had to come to terms with all of this. Your innocence is sweet. It's what I love so much about you."

He grips me close. "I didn't mean it when I said you had to move out."

I bury my face in his chest. "It's been such a . . . a difficult week."

"Yes," he says. "There's a lot to . . . sort through."

"Welcome to my world," I say.

We stay together like that for a while, Chase holding me tight in the kitchen. Even after everything that's happened, it's going to end up okay. We're back on track. And as I stand, letting Chase sway me, I hug the most important fact of all to myself. In only a matter of hours, Morris will bring Will over.

RUTH

Two hours after Family Services has stolen my baby, the hospital discharges me and Sully drives me home in his cruiser, a blanket over my knees. He takes me to his house, puts me in the spare room, lets Gravy sleep on the bed with me, even though I think he has rules about that kind of thing.

"I'm right next door," he says, "if you need anything." He pauses, his face racked. Then he pulls the door shut until it clicks.

The spare room is painted flint-gray, like pictures I've seen of stone walls in Scotland. There's an antique chair in one corner, and a black-and-white photo on the wall of a crow in a winter tree. For two days, it watches me while I try hard to sleep and eat. The only lifeline I still have to my son is the breast milk Family Services say they'll allow me to send to him, so I need to keep my body going. They've exchanged my living child for a breast pump, and they expect me to be okay with it. Morris hasn't even come by to pick up the milk yet. All night long I worry about what Will is being fed.

By the third day, Sully forces me out into the kitchen, where I sit and watch the rain, the bony trees beginning to rattle the windows. With my eyes open or closed, all I can see is my son. The chocolate-brown of his eyes, the soft curl of his hands. My desperation to see him is like a thirst. Everything about me is parched.

"They can't deny you access to your son," Sully says through the first week, putting cup after cup of coffee in front of me that I struggle to drink. "They might have removed him, but you have a right to see him. I don't know what's taking Morris so long."

Alex. She's what's taking him so long. I found out that they placed Will with her the same day they took him away from me, that he's there with her at the loft, and when Sully told me that, I felt sick to my stomach. The only hope at the moment is Chase, who seems to have fooled Alex into thinking that he's still on her side. He's a spy for us. But he's fighting an uphill battle. Everyone has played into Alex's hands. Even me. I came to Moses River so intent on mending things, so certain that, in spite of all that had gone wrong in the past, sisterhood was an inescapable bond. I wanted our relationship to change, and it has. It's found all new ways to get worse.

Seven days have gone by since I got out of the hospital, when Morris finally shows up at Sully's front door. He stands on the front step, holding a black umbrella over his head as the rain pounds. Once we've gotten Gravy under control, Sully invites him in. But Morris shakes his head.

"I can't stay, I'm afraid. I just popped by to see how everyone's managing." His eyes dart from me to Sully. "And to tell you that Will's fine. He's absolutely fine. Thriving. But if you've got any breast milk at all, I'd be very happy to drop it off."

"Access visits, Morris," Sully says, as I hurry to get all the glass jars I've stored for Will in the freezer—I've drawn a love heart on each one in red Sharpie.

"Do your job properly. This mother has rights."

"Yes, well, she does and she doesn't," Morris says. He takes the jars, his smile tight. "I'm working on it. Leave it with me."

But as I head into the second week without my son, I hear nothing. Feel nothing. I'm given nothing to hold on to.

The following Tuesday—nine days since I've been living in Sully's house—he makes me chicken soup from scratch while I sit at the kitchen table. It's lunchtime, although markers like that seem to have lost all purchase with me.

"Did you shower this morning?" Sully doesn't turn. The muscles in his back move under his shirt as he stirs. "You have to keep going, Ruth. It's not just enough to eat food and drink water. I know it's hard, but all the basics are really important. You have to keep your head up."

"I can't," I say. "I need my son. I need Will." I think of the smell of his hair when he slept against my throat, how his fingers gripped the front of my hospital gown when they pulled him away.

Sully stops stirring and turns. "We're going to get him back. You have to believe me. We're going to find a way."

I nod, my mouth pasty, and toy with the saltshaker on the place mat. Sully said he would dig into the things Alex has done, but clearly his investigation isn't yielding anything we can use. He isn't saying so directly, but it's been over a week now, and the inference is he's not making headway. I try to swallow, but my throat feels gummed. Any minute now, he'll hand me a bowl of soup and the steam that rises to meet my face will be nauseating.

"Hasn't Eli said anything at all?" I ask.

Sully shuts a cupboard door firmly. "He refuses to make a statement. So far I haven't been able to get him to admit to anything that's not already on his file."

My blinks feel heavy. "When will Morris let me see Will?"

Sully shakes his head by the stove. "Normally you'd have had access by now. Alex is blocking you."

By my feet, Gravy lets out an ancient sigh.

Sully sets a blue ceramic bowl onto the table, watches me wait to look down at the soup. "Give it a try, Ruth. Think of it all as fuel, and not just for breast milk. If you're going to fight for your son against someone as manipulative as Alex, you're going to need gas in the tank."

Sully is trying to help. Never before have I had his caliber of person on my side, even though I suspect most of what he's doing is simply an apology. He told me he'd encouraged Alex to report me. But when he admitted that, it wasn't anger I felt toward him. I just felt a part of a great, collective exhaustion. Alex reeled him in, just like she did with the rest of us, and now all we can do is try to fumble our way home.

I pick up the soup spoon as Sully sits across from me at the table, my hand trembling as a lift a mouthful of food to my lips. I manage to swallow a few spoonfuls of chicken, vegetables, and rice, when there's a loud knock at the front door. Sully looks at me for a second before he gets up and moves out of the kitchen, Gravy trying hard to be the first one into the living room. I stand, too, but hover with my hand on the kitchen door-frame. The only person I want it to be is Morris with Will. But it's never going to happen. Alex has full control.

Sully opens the door, and Chase is standing there. He looks tired. In the week and a half that's gone by, he's lost a lot of his beefiness.

"All good?" he asks, looking mostly at me, but I can tell he now knows the question is redundant. "I thought we should have a team talk."

"Of course. Come in." Sully steps aside for him, but there's a stiffness to his welcome. For a second I wonder if, deep down, they still feel like they're competing.

Chase moves through the living room and straight toward me, where he puts a hand on each of my shoulders, stares into my face, and then wraps me up in a hug. I exhale into it. For all that he's been through himself, he's still clinging to some kind of positivity about the world. Not everyone is good, he's learned, but those who remain need to be looked after.

"How are you holding up?" he asks me.

"How's Will?"

He nods, his mouth bunched reassuringly, and then he walks me back to my seat at the kitchen table. Sully follows, and so does Gravy.

"How's Alex?" It's impossible for me not to ask after her, and perhaps that's one of the cruelest parts. I love her, and she hasn't changed. Again and again she insists that it's me against her. The only thing that's evolved over the years is that the fights she forces me into have gotten more catastrophic.

"Alex is contained." Chase sits down next to me, his face grim and knowing in a way it wasn't back in June. "I think of her now as a viper, and my apartment is the tank. And I have to just grin and bear it all, trying not to let my disgust show."

"You're watching her carefully? Like we talked about?" Sully leans by the fridge with his arms crossed.

"I'm watching everything," Chase says. He puts a hand on my knee. "And Will is beautiful, by the way. He knows she's not his mom."

"He does?" Everything inside my body convulses, a great dragging ache of love.

"You want some soup?" Sully asks him. "I've made tons here, and Ruth is . . . she's not very hungry."

Chase looks at the bowl on the table that is losing heat. "I can't eat, either," he says. I think he means generally. "But I'll take a glass of water."

Sully pours him one, deposits it in from of him.

"How are we shaping up?" Chase says, stretching. He looks like he's slept very little, but still he's approaching the week like it's a run-up to a sports cup final.

"I've hit a wall," Sully says, shooting a guilty glance at me.

"Fingerprints on the coffee tin?" Chase asks.

"We ran those and they're on there. But so are ours. She could argue we moved the tin knowingly. Or that she moved it without knowing what was in it."

"The texts and voice mails?" Chase drinks his water like he's spent days in the desert.

"Nothing Eli said or did incriminates anyone. There's no specific mention of the drugs at all. That's good for Ruth, but it's also good for Alex."

"Shit," says Chase. He puts his hand on my knee again. "So what *can* we prove? The abortion?"

"Yes. But obviously that's not a crime. And her lying about it to you, Chase, is just a domestic issue."

"The attack on Eli?" Chase says.

Sully shrugs. "It'll be hard to prove. A known felon's word against hers. We're keeping those charges on the table, just to fluster her."

Chase sighs. I watch the side of his head, my gaze blurry as if I'm outside my body.

"I have a question," Chase says, "and it might be a stupid one. But are all drugs the same?"

Sully frowns. There's a chasm of life experience between them. "Not really, Chase," he says gently, as though he's talking to a child.

"It's just . . . Alex mentioned this case from work where cocaine was involved. And a kid, too. And there's something about all of it that just doesn't sit right."

"What case?" Sully's arms tighten across his chest. "Did she say?"

"The kid was called Buster. Buster Floyd, I think. The way she spoke about it was . . . just weird."

Sully moves to the table and sits down. "I know the Floyd case," he says. "I was in court when Morris presented it to the judge. The parents are troubled, but yeah, it was drugs that cinched the case." He stops drumming. "And to the very end they swore they had no knowledge of the drugs. They swore they were clean."

"You're not saying . . ." Chase's runs out of voice.

But Sully's breathing is quicker; his energy's up. "Even if I was, it would be near impossible to prove. Wouldn't it?"

I look from Chase to Sully, my eyebrows raised.

"Do you still have Eli's tin in evidence?" I ask, the fog in my head clearing for the first time in nine days. "When I got here, it had ten thousand dollars rolled up in it, and exactly twenty-four ounces of coke in separate dime bags." Both men stare at me. "It was a very precise amount. How much is in the tin now?"

Sully's eyes widen. "Less than that, I think. I mean, the money's all there. But . . . Jesus. I'd have to check the report." He stands up, sits down again. "Ruth, where does Eli get his product from?"

I hesitate.

"It's okay, Ruth. You're not going to get in trouble," Sully says.

"From a buddy in Philadelphia."

"Okay, that's a start. That's good." He stands up again, patting his pockets as if checking for car keys. "I can use that. Maybe Eli will get a little chattier." He looks uncertainly at each of us. I'm going back to the station. How about we meet back here later tonight?"

"Sounds good," says Chase. He half stands, glancing over at me as if he'd maybe like to hug me.

"Can you bring Will over when you next come?" I ask, squeezing his hand for an instant. "Say you're taking him for a walk? And bring him here?" I know my pitch is squeaky. I can't help it.

"You know I can't." Chase bites his lip.

"They have to be sanctioned visits, Ruth," Sully says softly. "We're doing our best."

"The only thing she's letting me do is stay back with Will while you have your conference thing in three weeks."

"It's too long away," I say.

"Hang tight, Ruth." Sully's voice is more confident than it was an hour ago. "We're going to get your son back."

———

It's five o'clock when Sully gets home again. For hours, I've been sitting in his living room with the television on, although I'm not sure what it is I'm watching. Mostly I've been staring at a patch of wall above the screen, or out the window at the neighbor's fence, which is starting to build up to a festive Halloween, that calendar holiday where families celebrate skeletons, ghouls, and disguise, as if none of it will ever pervade them.

When Sully rushes in, Gravy wakes from where she's been asleep on my foot, and her tail thumps once. She begins the long process of standing. Sully's carrying a huge pizza box, on top of which are a couple of sheets of flat white paper, pinned underneath his thumb. Probably the receipt for the takeout. He turns off the TV, sets the pizza box on the couch, and crouches in front of me, still in his jacket and shoes.

"What?" I say. "What's the matter?"

"I have to tell you two things." His eyes are deep brown like oak. "I'm so sorry I fell in love with your sister. It completely messed up my judgment."

"I know," I say. "I've already told you it isn't your fault."

"And two"—he passes me the white sheets of paper from on top of the pizza box—"look what I found."

232

I open them shakily, scan them as fast as I can. They're documents, headers over the top that look official and medical, data in a printout below. "What are these?"

He bumps his fist once against my knee in tiny triumph. "They're the key, Ruth. It's early days, but they really could be everything."

ALEX

Chase has never been so interested in my job. Since he apologized last week for not understanding it, he now asks me question after question about cases and procedure. I've slowed down on what I tell him—mainly because it's confidential—but I also have to be careful. As harmless as he is, he could blunder in and ruin everything. But I like that he's invested. It took him long enough.

When he's in the apartment, he's also extra attentive of Will, but he's been father-figure-obsessed with the notion of Ruth's pregnancy since the get-go, so probably it's all just an extension of that. If he asks to take Will out alone, I don't let him. Even if I feel a little worn-out from the demands of new motherhood, that child is not leaving my sight. If he goes outside, I'm the one who'll take him.

It's quiet around the loft, though, now that Chase's job has started to pick up again. He's having to attend meetings at the Spirit Ridge with clients from other resorts, and it's not like I have a job to go to. Morris signed me off work for a month the same day he placed Will at the loft.

"We're employing you as a foster parent now, Alex. That's your job. And word to the wise, you might find it's more full-time than ever."

"What about my caseload?" I asked, letting his warning roll off me.

"Minerva or the other protection workers will cover it."

I made him promise he'd oversee the decisions Minerva made. Since then, I've thrown myself wholeheartedly into the important job of being a parent. Day and night, it never stops—as it shouldn't, if you're doing it properly. There's so much cleaning to do—onesies, bottles, muslin cloths — and my knuckles are raw from all the water and soap. I get two hours' sleep in a row through the nights, but I'm certain the deprivation won't last forever. Will is a fussy baby—hungry, fitful, sometimes inconsolable— and Chase, who hovers a foot behind me and Will through most of the days, is noticeably absent during the night shift.

We're a tight-knit unit, Will and me. I've relocated to the living room. My bed is now exactly where Ruth's was, Will's bassinet right next to the coffee table. I spend nights with him, pacing the room, staring out the window into the night sky. It's a privilege, motherhood. I've earned it.

Morris comes by every week with more breastmilk he's collected from Ruth, as all good social workers should with a newborn baby they've removed. It's a steady conveyer-belt supply that I throw away as soon as he leaves. I can't even bear the smell of it as I pour it down the drain.

"How are we feeling about visits?" Morris asks me each time he comes over, and this week is no different. He's sitting on the couch, flanked by tiny socks and dirty laundry, drinking lukewarm tea while I stand with Will in my arms. "The baby's three weeks old now. Are we thinking we're ready to set something up with Mum yet?"

I wish he'd stop asking. And he can stop saying "we" like there's some kind of team. Or referring to Ruth as a mother.

"Morris, visits are not a good idea. You know what my sister is like. You've met her. She hasn't changed all of a sudden."

"No, but she's . . . she appears to be doing quite well. You know, with the right supports in place. And protocol states that birth mums are allowed access to—"

"I know what the rules are, Morris, but they don't apply if the birth mother is unsafe. If they're involved in—you know—*drug dealing*. Or if the father of the child isn't domestically violent ex-con who's broken all the conditions of his parole. Have you forgotten why we removed Will in the first place?"

"No." Morris sets down his cup, licks his teeth. "Okay, you're probably right. In extreme cases, we can still argue that—"

"This is an extreme case. Don't let Ruth guilt you into anything."

"Sully's pushing pretty hard is all. He's advocating."

"Well, don't let him!" It infuriates me that Sully moved Ruth in, that he's the one supporting her. I have to admit I didn't see that coming, but I should have. He loves to be the knight in shining armor, and Ruth is the real damsel in distress. I've tried texting Sully, but he only replies to one message in ten. Sorry, can't talk now. I'm busy with work. It's fine. Ruth can have him. I have what I need now.

Morris shifts uncomfortably peeling a sock from the side of his thigh. "Are you sleeping, Alex? You look tired. And can I ask, why have you moved your bedroom out here? Is everything with you and Chase okay?"

"Everything's fine." I jiggle and bounce from foot to foot. Why won't Will nap? He's had his formula.

"Alex, if your living situation changes at all, that's a paperwork issue. Family Services will need to know about it. We'd need to approve the new residence."

"I'm not moving out. Why the hell would I do that?" I roll my eyes mid-sway but Morris doesn't see it.

"The family conference is scheduled for next week," he goes on. "It might be a bit of a tricky one."

I stop swaying. "Why do you say that?"

"Well, there were no drugs located during the police sweep of this apartment. Eli Beck won't give any indication whatsoever as to the nature of his current relationship with your sister. Which means we can't prove his intention to co-parent. If anything, he seems rather surprised by the pregnancy at all."

"They're together," I say, sitting down and bouncing Will on my knee. He starts to cry. "Eli's here, isn't he? I mean, he's in police custody here *in our town*. They're together and he's violent."

"That's the other thing." Morris shifts uncomfortably against the cushions. "He's certainly here, but I've got wind that Beck might be pressing countercharges. Something about an attack in this apartment. Of course, it probably has no basis, and we'll try to throw it out, but—"

"But what?" I prod at Will's mouth, trying to make him stop fussing.

"It might be our word against his."

I laugh, but it comes out shrill above the clamor Will is making. "You're saying the judge will take a convicted criminal's word over mine?"

"I don't know. I can't say who we'll get. Hopefully it'll be Vickers, but . . . Look, are you doing okay? Is there anything I can help you with? Anything at all?" Morris stands, reaches out for the baby, but I turn my shoulder and take two steps away.

"I'm fine," I say. "I've got this. I'm a natural."

He waits, watching me. "If you need respite, Alex, you can ask for it. There are budgets in place for that kind of thing."

"I don't need it. I'm perfectly fine."

"Right. Right, okay." He glances at his wristwatch. "I'll push off, then. You have the new breast milk, yes? You should probably pop that in the fridge."

"I'll get to it."

"We'll see you at the office for the conference next week." He zips up his coat. "It'll be standard, I'm sure. I didn't mean to worry you. Everything will be just fine."

"I know," I say.

He walks to the door. I don't see him out.

I'm up at 3:00 a.m. It's as if Will heard everything Morris said earlier and has decided to add even more pressure. I pace by the bay window, the sky outside dark and shadowy. I've warmed up formula for Will in the microwave, but when he sucks at the bottle, his little nostrils flare momentarily—a sign he's unhappy. Well, it's the middle of the night, who isn't unhappy? I stifle a yawn and cast a glance toward the bedroom where Chase is sleeping soundly.

"Come on, Will," I say. "You're hungry. You have to eat."

He's holding on to that goddamn clothespin. She gave it to him to taunt me, even though letting him grip it is one of the surefire ways to soothe him when he cries. I hate that thing, but whenever I try to prize it from him, his tiny fingers only tighten.

As I watch him, he spits out the nozzle of the bottle. When I try to ease it back into his mouth, he turns his head so that yellow drags of formula streak his cheek. He's stubborn, his little neck twisting, so I sit him up and pat him for a while on the back. The light is wispy around us, and I feel almost delirious. How long is this going to take? Suddenly I hear footsteps outside our door. Someone taps softly. Who is it at this hour? Is it Sully, coming to tell me he's on my side after all?

I get up, still holding Will. But when I open the door, it's Ruth standing there on the mat, her eyes dark sockets of pain. She's so thin she's almost unrecognizable, as if in three weeks she's melted down to the wick. She's pasty, too, her hair unwashed. This is the real Ruth, in all her scarecrow ruin.

"You can't be here," I say. "It's the middle of the night. It's not a sanctioned visit."

"Hi," she says, trancelike and sweetly, and it takes me a second to figure out she's not talking to me. "Hi, my little bear."

I'm holding Will out like a display item, and the two of them have locked eyes. I half turn away, breaking their contact.

"What do you want, Ruth? The family conference is in seven days. You can make your complaints then."

"You'll be the one making complaints," she murmurs, soporific, hypnotized.

"What does that mean? What are you talking about, Ruth? And what did you do with the drugs?"

"What drugs? I thought you knew nothing about them?"

She tries to take a step into the loft, but I barricade the door with my foot.

"You can't be here. You know that."

She can't take her eyes off Will. Her left hand reaches out for his knee.

"Don't touch him," I say.

In the doorway, she tries to gather some height. "Sully is a good man," she says. "You were right about that. And a very good investigator."

It's a threat, and I know it. "Shut up," I say. "You're bluffing. And you're doomed. Ruth, do you think I give a single shit about the police?" I shift Will farther from her line of sight. "Let's talk about the power *I* have. I'm a child protection social worker. I can remove anyone's child—*anyone's from anywhere*. Even my own sister's."

She's still and silent now, her eyes reddening. "What is wrong with you?"

"Me?" I say. "Look in the mirror, sis."

"I protected you after Pim. I didn't want you to carry any of the blame. You were eight years old; you were a good girl, my little sister. And I did it again when you got yourself pregnant. I let you lie and get away with it. I walked away from our family so that you could stay. But you know what I realize now?" She's choking on the words, coughing them out like phlegm. "I should have just left you to hang."

"Fuck. You." The two of us stand in silence. I can feel my heart slamming in my chest. I recover my steadiness and find more words that come out treacly and sweet. "That's nice, isn't it, Will? Isn't she so caring? Your long-lost auntie?" I kiss him lightly on the forehead. "Lucky she'll never be your real mom."

I push forward and close the door in Ruth's face, locking it behind her. I walk back to the living room. There's not a sound from Chase's room. He's managed to sleep through all the disruption.

I put Will back into his bassinet by the couch and pull the blanket over him. He's staring at me, his eyes dark on mine. It's a face I've seen before, and I shake it from my memory. I won't go back there. Pim is gone.

"Stop it," I say. But he doesn't. I work the clothespin out of his grasp, throw it across the floor. Then I turn away from him, bury my face in my pillow, and try to sleep.

RUTH

Seven days later, Sully walks me into the Family Services building for the family conference. We ride the grinding elevator in silence, my stomach churning. Once we're inside their reception area, which is cruelly colorful, Morris shows us into the boardroom, hurrying to lower dusty vinyl blinds over a huge whiteboard that flanks one whole wall. I catch a glimpse of a few names before he does. Other taken children. I feel utterly queasy.

"Excuse me for a moment," Morris says. "Let me go and round up Minerva and Alex."

"They won't be long," Sully says once he's gone. He insisted on coming with me to the family conference, woke me up early, made sure I wore ironed clothes. He hands me a granola bar he got from the vending machine.

I stare at the snack, my insides slippery as eels. "Sully, what if they don't give him back?" I remember him on her chest at the door, his eyes wide and frightened. That was one week ago. He's my child. He needs me, and I need him. More than that—I'm more than fit to care for him. Can't anyone see that but me?

"Try to stay positive, Ruth. We'll have answers soon."

But Alex has stacked the cards against me. She's always been a cheater, and I'm wondering what she has up her sleeve this time.

Sully pulls out the folder he's been working on for the past two weeks, sets it down on the table.

"Do you really think we have all we need?" I'd been confident until now. Sully had convinced me we were more than safe. But now it's decision time, and it's all I can do not to vomit onto the carpet.

Sully goes to say something, but is cut off by the reentry of Morris and Minerva. They march in the same exact formation as when they came into my hospital room. Morris leads, his tie askew; Minerva trails behind. He takes a seat opposite us. She follows suit.

"I'm sorry for the wait," he says. "And may I just quickly reintroduce Minerva Cummins to you, although I'm sure you remember us both."

"Of course I do," I say. They came like reapers into my life; I'll never forget either of their faces, ever.

"Officer Mills, I hadn't actually been told you were coming to this meeting."

"I'm only here for Ruth," Sully says. He places a warm hand over top of mine. Minerva tracks it and briefly I wonder if everyone who works in Alex's office is in love with Sully.

"Where's Alex?" I ask.

"On her way. She's running a little bit late this morning." Morris smiles apologetically.

"Right," Sully says.

I shake my head. Is she doing it on purpose, to make an entrance? Will she bring my baby, or leave him at home with Chase?

Sully nudges me, and I focus on what Morris is saying. "I know it's been a tough month. But we're all here to see if we can find the best pathway forward for Will."

"Give him back, then," I say.

"Sometimes, the best solution for a child isn't always what you as a birth parent might—" Morris begins, but I can't hear him anymore, because Alex has arrived in a flurry into the boardroom. She's alone. No Chase. And no Will. I stare at her, my eyes hard. The last time I saw her she slammed the door in my face.

"Sorry," she says. "I was up all night and . . ." She stops short at the sight of Sully. "I've been working hard. Protecting the ones I can." Sully meets her gaze, but his face stays neutral.

"So now that we're all here," Morris says, placing both palms flat on the table, "let's outline the situation as it stands. As you know, concerns were brought to light about the safety of Will Van Ness."

Across the table, I watch my sister, the child protection worker, operating however she sees fit, abusing her power. All I feel for her is sadness and anger. But she sits placidly, as if protected by an invisible shield. How did we end up here?

"In the month that's gone by, Minerva and I have managed to gather collaterals regarding Eli Beck, the alleged father of Will—and in fact, Officer Mills, your department has been very helpful with that."

"Eli Beck has an extensive criminal record," Sully says. "It's not a secret."

"No, but the problem lies in the ongoing contact he has with Ms. Van Ness," Morris says. "We can't in good faith say that a child will be safe if he is in such close proximity to a known felon."

"He's not in close proximity," I say. "I left Eli behind in Pittsburgh."

"Did you?" Alex replies. It's all I can do not to launch across the table and beat her.

"We've had a look at the phone records," Morris says, "and there was ongoing contact."

"Of what nature?" Sully asks.

"I never answered his phone calls. I texted him, but that was to make sure he stayed away." Beside me, Sully's eyes are calm. He's willing me to stay calm with him.

"There's also the matter of the drugs," Morris says, changing direction. "The ones hidden by Ruth in her sister's loft apartment."

Alex keeps her hands neatly on the table. There's not even the slightest tremor in them.

Sully intervenes. "The drugs in question are in police custody. Although Ms. Van Ness admitted to hiding them originally, she turned the drugs in voluntarily. They were officially reported and seized."

"What?" Alex bolts upright in her seat.

Beside me, Sully, stoic as rock, flips open the folder. "On the fifth day of September, Ruth Van Ness, accompanied by Chase Kennedy, surrendered a quantity of drugs and cash to police custody of her own volition. These were not hers, and she did not want them. She has also been immensely helpful and cooperative in giving evidence against a known felon, Eli Beck. As such, her behavior has been extremely responsible, Morris, not criminal. It's someone else who's been acting illegally and untruthfully."

I stare at the side of Sully's face. He's so good at this. Never before have I had anyone fight in my corner.

"When any drugs are seized," Sully goes on, "we write a report on how they came into police possession. I wrote the report about these drugs, Morris. I took the liberty of bringing you a copy of it today." He slides the first of his pristine white sheets across the table. "You'll see I've documented the seizure of the drugs as just stated.

"Ruth surrendered the tin just before she went into labor. It was not where she had hidden it in the home of Alex and Chase. But she did locate it. This is all documented." Sully drums his fingers on the papers in front of him. "The drugs were behind a vent in your bedroom, Alex. Chase Kennedy has made an official statement about this, as he was there with Ruth when she located them. What was strange, though, is that Ruth claims this was not where she'd put the drugs originally. And Chase had never seen them before."

Alex looks at me. She knows only I could have directed Chase to that hiding spot.

Sully continues. "It was you, Alex, who first told me of the drugs. Did you move them, Alex? And if so, why? Eli Beck came to your apartment, hunting your sister down because she had fled from him. During that visit, you attacked him with a paring knife. I have a sworn statement from him to that effect. Forensics have traced particles of his blood in your entranceway. And yet Ruth and Chase claim to have no knowledge of this encounter."

"Why are you even *here*? You've been harboring Ruth in your home. What for? When you know that she and Eli are deadbeats, when—"

"He's here for Ruth." Minerva keeps her voice level even though her mouth curves slightly. "He said so."

"And I'm acting in an official capacity. I've been working hard, too, Alex," Sully says. "Protecting the ones I can." He teases out the remaining two sheets of white paper—lab reports. "When drugs are seized by our department, we run a toxicology report. It's standard procedure. We've had two batches of the same drug seized within a month of each other— one from the Floyd residence, one from the home of Chase Kennedy. I took the two reports. And I compared them."

I see a flash of disbelief cross Alex's face. It's the same look she had as a kid when we played Monopoly, when she knew her empire was crumbling.

"Cocaine is like a fingerprint. Each batch has additives that make it unique. That's actually helpful to us with investigations as we can often track a batch back to its source." Sully pushes the sheets of paper across to Morris, who picks them up and scans them. "Benzocaine." Sully points from one report to the other. "It's a numbing agent. It's rare to see it in powder form, rare to see it ever, in fact. But here, it's in both batches—in the drugs Ruth turned in and in the small amount found at the Floyd residence. So that really stood out to me."

All the blood drains from Alex's face.

Morris looks as though he's just been slapped. "I'm sorry . . . This is all new to me. Are you saying—"

"I'm saying that the drugs handed over to me by Ruth Van Ness are *definitely from the same batch* as those found at the Floyds', the drugs that were cited as the basis of removal of their child."

"So what? What does that prove? It just means that Eli Beck is their dealer. You already know he's been in town."

Sully sits taller, faces my sister. "Eli Beck was most certainly nowhere near here on July twenty-fourth, when you, Morris, and Minerva found drugs in their home. I have definitive proof that on that day, and for weeks before, he was turning up to his mandated hours of community service in Pittsburgh and logging in with his parole officer. I checked." Sully continues to look straight at my sister. "As far as I see, there's only one person who had access to both Chase Kennedy's loft apartment and the Floyd residence. Tell me, Alex, how far would you go to protect a child?"

And it's then, only then, as Alex withers in her seat, that I allow myself to exhale. Sully reaches under the table and grabs my arm, giving it a gentle squeeze. It's really happening. For once, the universe is on my side. Alex is paying for what she did. And me? I might actually get my baby boy back.

ALEX

My mind is racing, but if I can just stay focused, everything will turn out the way it should. I know it. I just need to stay calm and clear.

I've been trying so hard, trying to do everything right. Sometimes, though, the more you reach for something, the farther away it gets. Sometimes, you reach and reach, and you can't make contact. And everything slides away.

"Alex," Sully says, snapping me back into the moment. "Answer the question. How far would you go to protect a child?"

"You have to be kidding me," I say. "The Floyds could have bought those drugs from anyone, not necessarily this Eli guy. I have nothing to do with this, except the confiscation part, which tells you *exactly* how far I'd go to protect a child—as far as I possibly can." I practically spit the words in his face. I hate him, this man who I once had feelings for, another betrayer in my midst, yet another person letting me down.

"Alex, your fingerprints are on the baggies we confiscated from the Floyds." Sully folds his arms against his chest. "But their prints are not. Keep talking, though."

Morris is still holding the lab reports. His face is the same color as the paper. "Alex, how the hell did this happen?"

"Morris, you know whose side I'm on. You *know.*"

"You . . . you planted drugs in their home?" Minerva asks.

Her eyes are watery. I'm sickened by her weakness. I roll my eyes. "Oh, fuck off, Minerva. You've never been in this job to do actual work. If we did things your way, we'd lose children left and right."

She glares at me, and predictably, her tears start to fall. "How *dare* you," she says. "Evelyn Floyd has been through enough. I can't believe you'd do this to her. It's *unthinkable!*"

As if we're all meant to believe Minerva ever really cared about Evelyn or her son. That was me. She's a lost cause, always has been. It's Morris who will have my back. I turn to him.

"Morris, in this job, saving one person always means hurting another," I say. "Problems hide inside themselves like . . . like Russian dolls. There's no way to twist one closed without opening another. As social workers, we know this. We know that what matters most is child protection, and that has to come above all else."

"Above the law?" Sully asks.

"Above the truth?" Morris adds.

I set my jaw, clenching it. I think of Will, his tiny hand wrapped around that useless clothespin. I want to go home. I want to bury myself in the brand-new, fresh-chance smell of him. Soon. Soon I will be there.

Morris glares at me. He doesn't say anything. Instead, he walks toward the back of the room and yanks the string of the vinyl blinds behind us, exposing the whole whiteboard wall of children in care. "Are there others?" he asks. His whole face has gone gray.

"What do you mean 'others'?" I ask.

"Other cases where you've planted incriminating evidence that undermines not only the safety of children and families but the very essence of social work?" he roars, and the whole room goes rigid. "Are there more cases involving children other than Buster Floyd or Will Van Ness where you've *lied* to ensure a child's removal?"

We stare at each other in silence.

"Answer the goddamn question, Alex," Sully says.

But the answer is not so simple. The truth never is. Because the laws don't cut it. Dysfunctional families reproduce endlessly, while healthy ones lose their children through no fault of their own. It happened to us in Horizon. It happens every second of every day.

Sully stands up, handcuffs at his hip. "I'm arresting you, Alexandra Van Ness, for unlawful possession of a controlled substance and fabricating evidence. You have the right to remain silent. Anything you say can and will be used against you in a court of law. You have the right to an attorney. If you cannot afford an attorney, one will be provided for you."

"I loved you," I say. "I thought you were on my side."

"I could say the same thing to you." He grabs my elbow, urging me up from the chair.

"Ruth," I say. "Tell them. Tell them the truth. Tell them I only ever wanted to protect Pim."

"You mean Will, right, Alex? Will. My son."

Ruth's eyes fill with tears, but I don't believe them. I never have.

So what? I made a slip of the tongue. It's totally understandable, given my stress levels and lack of sleep. I've been mothering a child every minute, every hour of the day. And who knew they'd look so much alike?

"Sister," Ruth says. "There's nothing I'll ever be able to do to help you."

Sully is now by my side. He bends to click cuffs onto my hands.

"What? What are you doing?"

"It's for your own protection, Alex," he says.

My mind flash floods with the faces of children. All the ones I've rescued from horrible homes, all the ones who'll languish now that I'm not there to help them. Buster Floyd. Oh God, they'll give him back to his rancid, lowbrow parents, who'll fill him with toxins and ignorance. He'll suffocate in their dirt and misery.

"Morris, I'm your very best protection worker. You know this!" But it's as if I'm speaking buried under a great weight: nobody's listening. I feel Sully's hands on my wrists, moving me. Just five weeks ago, his touch felt electric with chemistry. Now it's cold and unplugged. He walks me toward the door.

"You are not my very best protection worker, Alex," Morris says. "You're a fraud."

Minerva sits in a chair, her fat body puddled around. I want to pull her hair as I pass, but I don't. Instead, as Sully leads me away, I jam my sneaker against the doorframe and lock eyes with Ruth.

"I'm the guarder," I say. "That's my job." It's the role I was given when Pim handed me the peg, and we never changed roles again.

She wipes a tear from her cheek. My sister sees me, sees my pain, but she'll leave me hanging, as always. It's Horizon all over again.

"I'm the guarder," I say again, this time more quietly, as Sully moves me through the doorway and out into the corridor. There's nothing more to be said.

RUTH

THREE WEEKS LATER

When they give Will back to me, it's like being handed my own heartbeat. I can't stop crying. But I feel more alive than I've felt in years. In the weeks that follow, we walk together through the streets of Moses River, his plum little body cocooned in a warm wrap against me. It's the end of October. The weather is clinging to a golden soulfulness, everything deepening, mellowing.

Most days we stop in at the Lovin' Oven bakery. Will's popular there, and the owner seems to like me. *My baker's gone mountain biking again,* she often tells me in a flurry of flour. *When are you going to come work for me?* I can't tell if she's joking. Will hears the little bell over the door of the bakery, blinkss up at the direction of it with his soft brown eyes as we go in. It's an easy place to go with him when I'm sleep-deprived—not that I mind, not that I'd change anything. Other women at the playgroups complain all the time about having to get up twice a night. I understand it, I even join in and laugh, but I don't tell them how lucky they are, how the loss of sleep is a blessing, how nearly I was robbed of it all. At 3:00 a.m. with Will, the light between us is spectered and silver, our own precious

253

metal. *Here I am*, I think as I feed him, *a mother in the world*. Beaten about but doing okay now.

Today when I enter the Lovin' Oven, Sully's there at a table by himself, reading a dog-eared novel, sipping black coffee from his Gravy mug. I fumble a little with my change. I don't know if he'll want to talk to me, but when I turn, he's closing his book. He's seen me. Of course he has.

"Hi." I head over and stand next to his table. His hair's an inch longer than when I last saw him, three weeks ago, when he helped me load my things into Chase's car. It makes him look scruffier. "Long time no see."

He nods. "How have you been, Ruth? You look well. Want to join me for a minute?"

I ease slowly onto the bench, turning so that Will also fits in. Sully tilts his head to take in Will's face, smiles a little.

"What's your book about?" I ask, because I don't know what else to say. We've lived through each other's worst days, witnessed each other's heartbreaks. It was too heavy to suddenly be light.

"It's about a stranger who comes to town." His smile is bittersweet.

"Oh," I say. And then: "Are you doing okay?"

"Yeah, I'm okay," he says. "So you're sticking around? Where are you living?"

"In one of the town houses near the bridge and the park. It's a short walk from Chase's loft." I pause. "It's not mine or anything. Morris found it for me—the government helps me pay rent."

"Morris is probably terrified you'll go to the press," Sully says. "You could, you know."

I shake my head. It's something I've been wondering about. It's on my mind. But right now, I have Will to take care of. I have to take care of him first.

Sully nods, as if he's heard my entire thought pattern. "So the town house is nice?"

"Chase helped me choose linens. They're far too fancy for me."

"That's good," Sully says. "You deserve some nice things."

I blush, although I'm not sure why. "Chase helped me move in, too. The house is little but clean, new, simple. I can't believe I have the key."

"There you go," Sully says, sad eyes smiling. "Not everything's a battle anymore."

We both sip our coffee while I wonder if there's anyone in his life who'll give him a hug. Chase has become my person. When he's in town, he hangs out for long afternoons with Will on his lap and sports on the television. Just like old times. Almost.

"And have you—" Sully begins, but he's distracted by someone behind me. I turn to see a woman with a child—a little boy with socks on but no shoes, something hard and yellow caked on the front of his shirt. The woman is thin, way too thin, and the smell of nicotine wafts from the fabric of her coat.

"Evelyn Floyd," Sully whispers, and I try not to stare—this stranger who was pivotal to me getting my son back. She looks tragically familiar. I've known women like her all my life, the ragged strays, the ones who've drunk more in their life than they've eaten.

"Buster," she's saying, running after him with his shoes. "Put these on. You're in public, you have to behave." She grabs him and kneels, helping him with his laces. "Right. One, two, buckle my shoe. Now, are you having a cookie or a muffin?" They wander to the far end of the bakery where the display cases are.

I turn back to Sully, hold Will a little tighter. "She's doing her best," I say.

He nods.

"I wanted to thank you," I say after a moment, "for everything you did. I couldn't have gotten Will back without you."

He rotates his coffee mug an inch. "It's okay. Once in a while, good wins out in the end."

I nibble at my scone and say nothing.

"Have you seen Alex at all?" I ask.

"No," he says. "She's awaiting trial. I don't think I can see her." He could. He means he doesn't want to.

"That's okay," I say. "I don't she'd be thrilled to see either of us." I don't know why I feel compelled to visit Alex, but I do. Perhaps I'm still trying to prove my worth, which is silly, I know, since I'm the one escaping with my freedom, while she's in all kinds of trouble. It's not only the drugs, now—there are other charges being laid against her involving children, harm, and fraud—when I saw Morris to get the forms for my housing, he told me everyone's coming out of the woodwork. The case against my sister is growing each day. He said it's a shit show. But even after everything Alex has done, it's not what I want for her.

"You don't want to see her, do you?" Sully looks shocked. And he's right: Why would I go back for more? It seems masochistic. But it's something deeper that drives me back to her—an instinct, a shared blood—hard to explain if you're not within it. Try as I might to hate her, I can't seem to sidestep feeling love.

"I know her," I say. I know exactly why she is the way she is.

"Is that why you decided to stay here?" he asks. "In Moses River, I mean?"

At my chest, Will makes the softest coo. *I stayed to fix things, to heal all the wrongs. To take my sister's place.*

But I don't say any of that. I just shrug.

"Right," Sully says. He swallows hard, and we both stare at the table, lost for a minute in the past. "There's something that's been nagging at me." His eyes bore into mine. "Alex said she was the guarder. What did she mean? Because of her job?"

I kiss Will on the bridge of his nose, adjust Pim's clothespin on the blanket wrapped around him. "It's her role in a game," I say. "Hurry home. The game we played as kids on the day my brother died."

I won't say that I ran from the tree line that day to see Pim on the ledge of that grain truck, his little toes hooked over the rim, the wooden clothespin in the dark of his fist. Or how I saw Alex at the very top of the ladder, flailing at the peg, grabbing at it, trying to become the guarder, shouting furiously, so mad at him that she shoved him, hard, and he fell down, down, down into the grain until he was out of sight. I wish I could tell him all of this, but I can't. I won't. Sometimes words aren't enough, or they just don't matter. And even when sisterhood is a prison, like it has been for me, it's always, always a vault.

DISCUSSION GUIDE QUESTIONS

1. Is this a story about the enduring bond of sisterhood or the constrictive shackles of it?
2. What might the writer be exploring about the relationship between a person's past and their present? How do memory and guilt play a part in this?
3. Who were you cheering for at the start of the book, the middle, and the end?
4. If you were in Alex or Ruth's shoes, how do you think you'd react to the death of a sibling? How would it impact your relationships with the sister you have left?
5. Alex took Ruth into her home in her time of need, granted, she had ulterior motives. What would you do if your troublemaker sibling dropped in one day with stolen drugs and money?
6. How does *Hurry Home* deal with established beliefs about family, love, parenthood and the protection of children?
7. Alex, Ruth and Minerva all have a different approach to parenting/child protection and set the bar at varying heights. Is there a correct height, do you think? Whose approach did you most align with?
8. Is *Hurry Home* a tragedy? If not, what other kind of story is it?

9. What motivates the villain(s) in Hurry Home? Is she a psychopath, narcissist, sociopath, or something else? How does this make her similar or different to villains we usually see in psychological thrillers?

10. With the exception of her brother, whose life do you think Alex ruins the most?

    a. father

    b. mother

    c. Ruth

    d. Chase

    e. Sully

    f. all of the above, she's a wrecking ball

ACKNOWLEDGMENTS

First and foremost, I need to thank my editors, Nita Pronovost and Sarah St. Pierre, who helped me through the maze of this book and kept telling me there was gold in it. Writing is without question a collaboration, and yet the fact of that remains largely unsung. Nita and Sarah, thank you for keeping me going, and for knowing me well enough to send up flares when I needed them.

To my agent, Carolyn Forde, whose honesty, dedication, and all-around total ability to *get it* makes me so happy to be on her team, and even allows me to overlook the New York rooftop parties she keeps going to without me. Thanks for everything, as always, and I look forward to more fun.

To the fantastic team at Simon & Schuster Canada—FQ., Adria Iwasutiak, my amazing publicist Rita Silva, Kevin Hanson, et al. Thanks also to Jenny Chen and the team at Crooked Lane for understanding this book so well.

I needed professional insight throughout this process, and in gleaning it, I realize how many strong, frontline women I know who are doing some of the world's most stressful jobs. Thank you to Karen Scott, Lois Lien, Christine Watson, Shannon Thast, Paula Gummerson, Lisa

Rutherglen, Lisa Schmidtke, Sophie McLean, Carrie Mowery, and Susan Barth for everything you told me and everything you know. Massive respect to all of you, and if I got anything wrong, it's my misrepresentation, not yours.

To the 24-Hour Chevy Stevens Help Line, which has been made available to me daily since 2017. Chevy, you're a legend, my friend, and I ADORE YOU. Look, I even wrote it in capitals.

To Jo Histed, Sal Burdon, Sue Watt, Jonathan Watt, Robbie Nay, Kerry Elkins, Robyn Harding, Bertrand Pirel, and those in the inner circle. Writers need a community of people they trust, be it other writers, readers, bloggers, friends, and Instagramers: thanks to all those who post and tag supportively. You'd be amazed how far a kind comment can carry a writer on a self-doubting day.

To Empire Coffee in Nelson, British Columbia, where I wrote almost all of this novel, willfully disregarding the *No Computer Camping* sign to my left. Thanks to Joanne and the team for not kicking me out.

And finally, most important, to Clint, Cash, and Ruby. Hey, I finished the book! Here it is with all my love.